TIDE LINES

STORIES OF CHANGE BY LESBIANS

May '92

To Alison & Lynn
Here's to rare connections
enduring friendships
and the power of change.
Much love,
Lee

EDITED BY LEE FLEMING

gynergy books

~

A singular thank you to Lynn Henry, gynergy books' senior editor, whose collaboration in editing this anthology has been essential and much appreciated.

~

Cover Design and Illustration: ZAB Design . MTL
Book Design: Catherine Matthews
Printed and Bound in Canada by: Les Éditions Marquis Ltée

~

With thanks to the Canada Council for its generous support.

~

gynergy books
p.o. box 2023
charlottetown
prince edward island
canada C1A 7N7

CANADIAN CATALOGUING IN PUBLICATION DATA
Main entry under title:
Tide lines
     ISBN 0-921881-15-0
1. Lesbians' writings, Canadian (English) *
2. Lesbianism — Fiction. 3. Short stories, Canadian (English) —
Women authors. * 4. Short stories, Canadian (English) —
20th century. *
I. Fleming, Lee, 1957–
PS8323.L47T53 1991   C813.0108353   C91-097657-0
PR9197.33.L47T53 1991

CONTENTS

INTRODUCTION

Living on a small island, surrounded by the Atlantic ocean, I am not surprised that the sea tends to exert her influence on how I think and feel about being a lesbian. Thus, the title of this new anthology of fiction: *Tide Lines: Stories of Change by Lesbians*. "Tide Lines" evokes many images for me, among them, the forces of an indefinable energy that surely and continually brings change, in all its manifestations. It implies a continual reshaping of inner and outer landscapes—complex, and inevitable as moon and tidal cycles.

As an editor, I need my family of friends: to bounce ideas around, and to share in discussion about lesbian existence, practice and culture. The original call for submissions for this book was for short stories "that explore turning points in the formation of lesbian identity and community." Certainly a more left brain theme than, let's say, lesbian erotica ... This new obsession with turning points (and editing a book surely becomes an obsession), required numerous nights of discussion around the communal kitchen table. By the time most of these stories had been selected, I was still without a title. It was as unsettling as birthing a baby who is, three months later, still without a name. Finally in the eleventh hour, at that same kitchen table and with a looming publisher's timetable testing my stress levels, Silver Frith, Cancerian artist extraordinaire, said "How about Tide Lines: Stories of Change by Lesbians?" A collective YES was released. We all looked at each other with that satisfied look. Our baby had the perfect name.

Fundamental questions I asked myself quite awhile back, and to which I sought responses by doing this book, are: What are the turning points in our lives as lesbians? Are they different from those of our straight sisters and friends? How do these changes form our identity, both individually and collectively? These twenty-seven stories, although very different in writing style and subject matter, have change as a common theme. Moreover, all the changes explored in these stories happen *because* we are lesbians. Rites of passage, turning points, beginnings and endings—these are universal themes, experienced by all human beings. What makes this anthology so intriguing and personal, is that each story speaks very directly about the experience of being a lesbian in these times.

Three stories in this anthology are lesbian "coming of age" stories. In **Cerisy's Sphinx, Invert Sugar** and **Cass, Goobers and Girlies,** our young lesbian heroines struggle with being different from the girls around them. Being different is exhilarating, scary, and sometimes even dangerous. But by the act of accepting their "differentness," these girls are forever changed.

Certainly one of the most profound and universal lesbian experiences is "coming out." **Closet Space, Tulips, Ice-time, The Milky Way, The Journey,** and **Door Crashing** explore the coming-to-clarity about one's essential identity. From the charged eroticism of one's first love affair, to the power of experiencing a political awakening, to the profound relief and pleasure of "coming home" to oneself after years of searching—these stories are both familiar and unique.

In the process of defining lesbian culture and community, we also question our place therein. Sometimes we find harmony together; we also clash and struggle. **The Perfect Guest, Dogs on the Land, Circle Dance, Because,** and **Irene** all have in common the theme of change as it manifests itself in our community.

Several stories deal with being different (i.e. being non-white, or non-christian or non able-bodied) *and* being a dyke. The lesbians in **Alma's Daughter, Hot Chicken Wings, Maintaining the Peace (and silence), Fluency Process, (Un)Expected** and **Darlene**, search for self-integration. The road each travels takes many unexpected bends ...

An interesting theme that emerged, (and one that I realize I strongly identify with) is what I have come to call "the mid-life stage" of self-examination. In **Love in the '90s, Rhesa, ... then to Fuchsia, Inside Outside, Full Circle, Yousheme** and **Rita**, the central character is seeking wholeness in her life. A quest for meaning deeply informs her actions and motives. Yet she is often waiting for someone or something to suddenly give that meaning to her life. Her turning point comes from one or a series of key events that forces her to realize that *she* ultimately holds the power to transform herself.

Story after story reminds me of the power, magic and potential in our lives. Ready or not, change comes to us, constantly teaching us that we control very little. But, we *can* forge lives of worth and grace, even as change (if I may steal a phrase from Louanne Armstrong's story **Tulips**) often "rips our lives from one end to another." I am proud to present this fine collection of stories. May we always welcome the goddess of change in our lives, however she presents herself!

~ *Lee Fleming* ~
Prince Edward Island
August 1991

ALMA'S DAUGHTER

K.LINDA KIVI

My food co-op doesn't carry lingonberry jam. I hunt it down in obscure, side-street delis. In delis that smell of sausages, rye, caraway and smoked fish. In delis that smell like home but rarely see the likes of me—feta- and tofu-eating, expatriate ethnic gone sapphic. I usually find my jam high up on spotless wooden shelves, sandwiched between Ryvita and plum preserves. I usually pay my pennies to a woman who looks like my mother and reminds me of home.

Home. Lingonberries don't grow in North America, not that I would recognize a lingonberry bush if I tripped over one. The jam jar that lives in my fridge door was imported from a place I've never been to. I speak the language and have lived the culture (folk dance and whatnot) without ever having stepped foot in far-off Estonia. Even so, I was brought up on Immigrant Blend, spoonfed blood-red berries laced with blinding patriotism and the politics of exile. Culture and politics, love and hate, so tightly entwined that their threads were loathe to separate. So, lingonberries and Mamma's hugs were abandoned at the back door as I headed out in search of different flavours.

I gave up blood sausage and folk dance for feta and lesbian poetry. I debated over their socialist bashing with lists of American atrocities. I gave up going to protests over Brezhnev's visits for International Women's Day marches, Lesbian and Gay Pride Day, Winter Solstice and Take Back the Night. I dashed their hopes of my marrying an Estonian chemical engineer with my love of Sappho's daughters. But, I've never been to Lesbos either. The time eventually comes to go back home.

I started buying lingonberry jam to remind me of the part of me that is Alma's child. The part of me that doesn't find voice in feta or tofu. The part of me that is the daughter of an immigrant. Daughter of a Displaced Person. A refugee. Daughter of a land I've never been to. Daughter of an intelligent woman who is called "functionally illiterate." I still write out her letters when I go home to visit, arguing as she dictates diatribes about Communism addressed to Members of Parliament and local newspapers. Anger wells up in us both for our lack of understanding of each other. My mother and I both live in places where we've never been accepted and now have to struggle to accept each other.

Younger, I used to wonder why Alma didn't make friends with the neighbours. Why my friends' mothers belonged to bridge groups and coffee klatches, but she did not. Why her English got suddenly worse when one of those "Moms" would call. Wince. That was before I tried to see her side. That was when I thought that a W.A.S.P. was just another kind of bumblebee, only scarier. That was before I realized just how hostile Alma's adoptive home had been. Before I recognized the subtle insults—foreigner, immigrant, ignorant, "what do you know?"—spoken sometimes, but more often written on peoples's faces.

Nobody ever says those things to me. I've never worked as an alteration-ist, fixing five-hundred-dollar Christian Dior suits for a wage of twenty-five dollars a week. Foreigner. Immigrant. Ignorant. Nobody ever looks those things at me. I'm white skinned, accent-less and literate. My origins are written only in my name and in the voices that answered the phone in my youth. "Was that the cleaning lady?" I was asked more than once.

"No," I would answer quietly and with a touch of shame, "that's my mother." Silence on the phone. Only now do I wonder how much dead air she's endured. How many of those assumptions, theirs and hers, have cast her aside. Foreigner. Immigrant. Ignorant. Woman. Worker.

Alma did work as a cleaning lady only she never told me about it. She was always off to work as a sales lady in a store that didn't have a phone. I never doubted her. Add to her list: ashamed, silent, isolated. She wanted something different for me: to move among those who rejected her so that I would not suffer the same. But still, a cacaphony of saws, hammers and the Singer sewing machine whirl inside my "middle class" head. She tried to root industrial noise and otherness out of my future and yet, I come back to it. She raised a daughter who has her own list: woman, yes, but also feminist, lesbian, shit disturber. Another world to be at sea in.

Not all of us were raised on pumpkin pie, Peter Rabbit, Mother Goose and wheat bread. People continue to eye some of my food suspiciously, turning their noses up at my "rasolja," asking "What is that purple slime? What kind of name is Kivi anyway? What is that ring you're wearing? You've never tasted Yorkshire Pudding?!" No explanation of location, language or history aptly gives an inkling of the flavour of home unless the questioner has a similarly strange or unpronounceable name. And then, we eye each other suspiciously to see what unravelling the other has done.

I no longer see the friends of my lingonberry childhood, for few have unravelled as I have. Somewhere, somehow, someone decided that some things are not to be unravelled and that lingonberries, feta and tofu just don't mix. They decided that I couldn't be daughter to more than one mother, to more than one world. Sappho. I've never been to Lesbos either. But, my love of women is one ground to expel me from their midst. My politics another. Enough to merit those familiar looks of hostility, assumptions and misunderstanding: dyke, pinko, "can't you get a man?" spoken sometimes, but more often written on people's faces. And Alma, older now, wonders why I don't make friends with the neighbours. Why I don't belong to those coffee klatches that eluded her. After all, I don't sew and I don't do windows.

I struggle not to add "ashamed, silent and isolated" to my list. On her list they left enough of a mark on me. It is enough that I am second generation homeless, displaced person of sorts. Caught in between. Where *is* the land that lies between a Grecian island, a Soviet Republic and the social movement of this land?

I lick lingonberry jam from my fingers and screw the lid back on the jar. Tightly. I put my jam back in the fridge door. I suppose to myself, as the fridge sucks shut, that lingonberry is the flavour that gets left out in the cold the most. It's the hardest piece to weave in. It's the hardest kid to care for when my sisters can't even see the lingonberry stains on my cheeks. Does anyone else out there get heartburn from feta?

HOT CHICKEN WINGS

JYL LYNN FELMAN

Esther wanted silence. It had been eight hours since she had met Channah and Saul in the *Air Florida* terminal for their flight to Jamaica, and Esther was afraid she wasn't going to last the whole ten days. She had waited months for this reconciliation. But growing inside her was the terrible feeling that she needed to be saved from her very own parents. Then she laughed out loud. Maybe it was really Channah and Saul who needed to be saved from her, their very own daughter.

Esther took the elevator down to the lobby of the Windsor Hotel. Walking out the back door, she found herself in the middle of a pink patio. Hot-pink lounge chairs were everywhere. Nothing was familiar. She was used to the Piccolo Porch, to all the Jews sitting in brown wicker chairs at the Doral Hotel in Miami Beach. But Channah said they should try someplace new, different, to give the family another chance.

"Hello, darlin. Welcome to Ja' *mai* ca." Esther turned around, smack into Jamaica's face.

"Charlotte Gurthrie, here." Charlotte was smiling a huge smile. Esther tried to smile back. She reached instead for the Jewish star hanging between her breasts.

"Esther Pearl Greenberg. I'm with my parents, we came here to talk." Charlotte wasn't just smiling. She was grinning from behind her eyes. But Esther could barely meet her smile, even though it was the smile itself she craved.

Charlotte was dressed in a uniform. A green military blouse covered her large round breasts. She wore a tight, khaki-coloured skirt, short above the knees, with black ankle socks and black tie shoes. "Are you the tour guide?"

"Girl, I guard the doors right here at the Hotel Windsor." The woman was laughing in Esther's face.

Esther thought fast. She knew she couldn't spend all ten days with her parents, no matter how much she'd missed them over the last seven months. She took a deep breath. "I want to travel with you."

"By me, honey, it's okay. When ya want to see me *beau'* ti ful country?"

"As soon as possible, I mean it ... and Charlotte," Esther swallowed hard before whispering into the big smile, "I go with girls."

"Girls be fine too, darlin." The guard reached out for Esther's hand. "Come by me, sweet darlin. I be waiting."

"Esther!" Channah walked out into the pink patio just as Esther's hand met the hand of the woman in the khaki-coloured skirt, who was already turning around, walking towards the hotel lobby.

"Who was that?" Channah wanted to know.

"My tour guide."

"Esther Greenberg, you don't need a tour guide in Montego Bay. We came here for the sun. And to talk."

"I need a tour guide wherever I am." Esther needed patience. It had only been a year since she had told her parents the wonderful news that she loved women. "I'll meet you for dinner—just tell me what time." Esther understood her parents' disappointment. Not one of their three daughters had turned out according to the family plan. Her parents felt they deserved better than a divorce from a French Jew, and a Freudian psychiatrist who didn't believe in standing under the *chupah*. The problem was that her parents didn't understand Esther's disappointment with them.

"Seven o'clock, sharp. We'll wait for you in the lobby." Esther tried to meet her mother's eyes; but when she did, all she saw was the flash of her mother's pain moving across her face. She wanted to hug Channah, to tell her she was glad they came to someplace new. But she was afraid Channah wouldn't hug her back. Instead she nodded, turned around, and walked back into the hotel, wondering which door Charlotte was guarding now.

Esther stood alone in front of the elevators. When the doors opened, Charlotte walked out, almost bumping into her.

"Estie, where ya be keeping ya sweet self?" The gold in Charlotte's teeth caught her eyes.

"When does the tour begin?"

"Tomorrow's me off day." Charlotte's whole body smiled when she spoke. Her feet tapped the hotel floor lightly. Esther felt the smile coming up through the earth itself. By tapping her foot, Charlotte returned what she borrowed. "What's so busy in ya head girl?"

"I was just watching you live." Esther winked at Charlotte. "So tomorrow's our day. What'll we do?"

"Whatever ya be wanting, sweet Estie. I be coming by early, us be having us the whole day."

"I want to eat Jamaican." Esther decided to take advantage of vacationing—for the first time in her life—beyond the brown wicker chairs of Miami Beach.

"Sure darlin, I be cooking. Wear ya walking shoes, girl. Us walking long to me house from the bus. Now this hotel here be needing a guard." After a quick nod goodbye, Charlotte walked away.

Alone in the elevator, Esther tried to understand what she wanted from this trip. She knew she had longed for her family. But she didn't miss the heartache that always followed being together as family, as Jews. Even studying at Brandeis, where most of the students were Jews and she was majoring in Judaic Studies, hadn't brought back that warm feeling of belonging to her people. It was only Sunday. She told herself to take one day at a time, hour by hour if she had to.

At seven sharp Esther met her parents in the hotel lobby. They walked towards her just like two ordinary human beings. Everyone had dressed for the evening. Channah had on her favourite skirt-and-blouse ensemble. Esther had to admit her mother had good taste—the material was a soft silk, light blue and sea-green. Channah's face was already tanned. Saul wore his summer suit, without a tie. He smiled at Esther.

"Where are we going for dinner?" Esther's voice was friendly.

"The Montego Bay Beach and Tennis Club, it's just up the road and comes highly recommended in the *Kosher Traveller*," Channah answered, not looking at Esther and not looking away, just looking.

Channah and Saul walked out of The Windsor in front of Esther. They formed a perfect triangle. Esther remembered her therapist always said to stay away from triangles—only Esther had thought she meant love triangles. Now she knew that any triangle was dangerous, and that there was no way out, but physically to step out. Besides, a triangle was only half a Jewish star.

Saul asked the bellman to get a cab. Esther felt a large movement behind her. Charlotte.

"These folks ya parents, sweet darlin?" Esther reeled around, hostile, until she realized no one had heard the love talk but she and Charlotte. "Introduce me, if ya please ... "

"These are my parents, Saul and Channah Greenberg."

"You're Esther's new friend, aren't you?" Channah said.

"Oh, Estie and me be knowing each other a very long time." Charlotte grinned. Esther didn't say a word.

"Cab's here." Saul called out. Charlotte walked with them.

For a minute Esther thought Charlotte was going to bend down and step right into the cab with her parents. But she didn't.

The cab pulled up at a giant ranch. As soon as they walked into the dining room, which was like an old cowboy movie—big round tables in huge circles circling a gigantic fireplace—Esther knew her mother was going to say that the dining room was a little too much. Saul looked around before making his announcement, "Not many of us in here."

"That's exactly what I was thinking." Channah looked at Esther for support. Esther knew her parents were uncomfortable in the strange *goyishe* dining room, and so was she. For a moment, they were a family again.

But Esther couldn't stop thinking about Charlotte. Where was she? What was she having for dinner? Was she with her lover ... Esther closed her eyes to see better: she felt the warmth of two big women sprawled out on a double bed, feeding each other and laughing as the food spilled onto the sheets. She decided to have the fresh local tuna. She had read in *National Geographic* that it was a Jamaican fish.

She knew that tuna was kosher—the mothers didn't eat their young or prey off other fish. Esther had always hated the image of a mother eating her children. Whenever she smelled *treif* she immediately saw the floor of the ocean in her head. She pictured big shrimps, scallops, and giant oysters devouring their babies and any other fish swimming in their path.

Keeping kosher had always been important to Esther. When she was thirteen, right after her *Bat Mitzvah*, Esther had immersed herself in the meaning of *kashrut*, in hallowing the very act of eating. It was a way for her to eat with Jews everywhere and have Jews everywhere eat at her table.

She closed her eyes, wishing that she was alone with Charlotte. Esther hadn't remembered how depressing it was to be with her parents. She had always wanted an adult relationship with Saul and Channah. *Well, here it is*, she told herself. Then she had to put her fork down and stop eating. "I'm going to the bathroom, the waiter can take my plate."

She looked at herself in the mirror, shaking her head, not wanting to believe that absolutely nothing had changed. She knew her parents were unhappy. They had told no one, not even Rabbi Schwartz, that their baby wanted their blessing to bring home a Sabbath bride instead of a groom. So no one had mentioned her life; no one had even asked her if she was happy.

Being a lesbian made life with Channah and Saul so difficult. Her mother had stopped inviting her home for the holiday's, and Saul had specifically said they weren't interested in any "details," not even Esther's new friends. She could still hear Channah's reaction to her good news: *But why did you have to go and spoil everything? Why tell us?* Esther knew then that the only way into the Greenberg family was to be like Channah and Saul. There really wasn't anything to talk about. Esther returned to the table. She looked straight at her parents for the first time since arriving on the island. "I want dessert. Is anyone going to join me?"

"We'll split something with you." Channah said.

"No, I want my own." Esther shut her eyes and waited. Nothing happened. When the waiter came back she ordered Baked Alaska because she had always loved the taste of the meringue on her tongue as it melted.

Saul paid the bill while Esther took a last look at the big round tables. She was back at Camp Ramah, sitting with hundreds of young campers, cutting their kosher, *Shabbas* chicken breasts simultaneously. She stood to bless the wine, surrounded by over two-hundred-and-fifty adolescent Jewish voices, singing as though their voices alone could call the prophet Elijah back to earth. That was the last time Esther had really felt at home.

Of course it never happened that the entire Camp Ramah dining room began eating at the exact same moment, but Esther used to fantasize, every *Shabbas*, that all her people, everywhere, were striking matches as the sun set, welcoming in the weekly festival. In her mind for one brief moment, she had brought peace to the Jews, and to her family. Finally, Esther had to admit that being Jewish and being a Greenberg weren't the same thing.

~ PART TWO ~

"Estie, Estie!" Charlotte was waving her hands and calling to Esther. But it didn't look like Charlotte at all. Her green military blouse and khaki-coloured skirt were gone. Instead, she wore a purple beret balanced just above her left eyebrow. Deep-red rouge was smoothed into brown skin; red lip gloss wet her mouth. Charlotte had hooped gold earrings, two and three, in each ear.

"Ya *finally* ready, girl?"

Esther nodded, following her out the lobby of the Windsor Hotel and down the road to the bus stop. In the hot sun, Charlotte's black pants shone and her white blouse looked like silk. She carried a red-and-green hand-woven pouch and a small, brown paper bag in her left hand.

Charlotte's legs moved fast on the gravel road. Esther had to run to keep up. This was a new Charlotte, quick, taking up space. On the bus, Charlotte sat down, stretched her legs out across an entire seat, and said hello whenever someone she knew walked by. Esther sat alone in the row directly behind Charlotte.

By the time they reached downtown, Charlotte was asleep and Esther's eyes were wide open. The bus stopped inside a huge open market decorated in banners of gold, green, shiny black and red. In booth after booth people sold food, clothes, records. The smells—red onions, ripe mango, dog shit—blended together, making Esther sick. Charlotte woke up, and motioned for Esther to follow.

They walked across the street to another bus stop, and waited ten minutes. They sat again in separate rows, as if they knew without speaking that both of them needed a lot of space before their afternoon together. Pulling against the force of gravity the bus climbed straight up into the Jamaican hills, while the town below got smaller and smaller.

Skinny, bone-thin dogs ran everywhere; the driver kept his hand on the horn. A baby sat crying right in the middle of the road, sprawled out on all fours, trying to crawl to the other side. The bus circled around the screaming infant. As the bus climbed up, the temperature rose inside. Esther was hot. Everywhere there were trees—large wide-leafed palm trees reaching out, shielding the villages and the people.

Green, all shades—Jamaica was divided into shades of dark, light and yellow greens. From the window, the Jamaican green reminded Esther of Israel. Slowly, she let in the yellow-green Jamaican hillside. But she heard her father's voice in her head, like a tape recorded message playing over and over again: *Israel is the most beautiful country in the whole world.*

"Okay, Estie. Me stop is here." Charlotte hadn't spoken for at least twenty minutes. Esther didn't recognize her voice, but she felt their two bodies rise in unison, a pair of woman-bodies bending and rising together in dance. "Ready for some walking, girl?" Charlotte looked at Esther for the first time since picking her up at the Windsor.

"What's in your bag?" Esther asked.

"Our supper, girl. I went I to the butcher this morning for the chicken wings and legs." Charlotte was impatient. Esther didn't say a word—how could she explain the laws of *kashrut* to Charlotte?

Even though she wanted to eat Jamaican, she hadn't planned to eat *treif*. She never ate meat in restaurants unless it had been ritually slaughtered and blessed. Out of respect for her people, and for the food itself, Esther separated the kosher from the unkosher, the holy from the unholy, and ate only what was permitted by Jewish law. When she ate, Esther belonged to Jerusalem.

"Me kids be waiting ... Estie, pick up your feet."

"Kids?"

"Oh yes, I has I three children, one boy and two female beauties, little ones, brown and beautiful." Esther didn't think she had heard right—this was the first time Charlotte had said anything about kids.

"Charlotte, you got a husband?"

Charlotte nodded, her purple beret moving up and down. They walked side by side now, their buttocks moving from right to left, hitting each other slightly because they were walking uphill while their bodies pulled them down. "Me man he come and go; be working in Miami Beach most of the time. Send I a letter before he do home."

"What about your woman?" Esther concentrated on walking straight uphill. Charlotte didn't owe her any explanations.

"Oh ya darlin, whenever me man he be travelling, me girl Caroline and I, we goes to the bed and has us a sweet time. Sometimes us don't be up for a whole day, just to feed the kids and then us be meeting sweet again." They were almost at the top of the hill.

"Me man he love me, Estie. I got I he picture at me home. You'll see, girl." Charlotte pointed to a path off the dirt road. They headed straight down the side of the hill, into the overgrown weeds, bushes and very green palm trees.

Holding back a big yellow-green bush, Charlotte showed Esther where to walk. A slight odour came up to Esther's nose—the same odour she smelled on her body whenever she was afraid. The path wasn't cleared well and the brush scratched her legs. They climbed down, deep into the underbrush. The deeper they went, the greener the leaves became, the stronger Esther's body smelled.

Looking up, she saw that Charlotte had taken them way off the main dirt road. They stood in the middle of a row of small wooden shacks. Walking over to the far end, they stopped in front of a silver tin door. Esther heard voices. As Charlotte whistled long and slow, a young boy came out of the bushes.

"Where are the beautiful ones?" Charlotte bent down to the size of her son, whispering and kissing inside each of his ears. "Are they with Caroline?" The boy nodded, standing almost at attention, watching Esther. His mother's eyes were in him.

"Let's go." Charlotte nodded towards the door.

The shack was a single room, as big as her Windsor closet and bathroom combined. In the centre of the room was a double bed. Charlotte sat herself at the head. The boy jumped up, circling his mother with his body, protecting her. Esther stayed in the doorway.

To the right of the entrance was a big dresser with a mirror attached. Next to the dresser were several plastic milk cartons piled one on top of the other. From where she stood Esther could see dishes and silverware arranged in neat rows inside the milk cartons. On top of the cartons was a double gas burner. Everywhere, clothes were folded into neat piles.

The floor of Charlotte's house was made of firmly packed brown dirt. A broom and a dust pan were in the left corner by the doorway. The only window was on the wall opposite the bed. The frame was empty, but the green from outside grew up around the glass-less hole, filling it with a thick green softness.

"Estie, sit down, ya impolite girl; we in me own home now."

Charlotte cooked. She poured water from a jug on the floor into a sauce pan and added a cup of uncooked rice. She made a work space on the bed by propping up a six-by-twelve wooden board with two bricks at each end. Taking the chicken parts out of the bag she had carried since early that morning, she separated the legs from the wings, making two piles, dipping and rolling each piece into a flour mixture. After flouring each piece, Charlotte covered the chicken with spices. Esther watched, trying to figure out what the great rabbis would tell her about eating Charlotte's unclean food.

Charlotte lit the burner. She poured oil into a frying pan, waited a few minutes, watching the oil sizzle and get hot. Then one by one, she placed the wings into the hot pan, stopping for only a second to stir the rice. Every few minutes she added spices—red, black, and green powders—to the hot oil. When she was done frying the wings, she started over with the legs. Charlotte's love went straight into the frying pan and into the steaming rice.

On the bed, Charlotte spread out a single straw mat painted red, filled one plate with hot rice and fried chicken wings then put it on the mat in front of Esther. "Eat."

"I don't want to eat alone."

"Sweet darlin, where ya manners be? In Ja' *mai* ca the guest eats before the family. Eat."

Esther picked up the fork. What did it mean that she was about to eat Jamaican chicken wings and rice? She reminded herself that she had arranged this day, she had made the date with Charlotte and even told her she wanted to eat Jamaican. So Esther put some rice on the end of her fork, added a piece of chicken, and brought the fork slowly up to her mouth. She was eating Charlotte's wings, *treif* and unclean that they were.

The food had lost its heat, but when Esther put it in her mouth, she tasted all the Jamaican spices that Charlotte had added while she cooked—spices Esther couldn't see by looking at the cooked food. She had to taste them to know that they were actually red hot and sweet all in the same bite. Like nothing she had ever tasted before.

Esther chewed. The spices were overpowering. This wasn't the first time that Esther had ever eaten *treif*, but in the past, whenever she brought unclean food to her lips, she had never been able to enjoy it as she did now. She remembered the first time she made love to a woman. That was the beginning. Esther had been afraid to bring her tongue down between Judith's legs. She had spent a long time kissing arms, shoulders, eyes, and face.

Finally there was nothing left to do but bring her wet tongue straight down Judith's breasts, stomach, and inside her thighs. Those first woman smells had been overpowering too, sweet and hot like Jamaican spices. When her tongue circled between Judith's small thighs, Esther told herself to open her eyes and look at the curly mound of dark, black hair protecting her lover's vagina, but she had been afraid to look.

"Tasting is the same as looking," Judith had said, reaching down to hold Esther's head close to her body. Esther had known she was right, so she let herself breathe in a little at a time, all the different smells hidden between Judith's legs. She remembered being surprised that the lips outside Judith's vagina had only a faint sweet smell. It was the inside that smelled strong and tasted so wet. Using her fingers to open Judith, Esther had to fight off the pious old Jew in her head. He was tearing apart a red, *treif*, steaming lobster. Then slowly, as though praying, he dipped the white, sweet, unholy fish into a pool of melted butter.

With her mouth inside Judith, Esther began to chew, taking small, gentle bites. Just as she was crossing over to join her lover, Channah and Saul pushed into her head. They stared at her, *their baby*, and Channah screamed, "Go! Wash yourself until you're clean, don't come into my house with any of that filthy *treif* still on your tongue. Get rid of the smell before you walk into my kitchen." Esther had had to stop, close her mouth before she gagged, and bring her head back up, next to Judith's.

They had held each other while Esther's whole body shook. But she wasn't shaking now. She was taking another bite out of Charlotte's sweet wing and thinking that all her life she had been afraid of new, unknown, and different spices; but now she was chewing, bite by bite, Charlotte's crisp Jamaican skin.

"This is good. How do you get the flavours hot and sweet at the same time?" Esther piled more rice on her plate. Stuffing her mouth full, she barely took time out to chew and swallow.

"Slow down, girl. Me knows ya had rice before. Ya eating like ya never ate in ya whole life." Charlotte shook her head. Her son was laughing.

"I feel like I haven't eaten for days, for weeks." She was eating, really eating, almost as if for the first time. She laughed at herself. This, then, was Charlotte and Esther making love.

"Want to see some good pictures? I have I pictures of me, me man, and Caroline." Charlotte reached into another pile.

"Sure." Esther talked with her mouth full. They sat on Charlotte's bed, Esther and Charlotte and her boy, looking at family pictures. They were in the living room now—Esther had finished eating and all the kitchen equipment had been pushed aside.

"This one me favourite, girl. Everybody I love and who love I be in here looking out at the world." Charlotte handed Esther a picture with three adults standing in the middle of the road. They held each other, looping their arms together behind their backs. Esther knew without asking who was in the picture.

"That's me woman Caroline, there on the end, me in the middle, and me man Samuel on the other end." Esther stared at the picture. Something was going on in there that Charlotte wanted her to see.

"Ya done yet, with ya looking?"

Esther shook her head. Then she knew—it was in their bodies. If she looked closely at the way they stood, with their hips lightly touching and their thighs and knees bending into each other, Esther saw what Charlotte had been trying to tell her since they met. All three of them—Samuel, Charlotte and Caroline—were lovers. Esther steadied herself on the bed. She needed a few minutes to let in this new piece of truth, because it wasn't just about the three of them, living and loving in Montego Bay.

"So, you're all three together?"

Charlotte nodded.

"Anybody know besides me?"

"Impossible, sweet darlin. In Ja' *mai* ca a person gots to be either/or, Estie, not both. They say there's not enough room in the world for us to be both. But I, girl, I hates to choose; I wants all there is. Ya the same, those hungry eyes, and that dancing mouth, told I right away. That's why me brought ya to me home. I been wanting someone from outside to talk to. So, I picked I sweet Estie." Charlotte reached for the picture.

"I girl, I separate in me own *beau* ti ful country. Me whole life, I be needing to tell somebody. Me opening doors, looking around, when I see ya coming into the Hotel Windsor. I knowing then, I found I somebody doing like I do."

So Charlotte was alone too, alone in green Jamaica. She had been eating unclean food, separate from her people, for years. Only she was doing just fine. It was Esther who had never learned that eating a little *treif* was necessary to survive.

Esther had never been free to eat whatever she wanted, because that meant eating alone, without the Jews. She had always been afraid to eat by herself—once she started she might never stop. There were too many things to taste, like Charlotte and Caroline and Samuel all at once.

"I've got to leave, Charlotte."

"I be waiting for ya to stand up, girl, saying ya had enough."

They looked at each other, closing out the boy, the hot chicken wings and rice, and the picture of Charlotte with her two lovers. Esther burned inside. This was only the second time in her whole life that she was full. The first time had been with Judith, her first woman lover. She had been unable to continue loving Judith like she wanted—every time she tried, she imagined her head turning into the red head of a steaming lobster whose antennae reached out to strangle her. But she didn't think that would happen anymore.

"I'll walk ya to the bus."

They walked then, back up the green path, past all the other shacks, and onto the road. When the bus came, Esther climbed the three steps by herself. In the centre of the open market where all the smells blended together, Esther walked off the bus. She took a deep breath, slowly breathing in the pungent blend of red onion and ripe mango.

LOVE IN THE '90S

HEATHER CONRAD

The sight of purple ink, the small controlled handwriting, stopped her cold. She looked again. It was a memo from the office manager. She sat at her desk. Okay. That proved it. The whole thing was too much. It had gotten so that just the sight of a handwritten note gave her a jolt in the pit of her stomach. Grace sat back in her chair and looked around her office. She was at work. It was all right. She was safe.

So far the count was fifty-two. Fifty-two handwritten letters in response to the personal ad she had put in *Out Now* last month. It wasn't that her ad was so remarkable; it seemed rather she had underestimated the number of lesbians in the world or the drawing power of the written word.

At first, responses had just dribbled in, five letters after two weeks and she'd thought that was it. They all seemed to be from reasonable women, and so curiously, and dutifully, she'd called up each one, left messages, talked directly, set up dates. It had taken hours. Then four days later twenty-two more letters arrived. As she'd sat at her kitchen table ripping open the envelopes one after another she had felt a dense weight of responsibility for each carefully written hand, for each woman, for each expression of need and desire.

The fact was, she had a date with one of those women in less than twenty minutes. The whole thing was absurdly scary.

No psychopaths had responded to her carefully-worded ad, not as far as she could tell—hers was of the "nice girl" variety, not anything that could even vaguely be construed as kinky. She'd just wanted a nice companion. So did everybody else in town, it seemed. It was phenomenal how many lesbians there were in Los Angeles. From Burbank to San Juan Capistrano, mothers, waitresses, doctors, electricians, artists, white, black, French, Asian. And it felt like they'd all written to her, sight unseen, with hope and longing, wanting to please. "I too like what you like ... and I like morning light ... world beat and funk ... Jungian archetypes ... lying around ... " Whatever seemed to fit the image they saw of themselves and herself in a hundred-word ad.

This was her ninth date coming up in—she looked at her watch—fifteen minutes now. She took a deep breath that was more like a gasp and bit her lip. It was much worse than high school, if that was possible.

In her ad she'd said that she was "attractive," assuming that everyone would take that with a grain of salt and know that she wasn't Elizabeth Taylor, but she wasn't Elephant Man either. She'd said it because she didn't want to attract people who thought of themselves as unattractive. She meant it subjectively. Who knew what it meant?

And so there was always the first moment of shock. Two absolute strangers, face to face, to see if they could fall in love. It wasn't exactly like being a mail-order bride. But it was close—except that you could always change your mind and get home in half an hour.

It didn't help that her very first date, Cindy, had arrived with more make-up on than she herself had worn altogether in the past ten years and that, after three minutes of conversation, Cindy had said she felt sick. They had been walking down Wilshire Boulevard and proceeded to sit down at the first available restaurant, where Cindy talked about her illnesses for the next twenty minutes then said she was feeling really sick and the two fled from each other as quickly and gracefully as possible.

She'd gone right home after that and looked in the mirror. Would people think she had lied in her ad? She threw the I-Ching. It said, "Keep Trying," more or less.

Her second date was much better. Intentionally she had suggested a dark restaurant for lunch. Neither of them could see each other clearly enough to detect flaws and they had had a good conversation. They talked about past relationships. Grace's had been infrequent and difficult; so had her date's. Grace felt she had grown in the past few years, might be ready to try again; so did her date. It was hardly enough for true love, though. Grace left it open about a second date.

There were so many of them. And, each time, she felt she needed to make a snap decision. They were all so different. How could she tell in an hour and a half who someone really was? Or if she might find them suddenly very beautiful after a night of making love.

She nearly jumped when Teresa knocked on her office door and stuck in her head.

"A Jillian James is here to see you, Grace. Are you free?"

"In a minute." She thought she sounded hysterical as she nodded at Teresa, who left and shut the door.

Jillian, Jillian—what a name. She's early; I hate her. Grace stood up. Quickly she glanced in the mirror on the wall, patting at her hair which was probably cut a little too punky for her age. Thirty-eight was not kid's stuff. Still, she liked to look modern. She was a painter, after all, in addition to running this little agency. She glanced back at herself in the mirror as she headed for the door, hoping that her urban hip look wasn't more farce than fact.

Jillian's face fell before Grace was even out the door.

"Shall we go?" Grace asked anyway, whisking in front of Jillian and leading her down the hall to the nearest exit, at the same time throwing back a couple of ice-breaking questions. Jillian responded, but her disappointment was palpable. Grace didn't even want to look at her. She was deciding not to take it personally but, since the sick woman, this was the worst response she'd received yet. Did she have dirt on her face or something? She hadn't seen it in the mirror.

On the street, Grace fell back in place with Jillian, walking side-by-side to the restaurant. She'd gotten Jillian talking about her work as a marine biologist and took a minute to study the woman. Well, she was pleasant looking enough, on the large side, but well put together. She wasn't a beauty queen though—what had she been expecting of Grace? Jillian's talk of her career was polite, but the fact that she was forcing herself through the pain of disillusion was evident.

Still, Grace questioned her about her work because she was actually fascinated by marine biology and, besides, she'd been through enough of these dates to know it would soon be over. There was always the unexpected, and the worst was over now.

"So what do you do?" Jillian finally asked over dessert.

"A couple of different things," Grace answered, debating over which to reveal. "I'm involved in research too, actually. Our agency is very small, but we receive contracts from the universities to study various social trends. Currently we're looking at psychic and intuitional healing." She waited for Jillian's scientific mind to gag.

Jillian's polite smile deepened. Her eyes became unquestioningly intrigued. In a few words she summarized her own psychic studies—she herself was a psychic reader.

Grace was stunned, she never would have guessed that this high-level scientist, wearing a polyester pant-suit, would announce herself as a psychic reader. Her awe must have shown clearly, to Jillian anyway, because Jillian looked carefully at Grace a moment, as if she were considering sharing her gift with her.

Finally, Jillian spoke, "I hope you don't mind me telling you, I feel a lot of anger in you. You seem very angry at me in particular, today." She waited for Grace's response.

Grace felt as if a chair had been pulled out from beneath her, as her centre of gravity dropped deep within and the dream she'd had last night flashed vividly in her mind: a milk carton turning into a swarm of snakes that she fought, then strangled, then hammered to death in rage. She had dreamt this dream—of strangling snakes—often in her life.

"You're right." Grace said it as if she'd always known it, though in fact she only now fully realized it. "I have a lot of anger. A lot. I had a dream last night about it." She told Jillian her dream and some of its recurring forms.

"You don't like having expectations put upon you, do you?" Jillian asked.
"I guess not."

"And you feel that every kind of relationship is a field of expectation?"
"Yes."

"But who is it who's really putting demands on you to perform or produce?"

Grace nodded. Herself of course.

"If you let the snake alone, she may bring you power, not take it away, as you seem to fear."

Grace took a breath. "How?"

"You can start slowly. Meditate on the image, without taking any action. Let the snake be, just a few seconds at a time if it's frightening."

"Of course," Grace nodded again. Her agency was surveying a program in imagery healing that could help her. It was so obvious, it astounded her that it had never occurred to her to participate in any of the programs her agency studied. She had simply produced the reports as contracted, with a sympathetic eye of course, but she had never actually let it all in.

"It's obvious why we were supposed to meet." Jillian was matter-of-fact.

Grace raised an eyebrow.

"You called me up to come and interpret your dream for you. That's pretty good." Jillian smiled and reached for the bill. "I've got to be getting back to the lab."

They said goodbye at the intersection. A handshake and smile. Jillian hadn't said a thing about ever seeing her again. Grace felt too stunned to go back up to the office. She walked around the block. It was true. She was angry, much of the time. The dreams she'd had of rage: they were about the demands of relationships. It was what her therapist had been trying to get her to see, to feel, all along. As a child, her parents had demanded too much of her. The price of love enraged her. Her tears felt hot, pushing at her throat as she bent her head to her hand and walked quickly to the corner, seeking somewhere to hide because she was crying now. She was livid.

~

It was 6:30 p.m. twelve days later when Grace looked up from her magazine in the waiting room. Melinda Dean, Ph.D., stood in the doorway. "Hi, Grace. Ready?"

Grace smiled and put down her magazine. Melinda always looked so present—it was amazing, given all the pain and confusion she had to listen to. Grace had never envied the life of a therapist, especially her own.

She sat across from Melinda. They'd already dealt with the Jillian incident, last week. Melinda had deemed it a major breakthrough. That had been six dates ago. Grace was exhausted from dating. And she was still far from falling in love with anyone. No one had interested her very much. Although, since Jillian, she'd managed to try not to be angry with her prospective dates before they'd even met her. Still, she found the stress of presenting herself to a complete stranger almost paralysing sometimes. She tried to explain it to Melinda.

"It's so nerve-wracking. I'm practically trembling those first few minutes. So are they. Once I poured a glass of water down my chin the second after I'd sat down with the woman. She didn't bat an eye. Then I lost my voice. She kept talking like I'd finished my sentence naturally. I excused myself and went to the restroom. When I came back, she just smiled. She was a nurse."

"How would it feel to you to acknowledge what's going on? To let the other woman know that you're feeling nervous or uncomfortable?"

"No, I can't do that, then everything would get even more uncomfortable. You can't do that. You can't go meet someone for the first time and say, 'Hi. How do you do? You know what? I feel like throwing up.'"

Melinda didn't smile. Grace was surprised that Melinda took her so seriously sometimes. It wasn't like they were unfamiliar—she had been in therapy with Melinda for two years; she loved Melinda. She had exposed herself entirely to Melinda and Melinda had always been there, comforting, loving, challenging, soothing. Melinda was close to forty herself, had been through a lot—that was evident by her understanding of pain and her courage in the face of it. She was a Taoist, a mother, a lesbian, and remarkably gifted as far as Grace could see. Her intuitive skills were phenomenal. She had beautiful, complex blue eyes and the kind of engaging look that was vulnerable and tough at the same time.

"I didn't say you should throw up on your date," Melinda answered. She seemed almost indignant. Lately, Grace felt, it seemed as if Melinda was taking personally some of the things Grace said. Maybe she was angry that Grace had placed her ad on an impulse last month without consulting her. But she was too good of a therapist for that. Grace couldn't help but laugh.

Melinda let her laugh. "What could you do to feel less tense in the situation?"

"I really don't know. I feel like I have to be cool, keep the conversation going. Some of these women, it seems like they don't know how to talk. They sit there while I ask them questions and they answer or I tell a little story or ask them more questions. If I weren't doing all the work we'd just sit there and stare at each other like bumps on a log."

"Would that be so horrible?"

Grace sighed.

"What would happen if you told them what you were feeling?"

"They would throw up."

"Really?" Melinda cocked her head. "Let's try it," she challenged. "Come on. Pretend you're on a date with me." Melinda sat back, waiting. Grace looked at her and felt as if someone had pulled a chair out from under her,

her centre of gravity dropping as Melinda's blue eyes filled her vision. Yes. Yes, Grace thought. You.

~

It had been three days since Grace had fallen in love with Melinda at her therapy appointment. For the life of her she could not get Melinda out of her mind. Even her brunch date that morning with a French film-maker hadn't distracted her for more than the two hours they were together and even then Grace found herself fantasizing that Melinda would come into the restaurant and see her deeply engaged in conversation with the beautiful French woman and be impressed.

Melinda. Oh Melinda. Okay, okay, Grace admonished herself, it was transference to the worst degree. The problem was, she'd already been through the transference thing with Melinda, over a year ago. She could remember how, back then, she might feel a little twinge of jealousy when she saw another client leave Melinda's office. Or how Melinda told her she was going on a ten-day retreat in the mountains and Grace found herself wishing she could go with her. A lot of little things like that, and then it had passed and she felt only a respect and professional caring for Melinda.

This time though, it felt like the real thing. Melinda was on Grace's mind from the minute Grace woke up in the morning until she fell asleep again at night, and Melinda was in Grace's dreams too. Sometimes she was in Grace's mind only lightly, in the background, and sometimes it was constant fantasy: long involved conversations, or Grace might even go so far as to imagine Melinda in her bed, lying there, languorous as her blue eyes gazed in pleasure and pain at her own deep desire. That complexity, in her eyes, that intricate and fragile light, the range of emotion and acceptance—it was Melinda's eyes that Grace kept seeing, that obsessed her.

~

It was the night of her nineteenth date, just thirty minutes before the woman was supposed to arrive, that Grace had the odd idea. She had gone into the bathroom to brush her hair, which was now in a more subdued style (she had decided to tone down the urban hip look as it didn't seem to be going over that well). She looked in the mirror with her brush lifted to her head, when it occurred to her—it seemed like a psychic flash—that one of the fifty-two letters she had received was from Melinda. It all made sense.

It was certainly possible—one of the earlier dates had been with a psychologist who had used a fake name in her letter. It wasn't until they'd met at a restaurant in Malibu that the woman had told Grace her real name, explaining that she'd been more than a little concerned about ending up on a blind date with one of her clients. Grace didn't laugh at that thought now—instead she was overcome with longing, intense on the image of Melinda as the stranger she was about to meet.

She set down the brush and walked out of the bathroom, moving toward her desk in the bedroom. It was stacked with papers, files, letters. She rummaged through, finding the file, pulling out the stack of letters. She sat down at her desk, then stood again and walked over to her file cabinet. She hurriedly pulled out a drawer, reaching to the back and pulling out another file, grabbing a handful of receipts, then looked through them until she found it: a medical receipt with Melinda's signature.

Back at her desk, she sat down with the stack of fifty-two envelopes before her, pulling out the contents of each one, examining them under the light: the shapes of the a's, l's, d's, the dots on i's, looking back and forth from Melinda's handwriting to the carefully written notes from the fifty-two women, one after another.

She was nearly done when she found it, an old letter, one of the first. From Miriam. Of course. Melinda. Miriam. The writing was identical. She sat perfectly still, stunned, thrilled. Oh, Melinda, Melinda. Quickly she read through the letter.

> Hi.
>
> You sound interesting—I almost feel like we've met before. Your ad hit me that way, it spoke to me. I especially liked what you said about the importance of honesty in relationships. I agree, it can make all the difference.
>
> I have an interest in psychic healing, too. You could say I work in that field—though it's too much for me to explain in a letter, really. I'd rather talk with you about it. I'm very involved in my work. I love it, and am glad that you're someone who seems to be happy with what you do.
>
> I'm very interested in contemporary painting, too, though I don't paint. Other than my work, I like to spend my time in meditation, being with my child, studying and various other pleasures I'd rather talk about with you than write about.
>
> Give me a call?
>
> Miriam

Grace sat with the letter in her hand, gazing at it in wonder. How could she have missed it? It was Melinda all over the place. And she hadn't even wanted to respond to this letter. Why not? What had she been thinking? Though of course she knew: she did not want to admit it now, but she remembered the sensation she had had when she first read it and then put it in her reject pile. It had irritated her totally—its insinuating tone; its implication that they were meant to meet; the expectation of compatibility, and intimacy. Oh! Grace held her breath, felt nauseous. It was true. It was all true. This was Melinda, and Grace hated her and she was also in love with Melinda.

She put her head on her desk and the doorbell rang. It was number nineteen. Grace sat up straight, then turned in her chair. She took a breath.

~

It was number twenty though, a week later, that was Grace's last blind date. And one year after that, Miriam and Grace decided to move in together. Of course Miriam wasn't really Melinda. It's amazing how similar their handwriting is, Grace still insists. Sometimes she likes to tell the story at a party, with intimate friends. Friends who would understand about therapists and ads and all that. It's just love in the '90s, she says.

ICE-TIME

LEAH MEREDITH

"**Y**ou're going for a beer? Sounds great," Andy said as she packed the last of her hockey gear into her bag. "I'll be ready in a sec."

Pat and Arlene exchanged glances. "Um ... you probably wouldn't want to go where we're going," Pat said evasively.

"What? You're just going for a beer, aren't ya?"

"Uh ... yeah, but I don't think we're going to the kind of place that you're used to," replied Pat, trying to end the conversation as quickly as possible. It was always difficult explaining to the rookies that they had joined a lesbian hockey team. It wasn't that the whole team was extremely closeted, but the fewer people that knew in a prairie city like Calgary, the better.

"Oh ... okay then," Andy said, trying not to let the hurt of being excluded from the festivities show. She could take a hint. "Well, I'll see you at Thursday's practice." She threw her gear bag over her shoulder and left the dressing room.

Pat felt the familiar feelings of guilt begin to rise up from within her.

"Shit, I hate that," she said, looking at Arlene as if she could give Pat some kind of reprieve from her actions. Arlene just shrugged her shoulders and turned to gather up the rest of her equipment, leaving Pat to let the guilt take a firm hold.

Andy opened the arena door and stepped out into the cold January night air. She checked her watch: 11:45. It was shitty the way the women got the worst ice times. As she walked through the parking lot, listening to the snow crunch beneath her boots, she let the cold envelop her. It felt good. It reminded her of the long walks home when she was a kid in Cold Lake. After supper she would go to the outdoor rink and skate until they turned the lights off and her body was drenched with sweat. During the walk home with her skates draped over her shoulder, she would dream of being the first woman to play in the NHL. She would play for Toronto or maybe Montreal and her team would win the Stanley Cup. She would win the Most Valuable Player award and bring it home to Cold Lake and shove it in the faces of everyone who said that girls couldn't play hockey. At the time, that dream had felt so close, so real. She was gonna do it.

She reached her puke-green '74 Chrysler that she lovingly referred to as her "boat," threw her gear into the trunk and turned to watch the rest of the women leave the arena. Why did she still feel so left out? This was the reason she had left Cold Lake. While the rest of the girls in high school had been going on dates to the local movie theatre or dances, or hanging out at the burger joint, Andy had spent every free moment skating or playing shinny hockey with any guy who happened to be at the rink that night. She never quite fit in. After graduation Andy had taken the night shift at a convenience store to get enough money to finally leave the town to which she felt no loyalty. She had arrived in Calgary just after Christmas and immediately joined the JFL hockey team in mid-season. Andy had been in heaven. Finally a women's hockey league. Yet, even they wouldn't accept her. She jumped in her car, gunned the engine and pulled out before her teammates reached the parking lot. She didn't need them, she just wanted to play hockey.

The two days until Thursday's practice seemed like months to Andy. She spent the time walking alone through the frozen streets until her body ached from the distance and the cold. When she could walk no farther, she'd drag herself up the three flights to her one-room apartment and fall into bed, dreaming fantasies of what could be. When Thursday evening arrived, Andy was in turmoil. The fear of rejection contrasted with her excitement for the game. But there was also a need inside her. A need she couldn't understand. She had to see these women again.

~

As Andy entered the arena, the familiar smell of rubber from the walkways mixing with the smell of sweat relaxed her. She knew why she was here. Hockey. She entered the dressing room, sat down on the bench and began organizing her equipment. Pat's gaze met hers as she looked up from her gear. Andy saw sympathy and caring in the warm brown eyes of the woman who had rejected her only two days before.

"How ya doin' rookie?"

Startled, Andy turned to see Arlene sitting beside her.

"I'm ... a ... doin' good ... thanks." Who were these women who could change so much in so little time? Confused, Andy quickly and silently put on her gear and headed for the ice. As her skates scraped new grooves in the fresh ice, her confidence returned. She knew who she was out here. The ice was her domain. She had skill. She was respected. She was good. The practice was hard and fast. Andy's legs burned as she raced for the puck. The sweat that flowed down from beneath her helmet stung her eyes and blurred her vision. The cracks of sticks connecting with the ice, and pucks slamming the boards, filled her ears. To Andy, nothing was better than this.

Exhausted, the women collapsed in the dressing room, breathing hard and saying little. As strength began to flow back into their bodies, criticism about the practice was thrown back and forth. Compliments were shouted at

Andy faster than she could comprehend them. Even if these women didn't accept her, they sure liked the way she played. Andy was so busy basking in her glory that she didn't see the handsome woman approach until her hand was on Andy's knee.

"Can I talk to you for a minute?" Andy turned to see the beautiful eyes that she had put out of her mind an hour ago.

"Sure Pat, just let me get my other skate off."

Andy followed Pat out of the dressing room towards the bleachers. As she stepped in a puddle of warmed ice she cursed herself for being too anxious to put on her boots. Together they climbed the bleachers until they reached the top and sat down, both preferring to watch the Zamboni clean the ice than to look at each other. Their ice time had been the last of the day so the arena was quiet except for the shouts and laughter that escaped from the dressing room each time the door was opened.

"I'm sorry about the other night."

"Huh?" Andy had been busy squeezing the water out of her sock.

"I'm sorry about the way I treated you on Tuesday," Pat pushed, wishing that Andy had heard her the first time.

"Oh, that's okay. I know that it's hard to get used to new people some-times."

"That's not exactly the reason," Pat said, not sure how to continue. After a brief pause she spoke softly. "Andy, do you know what our team's initials, JFL, stand for?"

"Well, on the score sheet it says Just For Laughs."

"That's what we tell everyone so we don't get any flack. When we started the team, the initials meant Just For Lesbians."

Andy felt like the butt end of a stick had been jabbed between her ribs. She turned, pretending to focus her attention on the Zamboni once again. Her mind was whirling. Had she heard Pat right? Of course she had known that there were lesbians in the world, but she had never met one in Cold Lake. At least she didn't think that she had. Women with women, was that possible? Did women really love women the way they loved men? Is that why she was more interested in hockey than she was in guys? She pushed the last thought down and looked into the eyes that had never left her. She didn't know what to say.

"Anyway, I just wanted to let you know that we were going to a womyn's bar and didn't think that you'd feel comfortable. It was nothing personal."

"Oh," was all Andy could mutter.

Pat rose and retraced her steps down the bleachers. When she reached the bottom she shouted back.

"Hey rookie!"

"Yeah?"

"Nice practice." She turned the corner and headed to the dressing room.

When Andy finally returned to the dressing room, she was relieved to find it empty. She took off the remainder of her equipment and stuffed it into her bag. She slipped on her jeans and sweatshirt and heaved her bag over her shoulder. She opened the dressing room door and walked into the darkness of the arena. The manager had left, not knowing that she was still there. She walked out into the night towards the lone car in the parking lot. This time she didn't feel the cold.

By the time Andy arrived at her apartment, she had reached a decision. After much deliberation over whether to quit the team or to keep playing, she chose the latter. After all, she had come to Calgary to play hockey and that was just what she was going to do. And anyway, she kind of liked these women, even if they were lesbians. She would treat them just like any other women. They could have their lives and she could have hers. With that settled, she put all thoughts of lesbians out her mind. Or at least she thought she did.

~

The woman seemed to be born out of the light. The white linen that covered her allowed her features to be hidden. Andy could see the outline of her body as she squinted into the brightness. The woman was drifting towards her. Almost floating. But slowly, ever so slowly. Andy waited. Her body was weightless. She was free—free for anything. She felt no chains here. Something familiar touched Andy as the woman approached. Soon she was so close that Andy could smell the fragrance of her skin. She could feel the power between them. She reached up and removed the woman's veil, being careful not to touch her face. The eyes—they were the beautiful green eyes of the woman who worked in the library in Cold Lake ... they were the cool blue eyes of the hitch-hiker she'd picked up on her way here ... they were Pat's warm brown caring eyes ... the eyes were her own ...

She woke with a jolt, cursing the alarm that had slammed a wall down on her vision. She hadn't meant to fall asleep. Good thing she had set the clock. It was Saturday night. Game time. Andy jumped out of bed and raced around the apartment collecting her equipment. It was her first regulation hockey game and she couldn't be late. Her dream forgotten, she headed to the arena. She was out of her car almost before she had turned the engine off. She hurried into the arena, slowing only to glance at the dressing room schedule before running to the assigned room. She found a spot on the bench, closed her eyes and prayed that she wouldn't pass out.

"Hey rookie, ya gonna live?" shouted one of the players.

Andy turned to her. Her eyes. Where had she seen them before? She looked at the woman next to her. The eyes were there too. Time stood still as she scanned the faces in the room. She spent eternity focused on each pair. They were blue, brown, green, gold, mixtures of the rainbow. But they were all the same. Was this how lesbians found each other? Was it this inexplicable something in their eyes that linked them all together? Was it the same thing she saw in her own eyes?

~

Andy stood on the bleachers, staring at the now quiet ice. Her hair was still damp and her legs still shaky from the night's practice. This was going to be her last year playing the sport that she loved. How many goals had she scored over the past twelve years? She couldn't remember. How many bones had she broken? Was it five or six? Six, including her thumb. How many wimmin had she loved? She stopped and smiled. She had loved all of them. The faces had changed, but the eyes had stayed the same. And they would still be the same long after she had retired.

Out of the corner of her eye, Andy saw the young womyn with a gear bag thrown over her shoulder leaving the arena.

"Hey rookie!" Andy shouted, remembering her first practice with the JFLs.

"How about goin' for a beer?"

CERISY'S SPHINX

BRENDA BROOKS

I have a photograph of her from that time. She's wearing: her favourite pair of cut-off jeans, a striped shirt, a pair of grey tennis socks (many odysseys removed from their original white) and a pair of grimy sneakers I can still smell. She also wears a braid of fine sweetgrass looped around her wrist. You can't see this in the picture but it's there—I remember because I'd woven it for her earlier that day.

The picture is taken from above, from the branch of a tree just across from the one her swing is tied to. The rest of the kids are down below, all smiles, staring up from the very nifty clubhouse we'd built a few months earlier out of old bits of board and tar-paper salvaged from the dump.

We had a chair too, found abandoned in the woods—a kitchen chair with rusty chrome legs and a ripped, turquoise plastic seat, the stuffing bursting forth like bullrush fluff. Despite its cuts and bruises, we'd found it sitting quietly under a chestnut tree looking oddly civilized, as if a well-spoken person in a torn coat had sat awhile reading from a book with missing pages, then continued on her way.

We kept the chair outside because it took up too much room in the clubhouse and, being the only one, caused a fair amount of division or more accurately, collision, among the members. Most often it was used by Shadow, my family's old black retriever, who would clamber up and observe our meetings through the window.

Shadow's in this picture too, just disappearing at bottom right, looking every bit the reason we named him as we did. But the photograph really belongs to Blue, looking the way I remember her. That's Evelyn "Blue" Winters. She's standing straight up on that swing, having pumped herself and her dusty cutoffs and her sister's second-hand sneakers as close as she could get to that most desirable place, that whispering, blue beguiling place, glittering between the oak leaves above her.

That's just the way her hair flew back in a tangle too, and how her hands gripped the swing's ropes and thrust them apart, as she opened her mouth wide to howl into the camera, her swing reaching the top of its arc—that precise moment when it stopped briefly and then began to fall back again towards the upturned, landed faces below.

I recall her holler and how I thought she would catapult herself right out of that swing from sheer desire and glide off over the trees, over the playing field and the high bush blueberries, over the hollyhocks in her mother's garden, high over the rooftops, past the foothills and disappear like a reckless kite over the forest and snowy mountains never to be seen by any of us, most especially me, again.

That would have struck me in the heart and left a piece of cold, white neon in its place, I'd realized then. Not entirely because I wanted her to stay. No, mostly because I was dying to go with her, my heart already belonging to some distant, dreamy realm at once vivid and obscure. A place about which I knew nothing for certain. A nameless place that pulled and drew me to it from somewhere infinite and shivering and equally nameless within myself.

I never talked to anyone about this place; it seemed to defy dialogue and all usual manner of understanding. I contented myself with receiving fleeting essences of it from my books about wildflowers and fish and planets and trees, as well as in moments spent traipsing through marsh and woods.

Afterwards, in bed at night, I'd bring out my books and flashlight and proceed to give names to the individual essences of that compelling larger thing, whatever it might be: wood nettle, featherfoil, wild pine. Spring peeper, swallowtail, blue-winged teal. Wild hyacinth, owl and otter. Nebula, galaxy, Andromeda.

Or I'd lay and think about plunging to the pond bottom, then looking back up through the duckweed at the liquid green sky, as if through the long, calm eye of a mottled, silent fish.

I'd think about Shadow—his fur spiked and wet from the river, black and shining in the sun like the oiled feathers on the necks of nine crows bathing.

Perhaps I'd touch myself softly and dream about the day just past: climbing the oak's dark branches, Blue flying away on her swing, past the foothills, over the forests and snowy mountains, never to be seen ...

But of course that didn't happen. The swing fell back in its predictable reversing arc and Blue finally came down, emptied of shouts for the time being and somewhat nauseous too. Shadow snorted and lapped her perennially roughed-up knees, his tail doing a wacky, circular sort of metronome. Then, by casting our spell across the doorless doorway, we closed up the clubhouse and all went home, secure and filled with faith in the strength of our own magic.

Unknowing.

Our mothers introduced "Evelyn" and me at her tenth birthday party. They were just getting acquainted themselves, since my family was new in town. One day they would be found murmuring over coffee that perhaps their daughters had a bit too liberating an effect on each other. But that was later.

At the party itself, Evelyn had no influence on me whatsoever. I'd been to a few parties by then, after all I was ten also, and I saw immediately that this was the usual stuff: Pin-the-tail, hotdogs, Kool-Aid, and a mix of ten boys and girls including a kid with a brush cut and horn rims wearing a tiny blue suit I envied—coveted even—from within the itchy confines of my miserable poodle skirt. By this I mean a skirt which, on the off-chance its overall effect wasn't silly enough, had a wretched poodle drawn on the front and a small rhinestone glued approximately where its eye might be.

I had resisted this skirt. I had resisted going to the party. My plan had been to explore my new environment by leaping onto the back of my best imaginary steed and doing a thorough scouting of the neighbourhood, in full western regalia.

My mother assured me throughout my protests that my skirt would be "a hit, a regular conversation piece," and she was right; I spent most of my time at the party smacking other children as a result.

Evelyn's party was in June and it was a hot one. We ate cake with pink icing and drank raspberry Kool-Aid under the linden trees while the lawn sprinklers whirled slowly, sending off lazy snake sounds in the heat.

My mother had brought Shadow to the party and I watched as he panted along behind my little sister, who was steadily eating her way through the hollyhocks in Mrs. Winters' garden. My mother caught her before she started on the petunias, but these weren't her favourites anyway. It was hollyhocks my little sister made a beeline for, drooling all the way—her eyes widening as she tripped toward them, her arms spread, her tiny fingers flexing like famished sea anemones, as if the magic of these flowers was such that it wasn't enough to simply eat them; they needed to be absorbed through the eyes and skin, attended by the whole body whose entire purpose was to open itself wide enough to consume them all—acres, hopefully.

And, once again, my mother found herself exclaiming that she didn't know what to do about this kid, and was there something vital missing from her diet, or what? All the while she apologized to Evelyn's mom for the pathetic stalks with no flowers left standing in the garden—the same way she'd apologized to Mrs. Merwin, another neighbour, the week before.

Up until this point I hadn't thought much about Evelyn. She'd mostly been pestering her mother to let her get into her bathing suit so she could run through the sprinkler and, "Get the show on the road," as she put it. All in all she was doing what I was usually doing just before somebody called me a pain in the butt.

But, as my sister was being chastised for munching the garden and my mother brushed the pollen from her child's chin and tried prying the remaining petals from her clutches (sea anemones turned to venus flytraps), I noticed that Evelyn was taking careful note of these goings-on too.

Although we hadn't spoken to each other yet, she caught my eye and mouthed several words I couldn't make out, though I was to become practiced at interpreting these signals in the future.

I knew chances were good she was saying something rude to me since that's how it sometimes goes when you're new in town and a stranger at the party. Especially if you're a stranger at the party and wearing a ridiculous outfit.

I squinted at her and frowned while weighing the possibility that she hadn't yet noticed the pooch on my skirt, then considered inching it around gradually to the back so it would be planted on my bum where I felt it belonged, if it belonged anywhere.

She mouthed the words again and I resigned myself to having to smack her, birthday girl or not. Just then she got up, plunked herself down next to me, leaned over, cupping her mouth with her hand, and she said:

"Hollyhockburgers and Petunia Pie."

"What?" I said, deciding to attack this head-on.

"Hollyhockburgers and Petunia Pie. That's what must be missing from your little sister's diet, don't you think? I'll ask my mom to make some for her next time she comes. And maybe a drink of milkweed too."

Pause. "Get it?" she smiled cheekily.

"Uh-huh. I get it," I answered, my own substantial cheekiness feeling vaguely stirred and encouraged.

Then, rewinding the band-aid on her finger, she asked if I liked horses (because she did) and remarked that I had on a real nice skirt, looking genuinely sorry I'd had to wear it on her behalf.

Three months later we'd drawn a secret map showing each one of our favourite haunts. Green arrows indicated their exact location and they were labelled MDPs, "most desirable places."

Six months after that we'd changed our names to "Skeezix" and "'Blue," both agreeing that our given names were the most boring and sickly ones that our parents could have dreamed up.

Promises we made: never tell our horses' names. Don't tell any boys about the beaver dam we found. Don't tell anyone else what part of the body we mean when we say the word "nature." Keep a secret that we touch and show each other our "nature" when we sleep over. If one of us moves away, meet the other in twenty-five years at the Moonlite Motel. If one of us dies, the other buries her in the most desirable place, at dusk. Say the same two words, at the exact same time as each other before going to bed every night.

Know each other forever.

The two words were: Cerisy's Sphinx.

Cerisy's Sphinx is a moth whose wings can spread three inches or more. My book showed these wings opened wide and filled with swirls of grey, amber, pink and tawny-brown, then set off by blue eyespots fringed with black. At thirteen I looked at it often and shivered; each time, the unnameable tug of the body.

Looking into its wings I saw the sweet, wet of the woods after rain, the ragged patches of soft moss we touched to our cheeks and lips, the slightest feather fallen from the wing of a sharp-tailed swallow. I saw mountains folding into each other and thunder and night and mist. Waves of rain passed through blue hills, sheer as desire. It spoke the language of my body and I listened eagerly, the way a hungry child listens to the language of red flowers.

During our last summer together, the summer of the swing and snowy mountains, Blue and I tried every night to find the Sphinx. We slept, whenever permitted, in a tent at the foot of her parents' garden and roamed the woods with our flashlights searching the spots we thought most likely. We'd return with pine gum on our fingers and flecks of bark in our hair, and climb into a sleeping bag together. We'd whisper and giggle together at the stickiness of our hands and fall asleep holding each other, intoning the Sphinx's name in hopes that it would find us. Dreaming the beautiful moth under the July moon.

And her neck smelled like the inside of a guitar.

It was August when something suddenly happened. Even now this is the only way I can think to say it: something happened. I suppose this is because that's the first thing my mother said when she came to my room early on a Sunday morning, before I was beginning to waken.

She came strangely and carefully, like someone bearing the most delicate thing in a small box, something struggling softly to be released. When I sat up in bed rubbing my eyes, she looked as if to place it next to me and quietly remove the lid to reveal what was inside.

"Something's happened," she said. And then, "Blue is .... " She stopped.

"Her mother and father have been looking all night. And the police. They found her this morning ... in the playing field."

She put her arms around me.

"Someone took her, stole her away, you see? And then they left her there."

She told me all she could bear to tell me right then and tucked the blankets around my shoulders, then she sat beside me, sometimes looking off to wherever the delicate thing in the box had flown.

I slept again, my dreams full, as they would be for some time, of Blue. Blue on a breaking swing, falling through the dark oak branches, her body shattered on the ground beneath me. My arms outstretched. Empty.

Shortly afterwards I started stealing things and hiding them away. Small items from department and grocery stores when I went shopping with my mother or friends: a green candle, two ballpoint pens, a button from a coat hanging on a rack in Eaton's, a handkerchief with blue embroidery along one edge.

At home I took things from the kitchen and hid them in my room. Cutlery, food, a cup and dish. I still wandered the forest and marsh, but now with the sole idea of finding the Sphinx. It seemed more important than ever to find it since I was convinced that was what Blue had been doing when something else, something dark that we hadn't suspected, hadn't measured the right magic for, had found her.

For awhile, though I looked the same, I lived as if alone in my parent's house—a furtive, thieving, thirteen-year-old insomniac with a piece of cold, white neon in her heart.

The next winter we moved away.

My mother tells a story about me, and shows a picture taken the winter I turned fourteen, just before we moved.

The way she explains it, I got up early one morning in February, put on my jacket, toque and mitts and headed for the park, which was deep and fresh from an overnight snowfall.

There I engaged (she tells the "friend" who sometimes visits home with me) in the energetic and purposeful task of making snow figures—"angels" she calls them—the impression you leave after falling backwards into the snow and then fanning your legs and arms.

She says I made dozens of them and some of the neighbours even came out and took pictures, they found it such an interesting sight, as if all the angels in heaven had fallen to earth at once, and they'd chosen our park to do it in.

It's always at this point that my mother asks me what could have gotten into my head to do that. It's become somewhat of a rhetorical question finally, since whenever she asks I pretend I can't remember.

But I do. I remember making twenty-five figures altogether, and that in my mind they weren't angels at all.

Maybe one of these times when my mother asks I'll find some words to tell her—about the swing and the most desirable place, about dusk and the

Moonlite Motel, about namelessness and knowing something forever. I'll tell her about the undeniable tug; about Blue and how I loved her.

"Cerisy's Sphinx," I hollered (just as Blue had, from her swing) and leapt up from the snowy field, from my flock of illusive, fluttering moths, and galloped off into the distant trees, my heart filled with moss and feather and mountains folding into each other.

TULIPS

LUANNE ARMSTRONG

I wasn't sure. It seemed an odd, bold step, buying her flowers, but what else—looking back from now—could I have done? I bought her red tulips. It was April. We'd had a conversation one day about flowers because she was taking a series of photographs of them, and that gave me the idea. Somehow, it seemed to make it more casual. I clenched my teeth against my own long resolve not to take this step, decided this could be seen, after all, as an ordinary thing to do, stepped into the florist's one day and bought them.

When I went by her house later, she wasn't there. She seldom was, even when she said she'd be. It was part of her charm. Unexpected. Ostensibly, we were friends. We had some things in common. But I was married, and she, what was she ... poet; woman who carried her loneliness around with her like a shield and wrote poetry I read as though it held some clue to my own existence.

I remember now—coming home that afternoon, the day I bought the tulips, and looking out of the window in my study, in the house I had helped build. I looked out my window at the yard and the kids' toys and the things we owned and had built, and suddenly, like a toy castle made out of straws, watched what I thought I was and what I knew—crumble.

I never meant this to happen. I said it out loud. I don't want this, I said, and knew it was a lie. What shall I do, I said to the silence. I was waiting, as always, for the kids to come up the driveway from the schoolbus. I watched for them every day. If they were five minutes late, I let thoughts of disaster, bus crashes, kidnappings, seep in. But nothing ever happened. They were safe. We were safe. When they came in the door, I met them with cookies and tea and questions about their day. They met me with secure indifference. After they had fled into TV, their rooms, and various stereo noises, I went outside. Usually, this was my time to garden, do yard work, go for a walk before making dinner. But today, there was nothing I wanted to do. I sat and stared at my tulips, which had recently pushed their arrogant and stubby selves through the ground. I stared at them because I knew I was afraid. I was blind and afraid. I didn't want to know this was happening. But I wanted to see her. I wanted to put my hand on her shoulder, around her shoulder. I wanted her to see me, and be glad.

I hunched over, sitting in the garden, crossing my arms around myself, sealing it in. I would have died of pure anger and frustration before I would have willingly said a word to her. Unasked. She wouldn't want to know, I thought. But I wanted to. That was what I couldn't help and couldn't stop.

The day I bought the tulips ... I spent part of it sitting in a restaurant with friends, having lunch, gossiping, in mutual and shared comradeship. Spring. Our talk was of gardens and children and work and houses. It was an ordinary thing to do, on an ordinary day in a small town. What could I have begun to say to them about why I kept shifting in my seat, unable to keep still, concentrating fiercely in order to breathe or move or think a coherent thought? I don't know what they knew. I don't even know what I knew. Except I couldn't breathe. And everytime I thought about what I was going to do—such a simple move, buy her tulips, go by her house, maybe we could have dinner—I almost doubled over.

So I bought the tulips ... I left the other two women in the restaurant, and went and wandered down the street, irrationally happy. The streets were dry and warm at last, and people smiled and said hello to one another in the spring sun. I didn't know any longer what I was doing, or why—had lost my fight for coherence, left it in the restaurant with the ordinary day. I was happier than I'd ever been. I didn't care what came next. I stood and looked in the window of the florist shop for a long time, alternating between absurd terror and absurd happiness, and I knew. And I went in and bought her red tulips anyway, walked across a line that I had not known existed until a few weeks before.

Two weeks before, we had sat up half the night together, drinking and playing ... we had both been reading poetry at a conference together, and then we sat with our friends, smoking and drinking and telling wilder and altogether more ridiculous stories, and I don't know what happened. I will never understand it. No one does, I suppose ... I went to my room and lay with my face pressed into my pillow, staring into darkness. I cried, for drunkenness, for silliness, because I had nowhere to go and nothing to say to anyone about her.

Tulips ... they were one of my favourite flowers. I used to plant tulip bulbs all around my house, loving their arrogant spiky flowers, asserting their brilliant reds and yellows against spring ... but I never stopped to think, didn't know why I loved them. Something about the way the petals curved around a central cup, something about those smooth dark rounded interiors, something about the way they nodded and hung on their long slender stems.

So, I bought them, not just one bunch, but four bunches, a mass of tulips, more than I could afford. Red tulips. I took them to her house, and went in and put them in a vase that I found and left them on the table, and went back and moved them to a corner where they wouldn't be so conspicuous, and left a note and went back and ripped it up, and left again.

And sat in the car, a foolishly sane, middle-aged, married woman. And gritted my teeth, holding it like a heavy child, this new feeling which felt similar to terror, similar to fear, but wasn't any of those, which followed me around all day and all night, which sent me to sleep thinking of her, and had me waking thinking of her ... and what was I thinking ... of touching her, of holding her, kissing her chastely on the forehead ... I didn't get much farther than that. Of taking her places, buying her things, serving her, taking care ... crossing a line, buying her tulips, unable to wake from it or think straight, but knowing ... gone over, gone somewhere I couldn't retreat from, though it ripped my life from one end to another. Drunk on it. Dizzy on it. On her.

CLOSET SPACE

PAT WOODS

Sometimes I leave the top button of my jeans undone. It makes it easier to breathe.

A guy at work asks me to go out with him. I don't want to. He's been bugging me for three weeks, and I tell my mother about it when she calls me.

"Why don't you go out with him?" she asks. "How do you expect to find a husband if you don't go out with guys that are interested in you? You're no beauty, you know. You can't afford to be so picky."

"Yes, Mother," I say.

I notice there's a new woman in accounting, but I go out with the guy from purchasing. We go to dinner at a seafood place, then catch a movie I've already seen. After the movie, he comes back to "my place," as he calls it, and wants to have sex. He loves me—my mother always said they should—so we have sex.

I imagine he's the woman from accounting. She touches my forehead with her thumbs and smooths out the wrinkles that gather there during the day. Later, she pushes the hair out of my eyes and kisses them shut. When I open them, she's gone. He lies on top of me, sweat running down the sides of his face.

"What are you smiling about?" he says, sounding like he's out of breath.

"I love you," I say to the woman. He smiles at this and rolls off me but doesn't say anything.

"I love you, too," says the woman. She comes out of the closet where she's been hiding and runs out the door. I try to go after her, but his arm is lying across my chest.

Back at work, I apply for a transfer to the accounting department. The application comes back, rejected.

"There are no openings at this time," it says. I suppose the one in my heart doesn't count. I put the rejection in the top drawer of my desk. Nobody else is in the office, so I undo the top button of my jeans.

At home, Janis Joplin screams from the stereo as I lie on the bed eating chocolate-covered cherries. I undo my jeans the rest of the way, and the woman from accounting comes in. She stands in the doorway in jeans, sings along with Janis and eats a cherry. The cream drips out, and she catches it with her tongue as it moves down her chin. When I wake, she is smiling. So am I. She doesn't ask why I'm smiling. The woman from accounting knows.

My phone rings, and she runs out the door like Cinderella at the stroke of midnight. It's the man from purchasing.

"Hi," he says, expecting me to know who he is.

"Who is this?" I say, wanting to punish him for chasing the woman away.

"It's me," he says, but doesn't sound as sure as when he first said "Hi."

"I know." I feel a little better. "What's up?"

"Are we still on for Friday?" he asks.

I call my mother and tell her again about this man from purchasing.

"Did you sleep with him?" she says.

"Yes, Mother," I tell her. "He loves me."

"Did he tell you that?" she asks.

"No, not really. But he was going to. He fell asleep before he got the chance."

"Well, if he asks you again, you'd better go out with him. You're not getting any younger, you know."

"Yes, Mother," I say.

We go out once a week. Usually on Friday or Saturday, and we always have sex. When we go to "his place," the woman doesn't show. I think the dirty dishes in his sink and the squeaking of his bed frighten her. Once, I did the dishes before we had sex, thinking that maybe she would reconsider.

"Don't do those on my account," he said.

Back at work, I re-apply for a position in accounting. It comes back again, but this time someone has scribbled a note on the bottom.

"Try purchasing. They have an opening right now."

I tear it up, throw it in the wastebasket and undo the top button of my jeans.

In the fall the company has its dress-up cocktail party. Jeans are not encouraged, so I don't want to go.

"If he wants to take you," my mother tells me, "let him take you. It sounds to me like he's getting serious. You can't spend the rest of your life in blue jeans."

"Yes, Mother," I say.

At the party I look for the woman from accounting, but I know she won't show. I don't think she'll trade in her jeans as easily as I do. We go to "my place" and I take off my dress and put on jeans. He laughs at this. The woman is there, but she runs to the closet to escape the grunts of the man from purchasing.

"I need you," I call out to her. The man moves faster, his grunts turn to snorts, then he's finished.

He looks at me, sweat dripping from his chin, and says, "I know."

One of the drops of sweat falls in my eye. I blink and see the woman standing half in, half out of the closet. She steps out and heads for the door.

"Don't go," I cry, tears mixing with sweat at the corner of my eye.

"I won't," he says. He wraps his arms tighter around me, and I can't go after the woman. I wait until his mouth falls open and the drool hits the pillow; then I slip out from under his arm, get out of bed and put on my jeans. They feel like they're getting tighter.

"He wants to get married," I tell my mother when she calls.

"I'll be damned," she says. "I didn't think you had it in you. What do you need me to do?"

"But Mother," I say, "I'm not sure I love him. In fact, I really don't like him much."

"That's normal," she says. "You're not going to find a Prince Charming. You're no princess yourself, you know."

"Yes, Mother," I say.

The date is set. He wants to do it in three months; I ask for two years. We compromise—I much more than he. We will be married in six months. I wonder if I should invite the woman from accounting. She can't be pleased with me, but Mother is.

Now that we're engaged, he brings his things to my place. At first it is just an extra pair of socks, a tie left forgotten on the back of a chair. Soon, it becomes entire outfits. Suits, shirts, ties, even the socks match. My jeans are being pushed to the back of the closet.

"Why don't you wear that skirt I've seen in there," he'll say. "You've got great legs, you ought to show them off."

"They're great," I tell him, "because I don't."

Mother calls even more frequently than before.

"Is it still on?" she asks me.

"Is what on, Mother?" I say innocently. I hope it drives her as crazy as it does me.

"Don't get smart with me, young lady. You haven't told your father, have you?"

"I haven't even told the woman in accounting," I say.

"Who?" my mother says.

Dishes are beginning to pile up in the sink. I don't have the energy to do them most of the time. It keeps the woman away, but I'm ashamed to have her see me like this. The wrinkles in my face are back, after she worked so hard to remove them. He finds my chocolate-covered cherries and eats them all while watching the football game. Led Zeppelin replaces Janis Joplin on the stereo, and I realize Janis wasn't screaming. Now I do most of the screaming, but most of it's inside my head.

At work, I apply for a position in accounting, and the application comes back with a note.

"We'll be happy to have you in our department. A position has been opened due to the resignation of one of our employees."

I start in two weeks, and my dreams dissolve into nightmares on my first day. My woman is gone. I have been selected to take her place.

We go to dinner at a Vietnamese restaurant. On the way to the car, we pass by two women walking towards a tiny bar on the corner. There's no sign out front. The women are holding hands. I stare after them, wondering if they might know where my woman is. He pulls on my hand to hurry me along. The women pause outside the bar and kiss, and I hear him snicker beside me.

"That's disgusting," he says.

"Oh, I don't know," I say, as I pull my hand from his, undo the top button of my jeans and follow a few steps behind him down the well-lighted street.

I glance back to the bar, but the women are no longer outside.

"They both had jeans on," I say. "Did you notice?"

"Who?" He turns to see why I'm walking behind him. "Hurry up, we can cross at the light."

The following weekend I tell him I have to go visit my sister across town, so I can't make dinner at home.

"I didn't know you had a sister," he says.

"I must have forgotten to mention her."

"What's her name?"

"Who?" I hurry to get my jeans on, making sure to leave the top button undone.

"Your sister," he says.

"You'll have to meet her someday," I say as I run out the door. I hear him saying "wait a minute," but slam the door so he thinks I can't hear.

I stand across the street from the bar watching women going in and coming out. It's hard to tell if any of them is my woman, but I know if I wait she'll show. I wonder what I should say to her when she comes. After a while, I decide to cross against the light and stand at the entrance where I can see better.

"Coming in?" someone behind me says.

"I don't know," I say, turning around to face the voice. "I'm looking for a woman."

"Well, you're in the right place. I have a feeling there just might be some women in this bar."

"No," I explain. "I'm looking for a certain woman."

"Aren't we all?" she says. "Come on in. I'll buy you a drink."

"I'm not really thirsty," I tell her.

"From where I'm standing," she says to me as she stands half in, half out of the door, "you look like you could use a drink."

She smiles and goes into the bar. I watch the door close slowly behind her, then reach for the handle to go inside.

CIRCLE DANCE

GABRIELLA GOLIGER

I'm supposed to be writing an editorial. A rousing editorial. A rousing editorial on lesbian community for the fourth anniversary issue of *Lavender News*.

Over at our cubbyhole of an office on the third floor of the Women's Centre, Martha is waiting for my piece so that she can finish off page two and send it to the typesetter. She's peering over her glasses at the cunning blank space she's constructed on the computer screen, humming a Rita MacNeil tune as she works. A twelve-hundred-word space surrounded by neat eleven-and-a-half-pica columns—letters to the editor, announcements, continuations from page one.

Or maybe she's taking a break, leaning back in the wobbly swivel chair to stretch her long, supple limbs. Hands clasped behind her head, one bare foot tucked under her bum, the other resting on an open drawer. The chair squeaks and rattles but she doesn't lose her balance, not for one moment. Her jacket, sneakers and balled-up socks are in a corner on the floor. "Buildings out here are overheated," she says. I see her finely-sculpted feet. Beige sandstone colour with deltas of blue veins. High arches that accentuate the separate spheres—ball of foot, heel, instep.

Any minute now she's likely to pick up the phone and dial my number. And I will have to say, "Just a few more hours." I, who pride myself on sticking to deadlines and who's never at a loss for a cool twelve-hundred words. Normally.

And she will say, "Hey, community was your idea for a theme."

So it was. Until last Friday it seemed like a simple, straightforward theme that would eat up a minimum of my after-work hours, make this month a little easier.

"Jesus Murphy! Don't tell me you've lost your faith because of this one silly incident," she'll say. "Try waking up one morning with your lover gone, your dole run out, your cat pregnant, your head feeling like a peeled grape between steel jaws ... "

No, she wouldn't want me to try it. And no, I haven't lost faith. Of course not. If I can put on a reasonably straight face (just enough make-up to pass) in the morning and put in a good day at the college it's because of the protective halo of community which is made up of ... (think of something).

One foot in Reeboks, the other in pumps and pantyhose. Part-time lesbian. But most of us are. Yvonne would say that's the problem. That's why we're always at the edge of burnout and *The Lav* is forever on the brink of collapse. Yvonne, at least, is out there on the progressive edge with her work at the sexual assault centre. Officially, it's twenty hours a week, but who's counting? Not Yvonne. Steady grey eyes with a slow burn behind them. Quiet voice that catches slightly when gusts of anger blow through. Undaunted by the "what you girls need" taunts and the grant that runs out at the end of the month.

But I do my bit too. I've put in hours for *The Lav*, how many hours this month alone? And too many of them at last night's meeting. Martha would say it's my own fault since I'm the one who made an issue of this business with my niggling doubts and wanting to be absolutely sure we were doing the right thing.

Community has always been the drumbeat of my articles. The answer to misogyny, homophobia, isolation, the parents who don't know, the parents who turfed you out, the parents who are okay as long as you and your lover don't touch in front of them. The answer, too, to our own divisive issues— monogamy versus non-monogamy, separatism versus working with the boys—issues that I like to tackle in calm, reasoned prose. Wherever you stand, there is middle ground and it's called community. Pull together. Build alliances. Remember the real enemies.

We have a good issue lined up, really. Yvonne's article on francophone dykes, the analysis of racism by the student in Montreal. Cartoons and poetry for balance. No one will miss "Ann Lavender." Though Martha can't see why we have to drop the column completely. My suggestion. My effort at compromise. If we can't deal with every letter, maybe we shouldn't deal with any. After all, it was supposed to be a light, almost tongue-in-cheek feature. An antidote to all the heavy political stuff and a way of reaching out to the unconnected women in the suburbs. The worst that could happen, we thought, was that no one would write in and we'd have to make up the letters ourselves.

Of course, it's not so simple. Community. Slippery, ephemeral. It "come together and it come apart," as the Ferron song goes. Still, it comes together. One moment, you're alone at the table with the ashtrays, the plastic beer glasses, the balloon that drifted down from the ceiling, watching the backs of couples on the dance floor, or a few women like Yvonne who whirl to their own rhythms. Next moment, the circle dance. Grip the hands of the women beside you, feel the tug of the human chain in your armpits, kick your feet with a hundred sisterly feet, whoop with a hundred voices and hear the echoes of thousands upon thousands crying yestogether, dykestogether, yes. From the Michigan Women's Music Festival to the Amsterdam Feminist

Book Fair to the underground clubs in Rio to the women's night in St. John's. From the Black lesbian alliance to the Asian lesbian alliance, the Native lesbian alliance, the Jewish lesbian alliance, the dykes with disabilities alliance. Who built these lifelines from sister to sister out of naked courage and despite millennia-long legacies of fear, hatred, guilt and invisibility? We did! We did! Who's that woman on the front lines, the picket line, the counselling line, the assembly line, the welfare line? Dykesister, dykesister, dykesister. (Good. Save to disk.)

~

Who built these lifelines, despite backbiting and infighting and discussions until after midnight in the overheated lounge of the Women's Centre? Despite too much coffee and stale Oreos that some other group left behind? (How could they? Doesn't Overeaters Anonymous meet in here?) "Despite picking at the foam in the torn couch-cushion," you want to say (but you're afraid to say because Yvonne's soft, urgent voice presses in talking about the images everywhere reminding women of their pain, about the need for safe space in our own community for those who are hurt and vulnerable). And then there are the discussions until after midnight about the letter (Crafty? Innocent? Deranged? Normal?) to "Ann Lavender" that came in Friday's mail signed "Confused," with just a postal box return address. Martha would have tossed it into the garbage after a quick first read. "Good grief, listen to this! Don't people have better things to do?" she said.

And I said, "But Martha, shouldn't the collective ... I mean, shouldn't we discuss ... ?"

And she said "Oh, Liz!" A hoax, she called it. Just some guy trying to get a rise out of us. A transsexual, maybe, Yvonne said later. In any case, beyond our mandate. Gentle words compared to what the others had to say. Male-identified. Self-oppressed. Mind-fucked.

I see Martha bent over the light table while she slices out superfluous lines with her Exacto knife. Twiddling her toes—long, flexible, expressive toes—as she works. Solid as granite despite the flotsam and jetsam of her past life. To have left Sydney in an ancient Honda with just her bags, cat and two-year sobriety medallion in the shirt pocket next to her heart. No job or contacts in Ottawa. Plenty to do for now just working the twelve steps, she said. Easy does it. One day at a time. She still had some savings. Oh lucky *Lavender News*! What a blessing that she came to the meeting six months ago, when we were going through one of our fragile periods, what with Marie having lost her sitter and Bev having moved to the States. Not that Martha doesn't drive me crazy sometimes. This business of sticking in *Big Book* quotations as fillers without a by-your-leave to anyone! If AA weren't riddled with sexism .... But that's another issue entirely.

She leaned forward, elbows on the table, and poured enthusiasm back into us from her glowing eyes. "I can do anything except write," she said. "Do you need someone to do layout? I once worked for a newspaper up North." Did we need someone for layout! The meeting over, she clasped each of us in her soon-to-be-famous bear hugs, and I felt the fine, sharp bones of her shoulder blades and smelled the sweet, woodsy scent of Bay Willow Body Oil for the first time. Great stuff for deadline-night massages. I could use her strong hands right now, as a matter of fact, to pummel my vertebrae back into shape. In return, I'd give her the best foot massage ever, working my thumbs around contours, into crevices, while she'd lie with eyes closed and utter contented grunts.

If she and I were lovers, I would run my fingers along sole, arch, instep, press my lips against the toe pads, each such a round, soft, perfect morsel. (Remember to erase.)

The point is, Martha is doing more than her share back at the office, keying in the pile of last-minute copy, while I sit here with that stupid letter at my elbow. Martha would say, "Why on earth did you take it home? We've made our decision." Because I needed to torment myself with it one more time, that's why. "Accept the things you can't change," she'd say.

Hey, here's an idea. We could just recycle that graphic of arms hugging the globe. Fill the whole editorial space with it. With a caption of course. I think it's on the bottom shelf in that pile of stuff left over from the International Women's Week issue. Yvonne would be annoyed but would forgive me, and what do we need another editorial for, anyway? We (I)'ve said it all before.

The letter is handwritten in neat, round (childlike? fearless?) characters. Here's what it would look like in the harsh anonymity of print:

> Dear Ann Lavender,
>
> I've been living with my lover for about two years now. We love each other a lot and have a good relationship. Everything is fine. I have an unusual fantasy, though, which I've never told anyone about. I dream I'm a man with a cock, fucking different women. Sometimes I can't come with my lover unless I imagine this cock and how it feels, sliding in and out, pushing deep into her cunt. I'm not butch. I don't wish I was a man. But maybe I do. What do you think? Does anyone else have this kind of fantasy?
>
> Yours,
>
> Confused

We are right! We are right not to print it. Oh, talk about stereotypes! Someone's bad Freudian dream. Ammunition for our enemies who crow "penis envy" when two women so much as smile at each other. And the hell that would break loose in the community! Last night's meeting repeated and amplified through the bars, the street corners, the kitchens for months, sapping precious energy, creating divisions. After all, even the word "fuck" is still problematic, still raises hackles because of male/violence associations. The outrage from women who are sick of dick worship. The accusations that we've let ourselves be duped, even if we could trace "Confused," drag her out of the shadows (supposing it's a "she"), produce her as evidence that the letter was genuine (if it is). Because, as Yvonne says, could someone who's so fixated on pricks really be a lesbian? None of us are pure ... but do we have to print every bit of writhing that some people go through to shed their conditioning and get comfortable with their sexual identity? And even if we printed a loving, sisterly answer to "Confused," reassured her that people have all kinds of fantasies and added a list of feminist counsellors, would she not have to endure the debate, the jokes, the expressions of disgust at dances, in bars? So what good would it do her? Better for her to receive no answer, to learn that the column was dropped, to draw her own conclusions which would be ... ?

Enough. Had enough. (See how these dumb issues drain us?) Forget about editorial. Too late. Graphic of arms hugging globe will do fine. Go over to office. Need to see Martha. Need to flop my head on her knees, let her work away the knots in my neck and shoulders with knowing fingers. I will kneel on the carpet. She will lean forward in her chair, balancing on the balls of her feet so that, glancing down, I'll be able to gaze at them to my heart's content without her noticing. If she and I were lovers, I would run my fingertips against the sensitive skin of the arches, suck each toe and slip my tongue between them to find the most exquisitely ticklish spots. I would press her big toe hard into my cunt, slide it in and out...

For the longest time now women's feet have turned me on. (Remember to erase.)

DARLENE

FRANCES ROONEY

"Have you ever slept with a woman?" Darlene asked.

"No, but it's coming." Claire's response surprised even herself.

Claire had finally managed to get her husband to leave, and she was flat, stinking broke. Darlene had answered feelers she'd put out for a roommate. Claire hadn't warmed to Dar, at first or since, but had heard from friends that she was many of the things a roommate needed to be: honest, quiet, good-natured, and, if not affluent, on time paying her bills. And she had been available—immediately. So here they were and had been for ten quiet, honest, good-natured, rent-paid months. But if Darlene wasn't going to run off with the wedding present silver, she was never going to be much fun, either.

She was, though, interesting in several ways. The child of poor prairie farmers, the youngest of five girls, she was the only homely one, and the only blind one. She could see to get around and, somehow, could read as long as the book was virtually rubbing against the end of her nose. But she was legally blind, and so close to totally blind that in familiar surroundings she frequently didn't bother to exert the effort to see, just closed her eyes and navigated using her other senses. The first thing she'd done when she'd moved in was rearrange the cupboards so that she'd be able to find things by memory rather than just by sight.

Claire found it unnerving at first to live with someone who tore around the apartment with her eyes closed and who bumped into fewer things than Claire did herself. It annoyed her that Darlene just assumed that she had the right to reorganize the kitchen, especially since Claire had it beautifully and left-handedly set up, an organization that tumbled before Darlene's right-handedness, but Claire didn't feel that she could legitimately complain. The other thing that bothered Claire, and yet was rather funny at the same time, was that Darlene was forever tripping over Sam, the cat. It happened only in the kitchen, and that because Sam was the same colour as the floor, but he took a couple of nasty kicks before he figured out that the kitchen was not a healthy place to be. When Claire moved his dish into the hall by the back door, life settled down to an ordinary routine.

Being homely and blind and the youngest had turned out to be a deadly combination for Darlene. When she was ten, her father had pulled her out of school and sent her to work as a maid/cook/general slave to a family down the road. When she ran away and tried to go home, he told her, with no thought for anybody's finer feelings, that he wasn't going to have no ugly blind kid—probably a bastard cuz all his kids were beauties, which she'd be able to see if she could see anydamnthing—in his house. He beat her silly, then beat her mother silly for trying to intervene, then dragged her back to her employers. They beat her a bit, too, fed her bread and water for two weeks, until she lost enough strength to interfere with her work, then relented. She stayed with them until she was nineteen.

It takes a lot of nerve for someone who lives in a world of blurred shadows and who thinks she's criminally ugly to walk away from her home of nine years with just the clothes on her back and hike to Edmonton, one-hundred-and-fifty miles away. But that's what she did. Her mother had become sick and Darlene went to visit. Her mother had thought she was dying. She wasn't, as it turns out, but she thought she was. She had never been any protection for Darlene, but she was the one person the kid had ever loved and been loved by. And now she told Darlene that she was dying and to get the hell away from there. She told Dar to take the grocery money, and she told her that she'd heard about a group of people who help blind people. Maybe Darlene could find them in the city.

So Darlene just kept walking. She didn't learn that her mother hadn't died then until eight years later when her father showed up on her doorstep, two weeks after the funeral. He was there to be taken care of—to have her do the things a woman does for a man, owes to a father. He was the reason she didn't want to live alone anymore.

It took her five days to get to Edmonton, and she arrived hot and sweaty and covered with prairie dust. But she got there in one piece. She told Claire that she guessed she was too ugly to rape. Or she was until that nice mobility instructor's friend decided differently, but that, as she told it, was another story.

The first place she went to was a truck stop on the edge of the city. She ordered coffee. Bacon and eggs arrived with it. The waitress said she looked as if she needed it. So she ate it, and because her system wasn't used to food and had never had so much at one time, she threw it all up. The waitress took her home with her, and made some phone calls, and that was how Darlene made contact with welfare and, eventually, with the Canadian National Institute for the Blind. She still wrote to the waitress.

Her social worker did an assessment of her, which meant that after a twenty-minute interview she wrote four pages about Darlene's personality, experience, and chances in life. The assessment said that Dar wasn't very bright and could hope for little more than to be self-supporting in a less-than-adequate sort of way—she could work as a housekeeper or a waitress in the kind of place she'd walked into her first day in Edmonton, not in a better place because of her looks. It recommended charm and grooming classes. So Dar spent almost an hour each morning for the next four years with her nose against the mirror trying to get mascara and lipstick on straight, and working as a housekeeper for one of the higher-ups at the CNIB.

Eventually that social worker left. Her replacement talked to Dar for another twenty minutes, decided she was close to brilliant, and that she had to go to university.

"I couldn't believe it. University. Me. I could be a social worker. I'd barely got through grade five. But she said that didn't matter, that I had the brains and was going to do it. She was particularly determined because it would be terrific for her career if I made it. I didn't mind being a guinea pig, university looked like heaven on earth to me, so I did everything she told me to."

Mobility training was the first step, and she learned, among other things, to use a white cane. She liked that, and did use one for a time—it made navigating easier—but mostly it told the world something about her that would never have been known otherwise. And she liked being identified as herself, as blind and getting along, rather than as just ugly and stupid. She gave up the cane after a while, though. People kept bumping into her—as if she were invisible and they couldn't see her, not the other way around. The cane seemed to give people licence to ignore her very presence on earth. Then one night she was hit by a car, crawled to the side of the road, and spent the night lying between two parked cars. Fortunately, it was July. If it had been January, she would have frozen to death. That was the end of the cane.

She was trained as a mobility instructor, too, which at least once meant taking a newly blind man to the top of a building and telling him, "So you're suicidal because you're blind. So jump." And then walking down the five flights of stairs and into the street with the sobbing man. What would she have done if he'd jumped?

The next step was to get her a part-time job at the CNIB booth and enrol her full-time at university. For some reason that also meant moving to Vancouver. So suddenly, after having received only five sporadic years of schooling ever in her life, and fourteen years away from books (except for the mobility readings), there she was in a new city. She didn't even know the bus routes, she lived in a damp basement room which was the best her living allowance would afford, she worked at a job where she knew nobody, she was enrolled in five courses, some of whose titles she didn't even understand, and her social worker was on a plane headed the other way, after she'd exhorted Darlene to succeed because if she did other blind kids would be given this chance and if she didn't they would all be condemned, and so would Darlene, to live lives of cleaning houses they couldn't see. Claire thought the social worker might have done the whole thing a little more humanely. Darlene considered the woman second only to God.

By the time Darlene moved in with Claire, she had two semesters to go for her B.A. The first year she'd spent in shock and near-catatonia, but then she got the hang of university and took off. She worked like a fiend, and was constantly in what looked like pretty severe back-and-neck pain from bending over her books and weaving back and forth between her books and notes, only some of which were in Braille.

Darlene had always been lonely, and thought she was used to it, but this was worse. Not only was she on her own, she was in a world where she'd never belong, a world where kids thought that no date on Saturday night was a problem. The polite awkwardness was awful, too, it was much worse than the abuse she was used to, abuse that was at least out in front of her and obvious and tangible, not the kind that denied its own existence and implied that her awareness of it showed that there was something wrong with her.

The only place she felt at home was the CNIB booth where she sold tobacco and magazines. And she was only there a few hours a week, with Willy, who, as well as being blind, was developmentally disabled. Much as she hated to admit it to herself, it made her feel better not only to be with someone with whom she could relax, but to be with somebody who belonged to this rarefied world even less than she did, who was even more disadvantaged than she was. She consoled herself by telling herself that he didn't even know he didn't belong, that he would have been his cheerful self anywhere, even though she knew that this was only partly true. She'd seen him clench his fist and growl after a retreating couple of pipe-smoking faculty who, though he didn't know it, patronized and condescended to everybody, not just him. She'd tried to tell him that, and he'd accepted what she said. But it didn't change the fact that he bridled at being treated as something less than human.

When Willy wasn't enough, when her deepened and broadened loneliness got to be too much, she went to the health service on campus and got valium. She hated taking it and never thought of it as anything more than a temporary and far-from-satisfactory solution, but she didn't have time for the therapy the doctor had recommended, that would have given her the courage to look for friends. She was using all her considerable courage to keep going. There were worse things than a mild drug crutch.

The two things that seemed inconsistent with all this, and that fascinated Claire, were Darlene's periodic trips to the Isle of Skye and then, a couple of weeks ago, this question about sleeping with women. "Periodic" was the wrong word for those trips—they were frequent. Every three months, for three weeks, like clockwork. And as Claire was coming to realize, it wasn't Darlene's question that was so perplexing, it was the answer—true, but until that moment, unrecognized—that had fallen out of her own mouth and heart and mind.

Claire sat in bed thinking about the trips and now the question. As had become more or less the habit, the door between the two bedrooms was open, and because the beds were on opposite walls and in a direct line of vision, she and Darlene had a clear view of each other. As had been happening more and more lately, Darlene was nude, sitting with the blankets gathered around her waist. Claire tried, yet again, not to notice that Darlene had the most beautiful breasts she had ever seen—they rose from a compact, smooth, wonderfully olive-skinned, slightly vulnerable and very inviting body.

Claire admitted to herself that the question made sense, that it had come as such a surprise not because the pieces of the puzzles that were herself and Darlene didn't fit together, but because she had been carefully not putting them together.

The last time that Darlene had gone to Skye, a letter had arrived from there the day after she'd left. She was planning to stay a few days in Montreal, and had asked Claire to phone if anything serious happened. She had also asked Claire to open any mail that looked important. So, with no more than casual interest, she told herself, Claire had opened the letter. Casual interest in a letter just like the pile of letters in Dar's sock drawer. Claire wasn't quite sure why she had to convince herself that her interest was casual, why the letters intrigued her so. Maybe it was the change in Darlene's complexion when she finished reading one. Maybe, Claire told herself, she imagined that change.

She knew she should stop reading when she got as far as "My dearest little Dar, I can hardly believe that in a week I'll be holding you, that we'll be lying out under the stars, leaning against our packs, making love to each other and the flowers."

So it was a love letter. Everybody gets love letters. She'd known it would be a love letter. She wasn't even very surprised that it was from a woman, somebody called Jenny. So why was it so important to her? Why was it so special? Why did it make her feel so good?

Had Darlene turned to women because she still considered herself too ugly for men? As she asked herself the question, Claire knew the answer. Now she knew the rest of the question, too, the part about herself: does the fact that I'm attractive to men protect me from being one of those? No, it doesn't, and I don't want it to. I don't want to be protected from what I've always wanted. I don't want to be attractive to men. And I don't want to pretend anymore.

Her mind jumped from one memory to another. The dream she'd had about Helen Henderson, her university roommate. They'd been standing in the lobby of the residence, their breasts pressed softly together, electricity running through them. Perfect peace and happiness. She'd had the dream many times since, usually when she was tired and discouraged, when she'd needed energy and courage and respite from the conflicts of her marriage.

The days she'd spent in the stacks of the university library in the section about sexual deviants. There wasn't much about lesbians, so she'd read everything she could find about both lesbians and homosexual men. Most of it talked of treatment and disease. None of the case studies had seemed very pathological to her. They'd been stories of people loving each other in a way that often made her feel warm and good inside, that sometimes tore her heart with their tragedies of suffering and self-hate. One day she'd met Fred Lamont there. She'd dated Fred and had always had fun: he'd never made a pass at her, and she'd felt safe to do things with him like go to the cemetery and make angels in the snow. They'd looked at each other and both turned the other way. They'd not gone out together again. She'd hardly seen him for the rest of her time there.

Her husband looming over her in bed, snarling, "You should sleep with women, then you could be the boss." His astonishment that she hadn't been insulted. Her laughing in his face. Her saying to him that he had it all wrong, that if she slept with women there wouldn't be a boss. The warm, calming feeling it had given her to think that.

Crushes on her teachers: her French teacher in grade nine; Miss Sullivan, the high school gym teacher whom only a few of the girls liked—she was too tough and sharp for most of them; Miss Kennedy, who hated the boys and liked the girls and made no secret of it, who was miserable until she went to teach at a women's college, and then was practically unrecognizable, so great was the change in her face and body.

Claire's biggest question about Dar's trips was where the money came from. She'd asked her several times, thinking that maybe if somebody on Dar's income could travel, she too might be able to travel, someday. Dar had a scholarship, but she was also on welfare, and obviously had very little money. The answers she gave to Claire's questions never seemed quite complete. She said she spent little and saved for the things that were important to her. She said that she lived on the welfare and saved the scholarship. She said that she got tips at the booth and saved them, that her books were second-hand, that her clothes came from the Sally Ann. All of those things made sense to Claire, but it just didn't seem possible, however frugal she might be, that Dar could save enough.

More puzzle pieces. Jenny. Darlene had talked about her friend Jenny, though she had never said where she lived. Claire had assumed that she was someone in Edmonton. Darlene's friend Jenny, the social worker. Who had a more-than-healthy salary and lived with her mother and whose only rent was the annual taxes on the house. Her friend Jenny whose picture Darlene kept in her mirror, whom Dar proudly showed to Claire saying, "Isn't she beautiful?" Claire didn't find her beautiful, but she was certainly an attractive woman. What Darlene didn't realize, probably never would, was that beautiful Jenny and ugly Darlene could have been twins. Jenny—Darlene's lover as well as her double. Jenny—who paid for these trips. Jenny—who from seven-thousand miles away could bring a flush to Darlene's cheek.

Four trips, twelve weeks, a year. Every year.

Darlene's voice wove into Claire's brain. "Huh? Sorry, I was daydreaming."

"I can tell. I was talking about you getting a new roommate."

"Why should I get a new roommate? Are you moving?"

"The lights are on but nobody's home. Yes, I told you."

"You did? When?"

"A couple of minutes ago."

"Oh. I guess I've been daydreaming for a long time. Why are you moving?"

"Try it one more time. Jenny's mother died a month ago, and she's moving here. I'm going to live with her."

Don't ask about immigration, Claire told herself. Don't show her how wonderful you think it is. Don't let her know that you know who Jenny is. Don't, for chrissake, be so jealous.

Trying to sound casual, she said, "Oh, that'll be nice for both of you. When is she coming?"

"It'll be a few months, she has to get everything cleared with immigration, but she's coming in eight weeks to look for a job, and we'll find a house then. Then I'll move into it until she comes, so I'll be leaving then. I'm giving my notice, I guess."

"Gee. I'll miss you."

"I'll miss you, too. I imagine that Jenny and I won't see much of other people at first, but then we can all get together."

"Sure. That'd be nice."

"What I was also saying was that I have a friend who's looking for a place to live. She's lesbian, but I don't think that should stop you. She's a good person, I think you'd like each other. Should I tell her to phone you?"

"Sure."

Claire thought for a minute. Living with a lesbian might be just what she needed. If nothing else, it would mean no boyfriends in and out and leaving their underwear in the bathroom. She could still hardly believe she'd been living with a lesbian for almost a year without even knowing it. But she'd not been ready to ask the questions that now crowded her head, she'd not been ready even to look at the answers that she was, apparently, carrying around inside her. Now she could see that Dar had been priming her for this. She'd known that she respected Darlene, but hadn't realized how much she liked her. And it had never crossed her mind that she needed her. Life would be very different without her.

Darlene took her silence as an objection. "She really is an okay person. You know, we all live among people whose secrets we don't know. I happen to know that you know four or five lesbians and don't know it. Give her a chance."

"Oh shut up, Dar. Of course give her the number. I was just thinking again."

"You sure?"

"Yes. Or give me her number. Do I know her?"

"I don't think so. Why don't we have her over for dinner?"

"Perfect."

"Good." After a minute she added, "You're going to do just fine, you know, Claire."

"Thanks. I think so too. Is everybody this slow?"

"Not everybody. And a whole lot are slower."

"How long ... for you?"

"I was fourteen. The woman I worked for. It made life worth living."

They turned off their lights. A quick image of Darlene sitting stripped to the waist in bed flashed through her mind. Then she thought for a moment about what Jenny must know of that body. And of the woman who lived in it. Claire cuddled down into her bed, smiling and hugging herself. "No, but it's coming," she heard herself say, again.

FLUENCY PROCESS

NANCY DARISSE

Twenty toes became wet gripping the slipping sand of Meech lake. Ten fingers caressed each other, discovered each other for the first time. Did anyone notice the falling star above them? Did anyone make a wish?

There was static in the air: an electricity that can only happen on the first date. A universal language that can only mean potential and desire. Connection. A language of secrecy and pride: erotic lesbian wanting. Even the silences bear messages.

She looked out at the starry sky and sighed. At least, I think she sighed from the sweet night air. Could it have been a sigh of boredom?

She had done most of the talking in a sweet broken English with what could only have been lavish French body language. I had many things to say but I feared I would break out in a stuttering panic as I exhibited my twenty-word French vocabulary. Still, since she was wearing a tee-shirt with a Quebec flag framing her gorgeous breasts in blue and white, I felt I should try something. Jesus! Did she have to wear the Quebec flag for me to realize the significance of her language?

She looked at me with a frown creasing her forehead. I must have looked perplexed, even worried ... this would definitely not make a good impression.

"*C'est si bon!* This night air, I mean." I found myself saying this spontaneously.

"*Oui, ça fait du bien,*" she answered, smiling. "With no car I cannot come here often."

How I love the accent! So sexy, so distinctive, so ... attentive ...

"Would you like to go camping sometime?"

~

The only time we went camping she insisted on canoeing to the site. This meant that, until we reached the site, there was nothing for me to do other than sit, watch and listen. My paddle was useless. I didn't know how to apply it to the water. Moreover, I had always feared drowning and my phobia was intensified by my proximity to the water. I certainly appreciated how she guided our canoe with agility and gentleness.

This was the only weekend we spent in this way—in a nylon tent, surrounded by a forest and facing a large, luminous lake. Yet, somehow, camping became the theme for our relationship.

Surrounded by my anglophone world, she came prepared for almost any weather. Her backpack of English contained many secret pockets and carried an impressive weight of tools and ideas. She communicated in my language with flair and agility, pronouncing opinions on most any subject, while recognizing theories, feminists, actors, musicians from my culture. She settled into my world as quickly as she left it.

L'autre camp was how she described her French world. It's literal meaning is "the other side," as in war. In *L'autre camp* I could barely survive. My backpack was embarrassing, tiny and fragile. When we were among her friends I could only sit and watch, while I lost her to the self-sufficiency of her French world. Translating would mean continually interrupting someone's train of thought or dragging the others to my level. And they all spoke English as a second language. I felt isolated and useless in my ignorance.

I concluded that there would be only two options: lose myself in unknown waters, or return to a familiar shore. I still feared drowning, yet I decided to plunge. Secretly, I hoped for calm waters.

~

There's a wildness to our loving. I find it assuring, magnetizing, bewitching. Through the storm we expand our access to each other. Here I can safely tame difference. The vibrancy of our bodies communicates one language that enriches our union and creates humour from our limits. I surrender easily to the passion, believing it melts us and warms our common bed.

Yet the same mouth that kisses me expresses the words and thoughts that separate me from her. Perhaps this is what I find wild.

Over a meal that is meant to be romantic, we break into the French-English discussion. This is the mid-point of the relationship. It is time to negotiate our participation in each other's cultures. I have been expecting this.

She begins by telling me about a couple of dykes who are both bilingual and bi-cultural, but were raised with different mother tongues. With a determination I have never heard before, she goes on to explain the details:

"They told me that the bilingualism creates *une solidarité* that is unique, special. That they don't feel the same solidarity with anglophones or francophones. They even claim that this *solidarité* resembles the one lesbians share ... and yet it can be more powerful *ou bien encore plus vraie*. They say that there are times when they feel closer to straight bilinguals than they do to unilingual lesbians. *Finalement* ... they link homophobia and francophobia as ... *en étant* ... cultures of the oppressors."

"Enough is enough!" I hear myself shouting impatiently. "Homophobia and francophobia are not the same thing! Let us not exaggerate here. Homophobia is all-pervasive, it's what every institution is built upon. On the other hand, English and French are just two different languages. No one says being French is abnormal or unnatural. Especially here in the Ottawa-Hull area, the French-English thing is common—everyone *adjusts* to it."

Candlelight accentuates the disappointment in her face. *"It is more common for a francophone to adjust.* Anglophones don't adjust ... they translate, they incorporate ... *Maudit!* They don't integrate the French into their lives. They don't need ... *ils ne sont pas obligés* ... to know French."

The silence is uncomfortable. I'm frustrated and confused by the intensity of her words. Isn't the homophobia enough work? Do we have to make an issue out of our language differences? Isn't the love between us enough to unite us beyond these differences? We can't compare cultures! This isn't a competition! Suddenly I feel very tired.

I watch as she leaves the table.

~

Later, without saying much, we concede that fresh air would help. We climb into the car and drive to Meech lake.

It's very late and, because it's Tuesday, the Lake is barren of swimmers and parties. An approaching storm slowly camouflages the stars. Spontaneously, we sit away from each other. I know that her silence since the meal indicates her need to be alone.

I had dared to dive into her culture, and I realize now that much of the experience was a struggle, not against her but against myself. The Lake is a depository for the stream of emotions and ideas that begin to well up inside of me from my unconscious. I want to let it pour out of me, I want to be cleansed.

I hear her crying and it draws me to her until I'm sitting there next to her and trying to wrap my arms around her pain. She refuses and pushes me away.

"What did I do? What did I say ... please, I need you to explain!"

"Explain! *Encore ... mais comment vas-tu finir par comprendre!"* She sighs heavily. "You, or the you created by your culture ... *conditionner* ... takes me for granted. You cannot listen to me. You listen to yourself listening to me! I'm tired of trying to be heard. I'm tired of translating ... for what seems to be your benefit only."

She takes a deep breath. "Please leave me alone for awhile. There is still some time left before the storm."

~

I stood up, feeling as though she had used her fist to punch me. Her anger created a presence stronger than words. I was stunned. Did I really take her for granted?

I stared out at the Lake.

Quiet, strong movement in the darkening Lake reflected the powerful motion of a transforming consciousness. Was it her consciousness, or mine?

Was she thinking of leaving me?

~

As with all endings, I do not know what happens next. I know only that there must be change. I let this flow through me, attempting to remove unconscious barriers.

I want to be a fluent speaker.

YOUSHEME

BETSY WARLAND

Yousheme was sitting by herself in the café. The clock, with a red knife and fork for hands, was at ten after eight. Funny, she thought, about a clock having hands. And a face. She wondered what that meant. Did it go back to when there were no clocks—when what you were doing with your hands and the accompanying expression on your face, at any particular moment, were the only human indicators of time? It struck her now that it was a bit like sign language, these hands moving in front of the face. Time, mute? Only our actions articulate it, give it meaning? Well, meaning as we know it. The hands of time. Time on my hands. She was off and running, as they say. Hands down. Yousheme loved to do this—play with a word or a saying or an icon. It wasn't just a game to pass the time, it was necessary for her sanity, her integrity. She was just beginning to understand all the whys of this instinct.

Her mind drifted to the invitation she'd just received, asking her to send fiction to a lesbian anthology. She didn't write fiction. She wrote an idiosyncratic brand of poetry and prose-poetry-essays. The thought of writing fiction seemed remote. She lacked a certain faith in it. Fiction writers often seemed to be clandestine conservatives. The "real world" by the "real writers" sort of thing, a belief that was fueled no doubt by the fact that novelists could actually earn royalties on their books, entertain the illusion that they were getting paid for a job well-done. Money and "reality" pretty much synonymous in the western world. But then, fiction writers had their misgivings about poets too.

The conversation in the next booth caught her attention. The people looked like parents (in their sixties) with their early-thirty-ish daughter. Mom and daughter on one side. Dad with his black-and-grey balding head on the other. Daughter was trying to rouse Father—get him involved, get him to talk. She was enthusing about the Blue Jays, with some obvious knowledge. He mumbled two semi-responses, got up, and left the café as if he had something more important to do. Since nothing was open in the village yet, except for the café, she surmised that this was a long-ingrained habit. Mom proceeded to get up and move across the table. Then daughter and mom began to talk animatedly.

She thought about the heterosexual couples she had known, remembered the frequent irritation between her parents in their latter years: classical and country and western playing at the same time. She puzzled about how people in these long-standing relationships often spoke about themselves with such clichés as: "We've never been happier" or "We're just like two kids," yet it was rare to witness this.

The scene around the Mendocino B & B's long colonial table: guests all eagerly consuming their breakfast and attempting pleasantries. The retired couple sitting next to Laurel and her—the wife making certain he had his muffin, his butter, his coffee, his cereal. Him groggy. Her repeating some question twice. Him ignoring her. Her sharply saying his name. Him surfacing: "Huh?" Her loud and exaggerated reply, "Read my lips." Red lipstick. Tense mouth. Silence all around the table. Him shrugging it off. Her shifting into public amicability, "Now, where did you say *you* come from?" Yousheme was mortified for both of them. This exchange seemed perfectly normal to them. It still sent shivers down her back.

She was so grateful for the way she and Laurel could talk. Sure, they got irritable with one another, but mostly they spoke I to I—all of them all there. Laurel. Where was she by now? She looked at the clock: 8:30. The ferry must be backing out of Otter Bay by now. Laurel would be on the mainland within the hour. That's why she was here in the café, having breakfast. She had driven Laurel to "the 6:40 a.m." Usually by this time they would be meditating. She had gone home after seeing Laurel off, had a shower, and after that, her mind was too engaged to meditate.

So, she was sitting here. No book. No paper. No notebook. No one across from her to talk with. Still an uncommon sight: a woman alone in a public place, content in her aloneness. Comfortable. Thinking. Looking at the sunlight through the fake lace half-curtains, that particular new radiance. Winter on the wane. This quality of light seduced her every year. She imagined when she first might have noticed it. At this time of the year she would been a two- or three-month-old baby then—old enough to see that far, get stoned on light and shadow.

Pippa came in, and noticing Yousheme, walked over to her booth. Yousheme asked her a number of "how's it going" questions. Typical. She always asked the questions. Most people seemed to like it that way. Besides, she was more interested in finding out about the other person. She already knew her story. Well, that wasn't exactly true. She was continually excavating her own narrative through her writing. But it was seldom anyone asked her a question that revealed anything during these kinds of exchanges.

There was another reason for her reluctance. She couldn't bear the thought of opening herself up to discover disinterest or distraction on her listener's part. She didn't fully understand this but she felt it deeply. It was odd—people thought of her as such a self-confident woman, yet she feared their indifference. Was it old incest dynamics again? No one listening to what she was saying? That frightening way in which your own words can be made to render you even more invisible? Better to keep them to yourself.

They were talking about buying houses. Yousheme said, "I was so tired of moving from apartment to apartment—I figured out that I had lived in twenty-two different places in ten years." Her acquaintance responded, "Candice and I lived in eleven different places in one year!"

Once again the fragility of their lives struck her.

"I heard your house is up for sale."

Yousheme's breath caught in her chest, "No way. We want to live there for a long time."

As she said this she looked nervously around and found a strip of wood to knock on—she wasn't about to cooperate with the possibility of bad luck. "Where did you hear that?"

Pippa floundered, giving the impression she couldn't remember. Yousheme imagined it was more a case of not wanting to say.

"Oh, I think it was at some party."

Oh well, it didn't really matter who said it.

Buying a house had felt like such a radical thing to do. On the outside, it was a very white, middle-class thing to do. On the inside, it still felt wildly radical to say to themselves and the world, "We have a right to a home." Not a hidden away, run-down flat where the landlord could raise the rent, tear down, or sell at any moment, but a pleasant one full of light. Yousheme, Laurel, and Yousheme's brother Timothy had bought the house together. For most acquaintances, this made it seem even more bizarre, but for visiting friends and close family members, their house had become a refuge.

It was a big house. Big enough for Timothy to have his own space when he came for visits and big enough for Laurel and Yousheme to have their own writing rooms. It gave Yousheme great pleasure to run full-tilt from one end of the house to the other after living in cramped flats for so long. It had been two years since they had moved in. The joy of having a spot on earth where they felt safe to breathe in the beauty around and within them was still remarkable. And when they made love, they revelled in their freedom to groan as loudly in orgasmic pleasure as they needed. No more muffling of their ecstasy. No more fear of offended, indignant neighbours yelling through thin walls, and no more landlord intimidation.

This was the first time in her forty-four years that Yousheme felt she had a home. Although she had been raised in "a good home," she had always felt uneasy there. She knew from an early age, as soon as she was able to put such thoughts together, that she was different—that she did not "belong." Her difference ran deeper than her sexual abuse. Even though she had no words for it like *writer, lesbian, feminist,* she knew she saw things differently. She learned it was dangerous to speak much of this. She knew if she stayed, she would literally die.

Now, when her mother told her the story of the nearby farmer's daughter shooting herself at the grave of her father three days after he mysteriously died and was buried, she wasn't shocked, she wasn't utterly bewildered like those who still lived in the area. She could all too easily imagine what the never-to-be-told story was.

The only place she had felt at home as a child was outside, beyond the confines of their family farm. She had roamed the fields, the nearby river and woods for hours on end, losing all sense of time. A small girl alone, on foot, on her horse, on her bike. Her mother's threats did not stop her. Eventually her mother conceded to her wanderings by saying she was a tomboy and stubborn.

These were among the few times in her childhood that Yousheme felt happy within herself and at peace with the world. She would climb up the windmill, leap onto the barn roof and sit staring at the horizon for hours. She would follow the river for miles or simply sit on a rock and watch its flow, sensing that there were other unknown ways of living which its water passed through and was going to. She clung to the river and the horizon. They promised places where she might be free to live wholly in herself.

It wasn't just their house that made Yousheme feel finally at home, it was Laurel. There had been several others before Laurel. She had learned much and felt very close to most of them. Her first woman lover was now like a sister to her. But Yousheme knew she could happily spend the rest of her life with Laurel. She had never known this before. There was a certainty and an expansiveness in their relationship which they knew was rare.

Timothy was one of her closest friends. He was also gay, and a Capricorn, and had begun to write seriously in the past couple of years. Timothy and Yousheme understood what they each had come out of, how it continued to subtly shape them. They were the continuum in each other's life stories and had always hoped they might live near each other. Although he was on the other side of the continent, at least they now shared a home part of each year.

Yousheme was sipping her tea now and unravelling the knife and fork from the serviette the waitress had brought. She had been so lost in her thoughts, it had surprised her to find the blanketed cutlery there. She was still struggling with the fear that Pippa's question had stirred up. For once in her life she wanted to stay where she lived, with whom she lived, for a very long time. Was it possible? Would fate or the homosexual-hostile world surrounding them allow such a luxury? Would her own political and spiritual commitments eventually propel her into passing it on to others?

Yousheme recited the litany of lesbianism: no homeland; no public visibility; no historically intact culture; practically no human (read heterosexual and white) rights under the law; no agreed upon way of amassing collective political power; no way of even identifying each other most of the time. There were even serious disagreements about whether the word lesbian was really representative of women who weren't white, and solidarity with most gay men seemed to be undercut by their unacknowledged sexism.

She remembered that literary panel at the Gay Games: two American lesbian writers had been talking about their commitment to gay men with AIDS, and one in particular had talked of her intense involvement with ACT UP. During the question period, a lesbian in the audience asked this writer if gay men would be there for lesbians "if the shoe was on the other foot?" There was a perched silence. "No, I don't think that gay men would be there for lesbians." No one refuted her.

The litany went on in her head. Racism and homophobia seemed to often choke out coalition politics with other racially oppressed people. And extricating ourselves from class into a lesbian-defined, shared future seemed still very remote. There were so many differences among us, and, considering the fierce penchant of lesbians for individual autonomy, it looked as though we might forever be at risk in our fragile microcosms.

Maybe this was it—isn't everyone ultimately at risk? Maybe as dykes we are just living closer to the edge of knowing this. Or maybe it was just the tea; it always got her synapses snapping at an incredible rate. She looked over her shoulder—still no scrambled eggs, hashbrowns and multi-grain in sight. Her mind galloped ahead. Well—if this is the case—we should give up the notion of securing a larger place for ourselves in the world. Our power would be in our vulnerability—a "nothing to lose" sort of thing. A freedom to do what is needed, to be what is longed for—instead of trying to belong, which, given our society, doesn't end up being all that different from "passing."

Laurel would be in Vancouver by now. Negotiating her way through tense, hurried bodies and anxious faces. And Vancouver was more "laid back" than most cities! The knife and fork were now in Yousheme's hands. Breakfast had arrived. It looked good. Food was definitely one of life's greater pleasures!

"Our power is in our vulnerability," she heard herself say out loud.

The eggs were great, almost as good as Jimmy's at the Mars. Suddenly, she knew that her vulnerability was the source of her lesbian power—here she had been wishing she could get rid of it! No, she hadn't left it behind years ago with her heterosexual life, she had only left her fearful dependence on men, which at the time, like most women, she had called by other names. As a lesbian, her vulnerability was hers.

No fiction. You. She. Me.

(Un)Expected

JOANNA KADI

I will never forget the night I first saw the vibrant colours of her imagination spilling around her—reds and blues and purples and browns and greens. We were sitting across from one another in separate jail cells in western Toronto. I noticed her immediately because she physically resembled so many of my relatives, although I found out later she was Latina and not Arab.

She sat alone in her cell, while mine was temporarily crammed with those of us who had been arrested while protesting at a nuclear weapons plant. As I heard the stories my cell-mates were exchanging, I suddenly realized most of these women were daughters of doctors, lawyers and businesspeople. The times we had met to plan the action I had noticed only our shared concerns about nuclear war. Now I noticed other things.

I let my mind drift back to the morning's activities. Before the protest two people briefed us, or rather, they "shared information" with us. The man called himself a feminist, although I found out later he had been cheating on his wife for years. The woman had seen fit to dye her hair a singularly unattractive shade of blue, and carried a stuffed piranha. Afterwards, we moved to the site of the action and were promptly arrested. I didn't see the attraction in being dragged so I walked with my arresting officer; I found out later this raised questions about my commitment to the cause.

And now I was in jail with fourteen other women. I knew we wouldn't be here long, and I was more thankful for that as every minute passed. Did we have anything in common? I seriously began to doubt that when a prominent lawyer's daughter (whose life story I was becoming quite familiar with) received a note.

"Oh, no," Mary Beth cried, "I can't believe it!"

Instantly the other women crowded around her. "What is it, Mary Beth?"

"My sister's going into labour, and I'm her labour coach. I promised her I'd be there for her, no matter what. What am I going to do?"

The other women made sympathetic noises and hugged her. I bit my lip to stop from asking the obvious question of why she had got herself arrested if her sister was almost due. I knew that wasn't what she wanted to hear.

Mary Beth moped for a few minutes, then moved into action. "Guard, guard," she called imperiously. The guard, a woman with a hard mouth and a dye job that didn't fool anyone, appeared. Mary Beth used the same tone. "I've got to speak with someone in charge. I must be released *immediately*. It's vitally important. My sister is about to give birth."

Blank astonishment covered my face. I waited for blank astonishment to cover the guard's face. Instead, the guard checked something in the office and then led Mary Beth down the corridor.

The women in my jail cell were thrilled. I was appalled. I looked across the way at the woman with the colours of her imagination spilling around her. The colours continued to spill although her face bore a smirk.

I pondered inventing a sister who was in labour and a father who was a prominent lawyer. But somehow I couldn't undo my sister's surprise hysterectomy, nor could I move my dad from the factory line to the law office. And how to replicate the tone of Mary Beth's voice?

I gave up trying to figure this out as the other women in my cell vied for sleeping positions. I claimed the spot nearest the woman with the colours.

~

She said her name was Juanita and added wryly, "Well, I know why you're here." We laughed, both of us having heard several speeches about our brave action and the potential risk to our "careers."

"I'm not worried about my 'career,'" I said. "I'm worried about whether Mr. Smith will be able to do without my sixty words a minute for a whole day."

"Well, as long as I'm out in time to service my johns before their male lust *forces* them to go berserk, I'm fine," Juanita said with the same wry tone, telling me she had been arrested the previous night after being entrapped by a cop.

"It's so satisfying to know my tax dollars are being used to go after the truly bad elements in society," I said sarcastically.

"Well then, you'll be glad to know that Toronto's finest also use those dollars to keep the police station cheerily decorated in sophisticated colours. Maroon and peach are this year's colour scheme."

"Sometimes I wish I had a job where I didn't have to pay any taxes," I sighed. Upon realizing what I had said I blushed furiously, hoping I hadn't offended Juanita.

But she only laughed, and said she wished they would use some tax money to redecorate in here. "It's too depressing being surrounded by this much grey."

It was the same shade as the walls in the drug treatment centre where I visited my brother; I told Juanita about his struggle to get off cocaine and heroin. It turned out her brother was also addicted. Juanita talked about him, her two older sisters, the way her parents doted on their children and the small corner store they managed, Juanita's fascination with organic gardening, and her unfulfilled ambition to attend university. I told her about my unfulfilled ambition to attend university, my father's job in the factory, the way my parents couldn't let a day go by without beating up at least one of their kids, my engagement at nineteen to Samuel followed by marriage at twenty-one, my love of reading. Then Juanita asked why I had taken part in the action.

"Well, the war-mongers are continuing to build nuclear bombs even though there's already enough to kill us all fifty times over, and sooner or later there'll be a war. If not a war an accident, and I don't want that to happen. We have to stop the military build-up. We have to get the Soviets and the Americans to stop seeing each other as enemies."

Juanita yawned. I was a trifle hurt. "Then what?" she asked.

"Huh?"

"Then what? Then will our brothers stop using drugs and our parents lead fulfilling lives and you and I will meet again in art school?"

This stymied me, and I was momentarily silenced. Juanita smiled gently. The colours of her imagination spilled out brighter, swirling around her like a cape caught in the wind. I stared, fixated. "What is it?" she asked.

I told her. She laughed in a way that made me catch my breath and want her to continue forever. "Hey," she said, "I thought your brother was the one on drugs."

We both laughed. She proceeded to tell me an amazing story that lasted through the night.

~

"You see this grey," she said, stroking the bricks, "that's what my imagination used to be. Your imagination is your interior landscape. I had this grey interior landscape for a long time. Even before I was born, really. It's been passed down in my family, generation after generation.

"There's nothing wrong with grey. It can be beautiful. The problem starts when that's all there is. Because," she spoke more slowly and her hands paused in mid-air, "the uninterrupted greyness of an imagination stifled over generations is not beautiful."

At that moment, a particularly brilliant stream of purple cascaded over Juanita's long black hair and down her back.

"Of course my imagination was a mess," Juanita said reflectively. "What else could it be? Poverty, lousy jobs, cramped quarters, being called a 'dirty spic,' ugly clothes." She laughed a little cynically. "Ugly clothes. I swear to God I'd do anything not to wear ugly clothes again."

Her words went directly to my gut. She could have been describing my life. So she had lived with "dirty spic." I'd been called a "dirty Arab," of course, but usually it was "greasy Arab." And clothes. Every day I wondered if I was destined to go through my entire life feeling like a frump wearing the wrong clothes.

73

Juanita continued, saying that before an imagination could create colours there had to be colours in your life. Not that life had to be perfect, she added, but you sure couldn't stay in places where depression was normal. She gave me a piercing glance as she said this.

"You need encouragement, nurturing, ideas, knowledge, dreams, history, a roof over your head, nice clothes, love, community pride, a wild spirit, and role models," Juanita stated passionately. "Then your imagination can come alive."

I didn't know exactly what she meant by this. History? I had done well in history in high school. A wild spirit? Was spirit the same as soul? Somehow I doubted that what the Catholic church meant by soul was what Juanita meant by spirit.

But I had no time to ponder this, because Juanita kept speaking.

"There's one sure place to get all these—certain women. *Mi abuelita* [My grandmother] was the first. She was poor, she cleaned houses all her life, and no one in this city thought much of her, but she had pride. She never let me forget the little plot of land our family farmed for generations in the hills of Argentina, how we always had enough. I would curl up in her lap—right up until she died, and I was twenty-one then—and she would hug me and rock me in her rocking chair, and tell me stories. Stories about women healing, about living close to the earth, about singing and dancing with the whole community to express the joy they had in living. She gave me stories. She gave me pride, after those damn history classes in high school did their best to take it away."

Oh. We seemed to have different thoughts on high school history. But whatever it had or had not done, history class had never given me stories like Juanita gave me that night, stories of women I hadn't heard of, stories of women from her own neighbourhood and stories of women she had read about. Stories about the warrior whose hands were chopped off when the FBI killed her. The rape survivor who refused to keep the words of her experience locked within. The domestic worker who walked miles to her job in an Atlanta house to support her people's strike against a racist bus system. The spinster who laughed heartily when others lamented her unwed state. The worker who stood up to the T. Eaton Company and said: "No More," the same words her sister had uttered to General Motors Corporation decades earlier.

These women inspired Juanita, touched her, and helped her realize she wanted to spend her life with and for women. And so she came out as a lesbian.

A lesbian? I'd never met any lesbians. I didn't know what to think.

"It's not like being a lesbian undoes the past or alters everything in the present," she explained, as a vivid streak of green mixed with blue fell across her body. "But it can do a lot. It can bring an imagination to life.

"I got to this place where all of me, the whole person, was alive with dreams and visions. I moved beyond what's here now and began creating something totally different.

"Don't you see?" Juanita spoke passionately and loudly and moved forward as if to grab me through the bars and force me to see. "In these hard times, it's our imaginations that can sustain us. It's the visions from our imaginations that get us through the horror. Once our imaginations are dead, forget it! There'll be no *revolución*! If we can't dream about it and know what we want, nothing will change."

Juanita sank back against the wall of the cell and was momentarily silent. I thought about what she said. I had no visions for the future, no images except one of being surrounded by Samuel and the four children he insisted we would have. At that moment my Aunt Rose came to mind, a tiny woman whose feet were deformed by the preposterously high heels she wore all her life. A year before her death from cancer, we were watching TV together, and the host asked his guest about her plans for the future. I can't remember what the woman with the blonde hair and mink coat said, but Aunt Rose sighed heavily and said in a devastatingly sad voice, "Oh, the future."

Juanita stirred. She said lesbians had given her dreams and that's when her imagination began producing colours. "In one dream, I was pregnant. Really pregnant! My gut stuck out to here, and the great event was going to happen soon. I asked who I was pregnant with, and this voice answered 'Your self.' Right after that, a little bit of purple arrived. Other colours came with other dreams.

"You know," Juanita said, "before this, the only question I ever asked about dreams was '¿Adonde van los sueños cuando mueren?' [Where do dreams go when they die?] But not now."

Now the dreams stayed and the colours stayed too, and colours came from other experiences. Red became most prominent when the raging women of her new community kindled the anger that had been dormant for years. "It's great being enraged," Juanita said with the same satisfied tone I had heard other women use to describe their engagement. "It's *so* much better than being depressed."

She told me that the longer she was with her new community, the more she began to feel pride in herself and her people, and sometimes she associated the browns with pride. Golden, light brown, beige, deep brown, yellow, earth brown, representing pride and, not incidentally, she pointed out, capturing the skin colour of most of the world's peoples. "We're not the minority," she said fiercely. "Whenever I hear a white person use that word to describe us, I want to go for the jugular."

Throughout the night I became more and more aware of the abundance of life in the cell across from mine. Quite simply, I had never met anyone as keenly alive as Juanita, who sparkled, felt, laughed, moved and told stories as she did, who emitted as much powerful rage, humorous cynicism and profound hope and love as she did. I wanted to be like that.

~

Our conversation ceased as my cell-mates woke. A prolonged discussion was held about what to do if first offenders were let go that morning and repeat offenders had to stay. Would the first offenders act in solidarity and remain until all could leave together?

The talk proceeded in its usual fashion until a guard told us our group would be released shortly. A general cheer went up. In the pause that followed, I said my first words to these women, suggesting we carry out our decision to act in solidarity by remaining with Juanita until she was free.

Juanita made a face that clearly said "Get real." My cell-mates had no idea who I was talking about, since they hadn't noticed we weren't alone in the jail. Finally one woman said, with assenting nods from the rest, we should remain focused on peace and not get caught in "less pressing, more murky" issues.

When the guard returned, I refused to go. Juanita told me I was crazy and to get out when I had the chance. I ignored her and settled in. I watched the vibrant colours of her imagination spill around her and felt the tiniest ray of green spill from my own.

DOOR CRASHING

RHONDA JAYNE OLSON

If you ever find yourself at a soiree where you do not know anyone, remain calm, assuming the pose of one who belongs. Act like you are looking for someone that you know, and eventually a forgiving face will greet you, one probably a lot like your own. Learn to recognize these people yourself. Give them a warm smile.

Indeed, be hopeful that this is not a clique party where everyone is content to know themselves. These people are less likely to be sympathetic to newcomers.

And finally, a little courtesy note. At outdoor parties it is acceptable to light up a cigarette. Maybe another person with your awful habit will join you.

Maybe not.

Against a fir tree, rough bark on her smooth back like a lover's nails, she squats during an Italian black-and-white exhale of her blue cigarette. Miss Manners made Claire boxy and probably didn't have a chapter on door crashing. If one had to do this, she would no doubt suggest, one should at least obtain the name of the host before arriving. Ahh ... speculation. Had Miss ever attended a lesbian party?

That is as much as she knows of these women whom she does not know, some of whom look to be twice her twenty-two years and may have really read Miss Manners. While she watches the congested Georgia Strait glimmering over their shoulders, a tubby sailor waves from a multi-coloured Laser.

Georgia, the strait, makes Claire think of large drag queens on the beaches donning 1930s resort wear flaunting their knees, and of her own hormonal imbalance, which makes her think of her thin, uptight grade ten French teacher. He spent a class espousing through his large nostrils that déjà vu was a momentary retardation of the brain. What was that supposed to mean? "Already been seen," he explained in translation, "is not a paranormal experience, is not a remembering of a previous life, is not a glimpse of our eternal re-occurrence, and is not an extrasensory perception." And he went on so about what it was not, that you thought his life was one big déjà vu, and he was losing control of it. If, at fifteen, she had really understood any of it, she would have transferred blocks.

Claire wants a drink.

She finds her forgiver—the hands reeling backwards—in a woman whom she likens to a bearer of milk and cookies from her childhood after a rainy walk home from school.

"It's like getting adjusted to a new pallet of colours," the stranger says looking around, her head moving quickly like she has an uncontrollable tick, like she sees original combinations of mixed oil paints on everyone's foreheads. "The changing of the seasons, that is. Would you like a glass of wine, Claire?" she says, handing the glass to her, knowing the answer, a formality question.

"Are you an artist or a gardener?" Claire asks, uncharacteristically appreciative, following the path of polite conversation, wondering if she might know her forgiver as well.

"No. I was sort of referring to how you tell a story," she begins again. "Like in melodrama (the soap opera being its ultimate example) the ending, or climax if we want to get technical, is always the wedding. That is the whole purpose of telling the story—warped wish fulfillment," tick, tick.

Claire wishes that she could look directly at this stranger, meet her eyes. But every time that Claire begins to focus on her features, the stranger shakes her head.

"I wish I knew who our host is," interrupts Claire, unable to discern if she has offended the ticker by the interruption or with the idea that she's unaware of whom the host is. "Where our host is."

"What if you dispense with it ... and started at the other side. Claire, do you remember in elementary school when we did the little skit for the talent show?" Jill reaches out and squeezes Claire's wrist, a little too hard. She doesn't want her to answer.

"Looking back on it, I think our little innocent misinterpretation was rather more sophisticated humour than anybody recognized. Maybe we satirized marriage because we thought romance was icky still. Huh." Her tick starts going faster, suggesting urgency.

Claire responds, "All I can remember about that, Jill, is that we mistakenly called it a soapbox opera, and that I played Brad who had the most pathetic dialogue."

Jill laughs her head off. She looks stupid without it, stumpy, like she can't breathe. "And I threw them at you when you ... attempted to propose to me." With that she leaves, still laughing her head off, always having the last word—as if laughter is shame, the last laugh just like in elementary school. Just like in elementary school.

Claire's happy to have snagged a glass of wine. Unwittingly her lack of lunch has allowed the spirit to take control, for her to be addled by and about Jill, who must imagine herself, with a flower garland in her hair, to be a sayer, initiating her into this bountiful scented rite. Déjà vu, Claire accused, must be a regular for Jill.

As she gazes around smiling at whomever's eyes she meets by chance—the drunk, the animated, the concentrated and the silent eyes—the party's disparate voices form a tunnel right through the crowd. Through these now silent voices she sees her mother's face. Claire thinks, we think, that she should be alarmed, but she's not. It's not often, after all, that you accidentally bump into your mother at a party. The gaze is not returned to her and for now that seems preferred. She'll have to make up an explanation for why she's here, who she knows, why she's smoking, and how much she's had to drink. "I'll have another glass of wine," she says to herself. "Maybe my grandmother will show up on a motor scooter," she thinks, unable to distinguish between humour and sarcasm.

She is watching her mom—who hasn't seen her and is socially immersed—through this huge viewer her location and the voices have provided. She feels devious like a voyeur, outfitted with the latest equipment. Her mom, her mother's friends and the *déjeuner-sur-l'herbe* setting resemble the sepia pictures of Natalie Barney and Djuna Barnes: the women of the left bank in Paris that she had once seen in a book. After reading this book, she casually proclaimed to her mother and her mother's new boyfriend—at Thanksgiving dinner, squashing cranberry sauce through her teeth, her brother and sister talking real estate—that all the great women writers were lesbians. How they did not manage to respond, how no one would challenge such a statement escaped her mind, but some subjects had always been like that. Now, before her eyes, her mother floats about like Maria Christina in a very nice silk French suit, a man's cut, but without a tie, her pants drooping fashionably at the bottom, down around her shoes, like Vishnu. If she had looked in a mirror, she would have laughed at herself. If she was herself.

Brilliant visions have been said to appear when the senses are inviting everything, when one is weak and hungry. A woman with no hair, or rather the shadow of hair, walks through the middle of the picture we know as the garden. She is on her tiptoes so that she won't be missed. It's an unfitting dance but beautiful all the same. Oh, it is Serene, her lover. Claire calls, but Serene disappears again into the crowd, just as she had appeared, a flash, a mirage. Damn.

A woman in turquoise leather pants shoves a tray of biscuits and dip into her face. Others flock towards the tray, two women with wavy hair that reaches their bottoms. Claire fills her free fist and feeds.

"The eggplant is great," crinkles the leather pants.

"Have you spoken with Trudell yet?" the two ask in unison, with high speaking voices, nodding their heads and tastefully licking their fingers. "We haven't seen her or Silvia since that party where they met. Doing the twist!"

continues the full-lipped of the two, her statements emphasized with a honk of a laugh, the twist always having amused mermaids.

"They announced it at one of our sunblock parties this summer," answered the leather horn-bearer, breaking into uproarious laughter. Claire doesn't know what is so fuckin' funny. That's her mother they're laughing about—Trudell, the one in the French suit.

Amidst the offensive laughter, Serene appears again. She's the one with the awful habit. She blows a ring of smoke atop her head. She looks like an angel, without hair.

"How's my girl?" sings the angel.

"Confused. When did you get here?"

"When you did. Great party, hey. Wanna funk?" Serene dances to the music, her body moving like limbs are for hugging.

"Wanna tell me what's going on?"

"What d'a ya mean? ... Lets dance," says Serene, dancing with her eyes closed now. She's totally into it. "Find your mom," she finishes, not having a chat anymore, and she blends into the gyrating swarm. Serene belongs whenever she wants to.

So close to expecting to see her grandmother pull up on a motor scooter wearing a jacket with a pink triangle with "Putka" inscribed on the back, Claire grapples with the thought that her mother is going to marry again. She remembers, like her own birth, that she had seen Trudell with this lover of hers, Silvia.

One afternoon while in a knobby tree, fancying herself a silky feathered bird, Trudell and Silvia walked into her keen view. Chatting too far away for her to hear of what they spoke, only their animated smiles and frowns were clear. Mother's face was puckered, a sponge, it wasn't obvious if she was holding back tears or trying to squeeze them out. Silvia faced Trudell, her back to the perched Claire. Silvia yelled at Trudell out of the side of her ear, slapping her face. Twice. The sound of these sharp slaps were like the crack of a whip on Claire's back. The crying stopped.

Oh, to leap down from the tree with the pointedness of a hawk in for the kill. Scooping Silvia in her claws, squeezing her tight. Through grit teeth Claire bellows with feathered sense, "Do harm to my mother again and I'll ram your long white body into every billboard I know of in the city." Full body slaps, for full psychological impact, she caws to herself.

There are shades of black and blue at this party, now wedding, and in the petals of a flower she holds. Folded in this lush space where there are many tall trees to perch and rescue from if necessary, she wobbles her head, searches about, emulates the tick, and tries to relax. The low, flowering, wild bushes surrounding the yard, the calm light fixing peace in this new age, or the occasional squirrel wandering by for eggplant dip are missed in anger.

She hasn't seen Silvia yet. She needs a kiss from Serene, since drinks don't matter anymore.

Her former life-constant continues about in that damn suit, chatting, hugging, kissing and laughing with her friends. It comes to Claire that she's not the mom right now that Claire knows and remembers. Like really. This is an impostor, whom she's growing to like. Claire thinks this woman, however, is only like her mother in appearance. It is hard for Claire to remember Mom, now that she has found herself mingling at her mom's lesbian wedding ceremony.

"There are times in your life when nothing seems to make sense at first," they kiss. "Have you ever understood something you read or somebody said to you, like ten years after you first heard of it?" they kiss again. "And then something happens, usually something really small, that makes it click," she kisses her shortly. "That little thing of the past makes sense. I think we all just have to be patient yet unrelenting when it comes to the confusing things," Serene finishes and dives on top of her.

Claire wishes she could respond to the soothing advice with something other than a kiss. But on second thought, what is so wrong with that? This community that at first had seemed so foreign to her has become, one by one, her past enlightened, emerging before her. Her own back yard.

And in walks Miss Greig on cue. She's an English woman who lived near Claire as a child—among neighbourhood gossip circles she was deviant because she lived alone. They, the gossips, had told six-year-old Claire that Miss Greig was strange. At that age, all Claire knew was that Miss Greig talked too much.

"Try one of these tomatoes," offers Miss Greig. She is generous. Perhaps that is strange too.

"Thank you, Miss Greig," responds Claire politely as if she were six again, the elastic waist band of her skirt itching. It isn't easy stumbling into a party and being confronted by your past. Miss Greig had been Jill's neighbour. They had both spied on her together.

"They're really quite lovely. Your mother is always looking at my fruit. These ones remind me of the tomatoes I had growing in the garden once. Well, they were the first I'd grown by myself. They were planted late, and fall was rushing in," she breathes deeply. "One of the ten or so green tomatoes growing there was starting to turn colour. She wasn't ripe yet. I couldn't help myself. Looking at her I had to caress her. I wasn't pushing hard mind you, but she fell off the vine," she says looking sad and troubled, but then perks right up. "I put her in the sunniest windowsill, and she ripened nice and red. We practically had a ceremony when we were going to eat her. Oh it was beautiful. So sweet," she smiles and her large brown eyes look about inside as if she were enjoying that very tomato now. Claire bites into her tomato wondering who "we" were. It tastes like candy.

The women Claire has met today come up to her. As they take turns uttering her questionable thoughts for her, they shrink. They become smaller with each syllable, and their voices become weaker and weaker. "Has your mother turned her affections to women because you never allowed her time to herself, time to go out and find a man?" Edna puts to her, knowing she is in charge of the most ridiculous question.

"Had she become so tired of caring for her greedy demanding children, that she turned to someone who could care for her?" says Miss Greig knowingly, like she had never really been alone.

And Serene asks her, as if she is wanting to start a fight with her, "Had you suppressed who she really was, forcing her to remain your aproned mother?"

Thus, Claire's thoughtless thoughts and ridiculousness aside, the only real question becomes: why has she kept this a secret from Claire, her own daughter?

Beginning to search for Trudell, Claire bumps into two smiling gentle women. Nothing is spilled. They seem to have been waiting for her. They both have short grey hair, rounded steel-rimmed glasses, wear slacks, and sip martinis with pink olives. One of this older couple speaks to her.

"It sure is wonderful that people can come out these days, like really come out," she chuckled, "You must be pretty excited for your mom, hey?"

For the first time, their eyes meet. Claire has been awaiting this moment. It is as if all the chatter at the party stops and a crescendo of violins has received the go signal. Today, she thinks to herself, as her mother smiles at her and excuses herself from the large Asian woman she has been talking to, today she will begin to talk to Trudell.

In an approach that seems to take forever, her mother comes to her. Without saying a word Trudell embraces her. The embrace that Claire is accustomed to, that particular amount of tension with which they usually hold each other, increases tenfold. She feels that her mother has become stronger and happier. Trudell squeezes an unexpected tear out of Claire, just one plump tear. Trudell laughs when she sees it, accusing her of being the most emotional one in the family but the least capable of self-perception. Then she throws back her head and screams, "I'm a lesbian. I love Silvia and I'm going to marry her."

Claire returns her cry, but through a cracking voice she barely recognizes: "I love Serene and we're going to live together." Trudell wipes away Claire's tear and asks her not to be angry with them. She'll explain later, if she needs to. And as if to punctuate her announcement, Trudell leaves, so that the proceedings may begin. She twirls around as she leaves, giving Claire the full view of the suit, making Claire choke on her undrawn tears and sniffles.

Claire doesn't see the ceremony, although she is standing right at the front, nearly pressed against Trudell and Silvia. She's concentrating on the wind that blows some leaves in little hurricanes around the yard. A kitten is chasing one of these little vortexes, laced with streamers and leaves, everywhere. She becomes dizzy and begins to make herself sick.

The kitten stumbles through a doorway to hide from the tides. Through this doorway Claire sees her mother in the kitchen doing dishes, looking and seeming as she had been when Claire was a girl. A door closes before her. The knob is really big, like in a child's drawing of a house. She reaches for it.

An arm around her waist pulls in her weeping body. A whisper tells her everything. Gentle hands hold her tears.

Awake now, she stares outside the bedroom window at the blue sky with its fluffy white clouds. She thinks of being in the back of the car with her brother and sister, with mom beside dad at the wheel. We're pointing out cloud formations to one another. There's a fluffy person in a skirt riding on a motor scooter. It's granny. We're all laughing.

Her lover's warm soft body touches her sleepily in every possible body point from head to toes. Claire giggles when her lover wiggles her toes at the arch of Claire's foot. Today is the day. She'll talk to her mother.

DOGS ON THE LAND

GARBO

"All right," said Oak's soft voice, "when you have crossed over the magic bridge, and rejoined us in the here and now, slowly open your eyes."

I blinked twice, and Susan's pretty ceiling came into view. She'd painted a sky-scene on it, fluffy clouds rolling across a soothing blue background. I sat up slowly—after years of these guided-visualization things, I knew how to take care of my back.

The art supplies were in a loose heap on Susan's moss-green carpet. Most of the women in the circle were still stretched out on their backs, but across the way Randi was already busy, sketching with an ordinary No. 2 pencil. She looked up from her drawing, gave me a little smile, and went back to work.

I considered watercolours, but decided coloured markers were less dangerous and splashy. I picked out a blue-violet marker, then pine-green, indigo, and red. After a moment I put back blue-violet for someone else to use, and pulled my sheet of newsprint close. As I filled in a few trees in one corner, the other women in Susan's living room began to sit up and gather art materials. Susan was the last to sit up, and I looked up over my glasses to make sure she had something to draw with. All the crayons left were earth tones, but there was also a set of watercolours, and Susan seemed content to select a brush and begin.

She was the last to finish, but the first to share her vision. She propped the limp sheet of newsprint against her chest, and looked down at it from the top edge. Her perspective was perfectly appropriate, since she had created an ariel view of a village. The roofs of all the buildings were not quite round, but spoked like umbrellas. A ring of mountain ridges protected the buildings. The middle building was largest, twice the size of the others. The other structures looked like offspring, huddled close by their parent's sheltering eaves. "This is where everyone eats," said Susan, pointing to the large building's roof, still wet with paint. "And the garden is behind there." Susan laid her drawing on the carpet, took a pretzel from the pretzel bowl and crunched into it.

No one spoke for a minute, then Oak looked at Susan's face carefully. "Did you want to say anything else?" said Oak, and Susan shook her head, smiling around the pretzel.

Oak's turn came next. During the guided visualization, she had seen rainbow clouds of light. Her sheet of newsprint was folded in half, and the pretty image didn't even fill half of the half-sheet. Inside a neatly defined circle, Oak had used felt-tip markers to shade in delicate changes in hue. Looking at the picture, I felt as if I'd just read all of Lynn Andrews' books straight through. "I'd wanted to make room for possibility" said Oak. "I don't know why I put this blue around the edge, but the green is for growth and the purple is for spirituality."

"That's really nice, Oak," said Susan.

Oak laid down her sheet of newsprint, and Debra quickly put the final touches on her vignette. A happy woman (probably Debra herself, since her brown hair was very curly) was lying in tufty waves of grass. She had stretched out comfortably on her back, and now surveyed a gorgeous sky. The picture had mountains too, I thought at first, then I recognized them as dwellings, pueblos with doorways at different levels.

My turn came after Debra's, and I grabbed the top of my drawing and held it up. I was wrinkling the picture and as I held it, the sides folded forward and almost met in the middle. "I can't see it like that," said Randi.

"That's all right," I said. "It didn't come out too well anyway."

"No, come on, hold it so we can see it," said Randi.

What I'd drawn looked like a poor imitation of Susan's umbrella-roofed village. I hadn't stuck with an ariel view, like Susan, but changed my point of view several times while I was colouring. The houses along the top edge of my sheet looked like they'd been viewed from an airplane, but the buildings in the bottom right-hand corner looked as though I'd stood very close, maybe on the front step. This house was tall and narrow, pine-green with a red, steeply-peaked roof. I'd drawn this house last and put in many details: a hanging plant, a curve of curtain behind a window, a set of stepping stones through the side yard. An indigo cat tiptoed through the yard, moving between the stones.

"So is that where you live?" said Oak, pointing to the narrow house on the corner. "The one that's kind of away from everything else?"

"Yeah," I said.

"Where do I live?" said Debra. "In the house with you, or do I have another house?"

"This is yours," I said, showing her a pine-green square house close to the narrow one. The indigo cat, walking between the stepping stones, seemed to be headed across the yard to Debra's house. Everyone nodded, and I put the picture down.

I'd put in the hanging plant and the cat to fake myself out. I wanted to fake out everyone else, too. When I was lying on my back on Susan's rug, visualizing an ideal environment for a lesbian community, what I saw was Camp Sycamore.

My ideal lesbian community was a summer camp, where tanned, healthy counsellors would schedule our days for us. They would make sure that food came into camp and waste went out. Perfectly-inflated volleyballs would sail over correctly-strung nets. Social activities would be scheduled for the evenings, and chores would be distributed equitably.

My attention had wandered, and everyone's focus had shifted around the circle to Randi. "And this is my house," she was saying, pointing to her pencil sketch, "and this is Ginger's little house."

Debra said, "Ginger, huh? When did this start?"

I said, "How come she gets the little house? I hope it's far away from yours if you're going to try your non-monogamy routine out on her."

"No, my German Shepherd and I are strictly monogamous," said Randi. "Ginger pitches a fit if she smells another dog on me."

"Dogs," said Oak. "There's something that goes on the Issue List." She reached for the clipboard and added a word.

"Oh, come on," said Randi. "We've all got dogs and cats and stuff. We *have* to have *dogs*."

"I'll be really happy to talk about this when we get to Issues Clarification," said Oak pleasantly. "Do you want to finish showing us your picture?"

~

I was scared about Issues Clarification, so I was glad we were putting it off till after lunch.

I assumed that we'd be ordering pizzas, and I organized my vote in my mind: one pizza with extra cheese, mushrooms and black olives, and one pizza with onion and green peppers. But Randi and Oak went out to their cars and came back with covered dishes, and Susan produced an enormous fruit salad from her refrigerator.

I looked at Debra. "Is this a potluck? Shit, did you know that?"

"No," she said. "Nobody said anything to me about it."

I went into the kitchen, where Susan was taking forks out of a drawer and dropping them handle-down into a plastic glass.

"Debra and I didn't know this was a potluck," I said. "Should I run down to the convenience store and pick up something? Or is there a deli or—"

"Here you go," said Susan. She reached up and took a pan down from the top of the refrigerator. I looked into it and saw fudge brownies. "I figured somebody would forget," she said. "Nice of you and Debra to bring brownies."

"Thanks," I said, and carried the pan out to the dining room table. Susan followed me out, carrying her fork bouquet.

~

Issues Clarification started right after lunch. Oak, as facilitator for the day, picked up her clipboard. She said, "The topics have been alphabetically arranged—"

"Oh, no," I said. "We have to talk about boys first thing?"

"We're using the term 'Men'," said Oak. "Some of us have male partners."

"That's their problem," I said. Oak looked at me and made her lips very tight. I said, "Just kidding, just kidding."

"Okay," said Oak, looking down at the clipboard, "Our first topic is Dogs."

"How are we doing this?" said Randi. "Are we just saying what we think?"

"That's what we said we were going to do," said Oak. She held up a miniature hourglass. "This egg timer goes three minutes. No cross-talking, and we move around the circle. Do you want to start, Randi?" She turned the egg timer over, and the sand began to sift down.

"Uh, what?" said Randi, startled. She stared at the sand grains slipping down to the hourglass base. "Well, this whole thing is silly, I think. I mean, why do we need to sit here trying to make rules about dogs? We need to be talking about real stuff, money, land, cars and trucks." She glanced at Oak, who was watching her with interest. A third of the sand in the glass was gone already. "Okay, so dogs. Are we doing cats, too? Both of those, dogs and cats?"

Oak reached for the clipboard, but Randi said quickly, "Okay with everybody, we do dogs and cats together?" Susan and I nodded, and Randi rushed on, her eyes on the timer. "I just feel like this dog question isn't necessary. That's a personal right, having a pet. Everybody should just have whatever they want, a cat or dog or whatever they want. They have to take care of their own, buy their own food, unless a couple of them want to—"

"Time," said Oak. She was the person to Randi's left, and everyone was looking at her. "Okay, we're going this way?" She gestured with the miniature hourglass. "So, here's a couple of things to think about. One is, Third World nations—"

"The timer," Susan and I said together.

"Oh," said Oak. "Thank you." She turned the timer over and began quickly, "Third World nations are struggling for daily necessities, and I'm not sure a policy of feeding household pets is consistent with our concerns for the poor. Americans feed their dogs and cats with resources that need to be directed to areas that are drought-stricken and so on. Second, there's the question of allergies. Many people are allergic to the hair and to the dander of domestic animals, and they will be affected by the pet policy." There was a short intake of breath from Randi, as though she was going to say something. "Even if dogs are kept in restricted areas," Oak continued, "the hair and dander will travel into communal areas on the clothing of the owners." She looked at the timer, and said, "There are other questions, such as licencing, leashes, and so many other concerns that it just makes sense to adopt a humans-only policy." The last grain of sand dropped.

Oak handed the baby hourglass to Susan, who said, "I like dogs," and handed the hourglass to me.

"Is that *it?*" I said.

Susan looked down and stretched her skirt over her knees, then let it drop. She reached for a brownie. "I haven't got anything against dogs."

I held out the hourglass, but Susan shook her head. "That's all, I guess." She took a bite of brownie.

I turned the hourglass over and stared at it. "Well, there's got to be a way for everybody to coexist," I said. "Maybe we need to divide the community into zones where dogs are allowed or not allowed." I looked around, but couldn't tell what anybody else thought. "Maybe we could set a limit on the number of pets at any one time. I just hate to see this community torn apart by such a little issue. Maybe there could be a committee, and we could draw up some proposals." I looked at Susan, who nodded. I felt better, and went on. "We could bring the proposals to the next meeting, and then pick out four or five to vote on. I don't know if we should go with a majority vote on that, or consensus, or what. It just seems like we're all capable of reaching a compromise, finding some way that everyone can live together peacefully." I looked around. "I just need for us to have peace in our own community. I mean, out in the world people are killing each other. In our own community, why can't we agree and get along?" I still had a little sand left, but I handed the timer to Debra.

"Getting along isn't the same as agreeing," said Debra. "Probably, whatever we decide, one or two of us won't agree." She paused to gather her thoughts. "This isn't something we can have both ways. We could try and fake ourselves out by trying to make a policy that allows dogs but doesn't allow dogs." Everyone laughed. "But, folks, either we're going to have dogs or we're not going to have dogs." I caught myself nodding, and stopped. "On something like this, consensus is impossible. It's a majority-vote issue, keeping the rights of the minority in mind." Everyone was looking at the floor. "I suggest, Oak, that we call for a vote. Will you facilitate?"

"All right," said Oak. "We'll go around and everyone will say if she wants dogs or no dogs. I'll start. No dogs." She made a mark on the clipboard.

"Dogs," said Randi.

"No dogs," said Debra.

"Dogs," I said.

Susan stretched her skirt over her kneecaps, tighter than a trampoline. "No dogs," she said in a very small voice.

"Shit," said Randi, and we all looked at her. "I guess that's it for now. If we get more people, though, can we vote again?"

"Yes," said Oak.

"I can see her now," I said, reaching for a brownie. "Standing in front of Arlington Pet Supply, passing out flyers to strange women. 'How would you like to join a lesbian community and vote Yes on the dog issue?' "

Oak picked up the clipboard. "Okay, the next item for Issue Clarification is Environment. This will include the recycling policy, and whether or not we will install electrical lines."

Susan left for the kitchen. I put my head in Debra's lap.

"How are we going to live without electricity?" said Randi, disgusted. "We *have* to have *electricity*."

IRENE

BETH FOLLETT

You. Naked at the bedroom window. A week ago you and I in Cuba. Burning skin. Brilliant turquoise ocean.

You look out to the maple tree. Grey. Bare.

You sift through your top drawer seeking clean underwear, the familiar knitting of your shoulder blades. I want to tell you to breathe. You turn, see me watching. Burst. Tears explode from your eyes.

You come back under the cool sheets and we stare the truth down.

Irene. Has been given. Two months to live.

You doodle in the corner of your grocery list. Irene and her old friend Rae are coming for supper. Irene says that since losing the last of her hair, chocolate tastes like shit and red wine tastes pretty damn good. So Irene drinks wine, lots of it.

Your pencil breaks. You push back hard in your chair, the scream of wood on wood. You nab the list as it lifts off the table, grab your leather jacket and head for the door. God! Fuck! you curse, slamming the door between us.

Great soup, Irene says.
She pushes away from the table and hauls herself to the counter to get more wine. She moves in waves, as if not all of a part. As if she had forgotten about muscle, about breathing.

C'mon, Irene! You only had three mouthfuls, you say.

Yeah, well. Irene's bald head drifts, her fingers remove the cork from the bottle. Do you think this stuff kills? she asks. The tumbler accepts three, now four red ounces.

You rise. The tears have come again.

Rae goes out back to smoke a cigarette.

With her back towards you, Irene says, I'm finished. I've no appetite. They tell me it's normal. She drains the glass.

You step up to her and place the heel of your palm against the small of her back, your other hand on her chest. You lay your forehead on her shoulder.

Tell me what to do now?

In bed you ask questions. I lay my head on your breast, stroking the taut nipple, cross-eyed, losing your question. What do you mean?

I sit up in the bed and rearrange the sheets. I stay sitting, my back to you.

Irene wants to die in her father's house. Any one of us could have made a place for her. She chooses him. How will she get to the hospital for her treatment? It's a two hour drive. He doesn't drive. He's an old man. It would be better if she stayed in her own apartment. Who cares more than us? Who knows that?

I puff up the sheets, watch them settle around my legs. Repeat this.

Irene can't live with herself, lover.

June. You examine your nails while listening to the news. One thousand dead in Tiananmen Square. Fallen. The red of the flags, challenges falling into a stony madness. The official report: we did not shoot any students.

June. Irene in hospital for two days.

Renal failure, she says.

June. The maple tree outside the bedroom window is bright with new leaves.

You ask me, When is Irene going to talk to us about dying?

I am changing the sheets on the bed. They carry the smell of our sex. I put my face to the bundle and begin to sob.

Rae calls for the third time this morning. Her voice is low and sensuous and full of treachery.

I don't know, what do you think? Irene wants to leave me her car. And the pearls I gave her. I can't take that car. I told her I can't take it. She says, Rae, take the fucking car. I can't take it. It reeks.

Take the car, honey. You can always sell it.

Do you think I could? I mean, god, Irene's car!

Take the car, honey.

June. Irene has moved to the country. Her father is afraid. He is afraid of what she might do. He is afraid of what her friends might do. He hires a nurse, a friend of his nephew's wife. I give the orders here, he says. When a man's wife is dead and his only daughter is dying, he needs order in his house.

But why am I telling you this? he adds. You're a nurse.

There once was a cousin who put his penis between Irene's young breasts. Now he's married. Cousin has a young daughter. Daughter draws a penis, puts it upside down on her bulletin board. Daughter has a man's shirt pinned above her bed. In its make-believe hand is a flimsy scarf shaped like the word Mom. You and I lay stiff together on Daughter's bed, holding hands, not sleeping. Cousin and his family are away for the weekend, have offered their country home to you, Rae, me. Just ten minutes to Irene, and she's feeling up to a swim in their pool, she says. Keep the air conditioning on, Cousin instructs in a note. Immediately, Rae turns it off. Now, in the false quiet of a sealed night, we sweat. Disabled.

Irene, what shall we do with your journals?

Burn them, she replies from the air mattress on which she drifts in the pool, in the yard surrounded by evergreens.

Belonging to her cousin.

The toll bridge out of the city. To Irene. Exact change. You hurl your rage into each quarter going, your despair into each returning. The drive to the townships, to Irene's bed, to her father's pale yearning, like dreams without memory. Wanting memory. The body rigid with wanting. Grasping. This bridge washed out before our eyes.

Irene tells you, I've given my cousin all my computer disks. The story. About the incest. It's on one of the disks.

Why? What made you do it?

I don't remember. The morphine? I get scrambled.

This is going to make trouble.

You think so?

Has he read it?

He says he doesn't know how to access it. He says the computers aren't compatible.

For Christ's sake. He just has to shove it in.

Well, Irene whispers, bowing her head. He knows how to do that.

You stand before the mirror in the front hall. I watch you, watch the way your eyes narrow and search. I have to speak, to say, You knew. We suspected. She's just written her story. He hasn't done anything yet.

I can hear your dry rage, the grating of hate against fear. I can see your muscles shorten. I imagine your black eyes wide in the growing darkness. I watch. Then turn towards the kitchen to make a pot of tea.

In the dark you fold your leg across my belly and I stroke your calf. My breasts ache. Your hair is soft against my chin.

You tell me, Irene lived with Phyllis for eight years. She hasn't called Irene. She won't. Once Phyllis locked Irene out of their house. While Irene was at work she had the locks changed.

Jesus.

Spoon me?

We realign our bodies. Over the top of your head I can make out the silhouette of the maple tree.

Did they ever really try to be friends after their break-up?

They never were. Friends.

I trace the path from your hip to inner thigh, my hand falling with its own weight. You are thinner. Sharper in the bone. Closed.

Don't, honey. I don't feel like it. I'm sorry.

You try to turn your head around to see my eyes. Maybe you do. Maybe the stars give just enough light. My eyes reflect just enough.

You tell me, Irene wants us with her on her birthday. She wants to try her cousin's pool again. His wife will bake her a cake, her favourite chocolate cake. I told her to go ahead. I said, Let her throw it up.

I can't imagine how Irene does it.

She used to stick her fingers down her throat. She was doing that for years.

Oh. I meant, how she keeps living.

Oh.

Irene vomits. The stench is a mixture of morphine, Coke and something else.

A knot of pain in stagnant water.

She calls, Daddy! Bring a washcloth!

I hold her forehead and she spits the last of it, swearing between spits.

It's the water, I tell you. She shouldn't have so much water, her father insists as he stands awkwardly in the doorway of her room. He doesn't know about the Coke. Doesn't ask about the colour in the pail.

Irene says, I want to go to the pool now.

Oh Irene!

You gather her towel and a new nightgown under one arm, offering your hand to her. Her legs, her naked arms as she pulls herself up from the wrinkled sheets, like a tree bare of its leaves.

Hurry! Cover me up.

Her breath is horrible. She spins the room.

Irene watches you from her deck chair as you and Rae play in the pool. She is surrounded by her birthday gifts. Embroidered pillowcase. Purple balloons. Crystal vase. Birds of Paradise. She's had her cake.

We applaud. Then she throws up.

I love you, she shouts to you. Out of the blue.
Don't let me stop telling you. She waves her hand to keep us silent, closes her eyes, smiles.

I take her photograph.

She wants me to drive her back to her father's. I bring the car across the lawn. We carry her on the deck chair to the front seat.

Her eyes are closed. You don't look at me. I'll follow in Irene's car, you say.

Before reaching the mailboxes on the main road, you slow then stop. You are waving and pointing into the rolling country to our left.

A deer.

I stop the car, glance at Irene, back up slightly. Yes, there! By the side of the wood, bent down to the grasses. Sleek and brown. Do you see it, Irene?
No.
I back up again. Now!
No.
And again.
I guess I'm not meant to see it, she sighs, looking straight ahead. I back up once more. There, Irene!

Yes! I see it!

We continue on through rolling farm land. My eyes wander to the fields, searching for another.

Desperate. Feeling body incline towards body. Like swallowing a divining stick.

Are you frightened Irene?

Yes.

A thrush flies straight for the windshield then veers off to the left at the last second.

I don't want to talk about it.

All our lines are busy. We are asking each other if Irene has talked about dying. While Irene rambles, Forever, To ever, Whatever, Hey! in her hospital bed. All our lines are busy. We are asking each other if Irene knows she has been taken to hospital from her father's house. Her few last wishes: to die at her father's house, to have a pine coffin, that there be no mention of God in the days following her death.

All our lines are busy.

July 25, 1989
9 a.m.
Alone. In her hospital bed.

Beautiful day! the cousin says as we get out of the car. Rae glares at him. You spot the coffin.

Fucking hell.

You veer off to the only green grass in a parched cemetery. It has not rained for twenty-one days.

Irene's father arrives. He moves around the semi-circle kissing her friends. He is wearing black sunglasses that cover his eyes from all angles. His lips are cracked and dry.

The cousin's wife reads the twenty-third psalm. Then she and the cousin intone the lord's prayer. The friends look to each other. Look at the ground. I read from *The Work of a Common Woman*.

Then the coffin is lowered into the hard earth and an old man in trousers and a baseball cap begins the slow replacing of the dirt, shovelful by shovelful. He is careful and silent. You never take your eyes from him.

Irene would have loved him, Rae says as she climbs into the back seat.

The past tense hangs between us.

When we get to the reception at the cousin's house, Rae discovers Irene's car in the driveway. With new plates.

We go back to the cemetery the next day, our arms loaded with fireweed and rushes. We take apart the formal bouquet, stand the carnations and yellow daisies upright in the sod. The rushes wave like prairie wheat under the twenty-second-sun. We make a joyful noise because we know how. Our hearts are beating fast and breaking all at once. Rae turns a cartwheel. You shout something. I place my open hand on the side of your neck where your vein jumps. We remember. Irene.

You sit on the back porch looking up at the sky. You tell Irene you don't know why you are looking there, you don't believe in heaven. You look at your garden. I believe in purple basil, you say.

I go inside.

You call after me, She was a lesbian.

I come back and stand with my foot on the doorstep.

Once Irene and I went to a Chinese palm reader. She saw a break in Irene's lifeline.

What did she think it meant?

I don't know. She kept saying she was waiting for her big break.

I lean over to examine the grey in your hair. Are you going to burn Irene's journals?

No.

I stretch my arms over my head until I hear my back crack. I move my gaze to your small garden, looking at the purple basil almost white in the sun. I think of how you tend the delicate leaves, how thoughtful you are when you water the dry earth. Your little garden; small clay pots on this narrow porch.

I imagine I'm looking at the basil for the first time, I tell you, after awhile.

BECAUSE

CANDIS J. GRAHAM

Rosa is afraid to open her mouth and speak the thoughts in her head. Anxiety, tight and painful like a clenched fist, sits in her stomach.

The next berry is hard and she has to force the needle through, jabbing her finger in the process. Rosa pauses to suck her sore finger and thinks, I have to tell her. But how can I say what I am thinking in such a way that she won't take offence? How can I get her to listen? How can I get her to understand my feelings, without the conversation turning into a quarrel?

"You're taking a long time with those berries."

Rosa looks up, her finger still in her mouth. Maud is frowning and standing back from the tree to study the arrangement of lights.

Rosa loathes the fear in herself. She removes the finger from her mouth and examines the sore.

"I'm thinking," she says, hoping Maud will ask her what she is thinking about.

"Yeah, well, I'm just about ready to put the cranberries on the tree. Could you think a little faster."

Rosa hears the command behind the words. The fist in her stomach grows and tightens at the same time. She is trying to think of a tactful way to tell Maud their relationship is a fraud. She wants to say to her, We are impostors. We are liars. We pretend and pretend until we don't know what's real anymore and, worst of all, we deceive ourselves.

Rosa takes a cigarette from the pack on the coffee table and lights it with an inch-high flame from an orange lighter. Maud feels no need for tact when she speaks. Rosa wonders, not for the first time, if Maud's forthright approach is more honest. It seems more effective.

She inhales deeply and watches Maud attach a row of lights to the branches. Each detail is important to Maud, from the shape of the carefully chosen tree to the arrangement of hanging white balls. Maud insists on buying a Scots pine. Rosa can't remember why it has to be a Scots pine, although each year they drive around to Christmas tree lots searching for the ideal one at a bargain price. Maud never looks at the spruce trees or the balsams. There is never any discussion, except about whether or not a particular Scots pine is really worth twenty or twenty-five dollars.

Their first year together, Rosa protested. They were standing in the parking lot of a shopping centre, surrounded by evergreens of every shape and size. Rosa's fingers were stiff from the frosty December cold, although she was wearing handmade mittens over her leather gloves, and she was hungry because she had eaten only one piece of toast for breakfast.

She had said, somewhat impatiently, "It's sinful to buy a tree and a week or two later turn it into garbage."

Maud pulled a frozen Scots pine to an upright position. "What do you think of this one? Did he say everything in this row is eighteen dollars?" She looked over her right shoulder at Rosa. "Will you hold it so I can see how it looks?"

Rosa took hold of the tree trunk and Maud stood back.

"These conifers are for the Christmas market."

Rosa said, "That may be ... " but Maud interrupted her.

"There are farmers who plant trees especially for Christmas. It's how they make their living. We're not destroying any natural resources or harming the environment by buying one because the trees come from Christmas-tree farms. If we don't buy them, the farmers will lose their income."

Rosa was appeased but not entirely convinced. She chewed the corner of her lip as she helped Maud carry the tree to the car.

She exhales a cloud of grey smoke and looks at the tree Maud picked this year. When she was growing up, her mother used to say that Rosa only remembered what she chose to remember. Her mother would sigh, a small sigh filled with reproach, and mutter about Rosa's selective memory. Rosa has never entirely believed her mother. But, she cannot totally disregard her mother's point of view either.

She wants to remember why Maud insists they buy a Scots pine every year. Why can't she remember?

Rosa inhales. This one must be seven feet tall. It is a pleasant looking tree with a symmetrical shape. Maud has a good eye for picking trees and now she is decorating it with her usual meticulous attention to detail. Each year Maud performs her Christmas-tree-decorating ritual. First, she puts the lights on the tree. Next, she hangs the round white satin balls. Then she winds two strings of cranberries around and around.

Every December, two weeks before Christmas, Rosa sits a tin bowl filled with fresh cranberries on her lap and holds a needle with a double string of thread in her right hand—forcing one cranberry after another onto the needle and along the thread. This is Rosa's part in the ritual: she puts the Peter, Paul and Mary holiday-concert cassette in the stereo, while Maud gets the box of decorations from their locker in the basement; she makes the long strings of cranberries, while Maud puts the lights on the tree and then hangs the white balls.

Rosa exhales, forcing grey smoke out through rounded lips. Once the strings of sour red berries are in place, Maud drapes the icicles—those delicate shimmering threads of silver that remind Rosa of Christmas trees from when she was growing up—over the branches. Then it is time to sit back and drink hot chocolate with whipped cream and admire their creation.

In the evenings, over the next week, they will wrap their gifts and place them beneath the tree. Maud, a lawyer by profession but an artist at heart, usually wraps Rosa's gifts when she has finished with her own. Maud takes pride in decorating the presents to look extraordinary, with green or red wool wrapped around the shiny silver foil paper and fashioned into slender bows on top. Sometimes she ties miniature candy canes into the bows. Last year she used tiny chocolate Santas to decorate the gifts.

Rosa, a social worker by profession and a social worker at heart, finds December the most exhausting month of the year. She comes home tired every evening. Her clients, mostly women (and their children), are despondent because they can't afford toys for their children, can't afford the traditional Christmas feast, can't afford warm boots and snowsuits and hats and mittens. They worry about paying the rent and the phone bill, worry about having enough money to buy food as they struggle through the weeks of each long month. They are perpetually weary and nervous from worry.

Rosa patiently explains the latest budget cuts in social services to each woman and refers her to one or two of the over-burdened community groups that offer assistance at Christmas. Occasionally she also suggests a disheartened woman contact the local advocacy group and join the fight against poverty. Rosa urges her to educate herself and to rebel against her demeaning situation, at the same time feeling as pessimistic as the helpless woman. They both know that governments are made up of wealthy white males, lawyers and businesspeople who never listen to the poor. Rosa comes home from work each evening feeling so very tired and thoroughly inadequate.

Rosa inhales and puts the cigarette in the ashtray. Maud is singing along with Peter, Paul and Mary as she works on the tree. "Once in a year it is not thought amiss, to visit our neighbours and sing out like thissss." She is a little off key but sings with feeling. "Of friendship and love, good neighbours abound, and peace and goodwill the whole year a-ro-undddd."

Maud adores the Christmas season and all the rituals. Rosa thinks of her as being childlike in her devotion to the holiday. Maud watches every Christmas show on television, the made-for-TV movies, the cartoon shows, the Christmas episodes of all the regular shows, and the old Christmas movies like *It's a Wonderful Life* and *White Christmas*.

The only part of the ritual Maud dislikes is shopping for Christmas gifts. Rosa agrees wholeheartedly. Buying gifts is the most commercial aspect of Christmas, and the most stressful. She wants her gifts to give pleasure. But it is not as easy as it sounds, to know what will please others. And she always feels guilty when she spends money on expensive presents, on luxuries like black kid gloves for her mother and brightly-patterned silk scarves for

Maud's sisters, knowing her clients are struggling just to feed themselves and their children.

Rosa stares at the bowl of cranberries and feels like crying. We demean our relationship by separating at Christmas, she says to Maud in her head. Do you think we would spend Christmas apart if we were a woman-man couple? Be honest with me. Rosa shoves the needle through a soft cranberry, keeping her head bent forward to hide the tears in her eyes. To say it like that might seem like she is criticizing Maud. Juice squishes onto her fingers, leaving a dark red stain. She sniffs quietly and clears away a tear with her thumb.

Crying feels like a weakness within her. Especially when Maud sits two feet away from her and watches calmly, talking, seeming to ignore the tears, the way she did a few weeks ago when Rosa was crying about a client, Janet Powers.

On a day when she was feeling especially desperate, Janet Powers used her sister's credit card to buy winter coats for herself and her son, plus a set of pretty sheets and two down-filled pillows for her bed. She had never, she explained later to Rosa, bought sheets in her entire life. She always used hand-me-down sheets. She didn't mind hand-me-downs, it was just that for once she wanted brand new sheets that pleased her. And she'd been having trouble sleeping at night and thought maybe the soft pillows would help. Now her sister had to make the monthly payments to the bank and was furious and had told their whole family that Janet was a thief and was threatening to have her charged with stealing the credit card. What could she do? She didn't have the money to pay her sister back. She was so depressed she couldn't get out of bed some days. Her son sat on her lap, never uttering a sound. His skinny hair and pinched face worried Rosa.

She couldn't stop thinking about Janet Powers and her small son. By the time she opened the front door of the apartment that evening, there were tears in her eyes. Within the safety of her home, the sobs started and she couldn't seem to stop.

Maud sat across from her, in the wicker chair, and said, "You don't do them any good when you get so emotionally involved. Because that's not what they need. Where would I be if I got emotional about every client? And I could, believe you me. Soon I'll be swamped with calls from women whose former spouses are demanding custody. These men ignore their kids all year but when Christmas rolls around suddenly they want them. Just because it's Christmas. You should get out of social work," Maud said sternly. "You should get out of direct service. You care too much."

Rosa picks up the cigarette and inhales. She hates crying. Maud never cries. Not once in their four years together has she known Maud to cry. What does Maud do with her pain and tears?

Rosa exhales and puts the cigarette out in the ashtray with rapid stabbing motions. She understands that Maud wants to solve her problems for her and take away the pain, but she wishes Maud would say, instead, No wonder you're crying. You must feel awful for Janet Powers. Isn't life a bummer sometimes.

She wishes Maud would put her arms around her and say, Cry, let it all out.

But that is not Maud's way.

Rosa bends her head and forces herself to concentrate on her own problems. I love Maud. I want to spend Christmas with her. Is that asking so much?

So many of their friends do the same thing. They ignore their relationship, ignore their partner, to spend Christmas with their families. They act as if they are single women without any ties except to family—ties to their biological family, not to their family of lesbian friends. It's not fair.

Maybe it is the feeling of despair that makes Rose speak the first words that enter her mind. "Why do we bother with a tree when we won't be here for Christmas?" She looks up, watching Maud and waiting for her response.

Maud does not seem to hear the anger. "We have to have a tree," she says calmly, as if it were a fact of life like November leading to December. "It's Christmas." She opens a small box and places a white ball in the palm of her hand. "Are those berries ready yet?"

"No." Rose shoves the needle through a soft berry and slides the berry down the thread. She has started and she can't stop. "This is a fraud," she says, not looking at Maud. "Are we a couple or are we not? Your sisters and their husbands don't spend Christmas apart. They wouldn't dream of separating at Christmas. Why do we?" She didn't mean to say it like that. She looks up.

Maud is cradling the white ornament in her hand, stroking the soft satin with a forefinger. "We've been through this before. Do we have to go through it every year? Why do you have to spoil everything!"

Rose watches Maud hang the white ball from a branch, then take another ball from the box and move to the other side of the tree.

"I don't want to spoil everything, but I want to talk about it. I don't understand why we have to spend Christmas apart."

Maud turns to look at her. "You know why we have to. Talk! It never ends. We talk and talk, but what does it do? Everything's been arranged. Why are you making an issue of this? Why are you doing this? Because Helen and her new lover are spending Christmas together? Is that it?"

Rose picks up a berry and pushes the needle into the soft centre. "This has nothing to do with Helen and Nawal. And don't raise your voice to me. If you don't want to talk about it, say so, and tell me why you don't want to talk about it. But don't yell."

There is silence in the room. Maud hangs white balls on the tree. Rose bends forward and works on the growing chain of berries.

I tried, Rosa thinks. Maud doesn't want to deal with it. So, we will pretend. Always pretending that nothing is wrong. There's no problem. We're lesbians, but let's not make a big deal of it. No fuss, no muss, no disturbance. Let's just pretend we are two women who live together because it's convenient. It's cheaper this way, sharing expenses. And we have each other for company. It's simply companionship. Whatever we do, don't demand that we act like a couple or be treated like a couple. We are not married. We can't marry. We have no status, no recognition, nothing. That's it. We're nothing. We're just two women who happen to live together. Good friends, that's us. Nothing more. Nothing.

Rosa's hands move quickly, forcing one berry after another onto the needle and along the thread. Her throat aches. Why am I making this fuss? That's all we are. Why pretend? We are simply two women living together. Nothing more.

Her hands stop moving. But we are more. We're much more. We love each other. We are a couple. Except at Christmas. The tears are back, threatening to spill down her cheeks.

She sets the bowl on the floor and goes into the bathroom. Closing the door behind her, she leans across the sink. Her face, reflected in the mirror, looks grim. Am I always this pale? She bends forward to study the colour of her skin. Maybe it does have something to do with Helen and her new lover spending Christmas together. I envy them, envy the excitement of their loving feelings and their easy decision to spend Christmas with each other.

There is a knock at the door. "Are you okay?"

Rosa clears her throat and watches herself answer. "I'm alive and breathing."

That's nasty. I'm sorry Maud. You don't deserve it. The white face is motionless, staring back at her. There is silence in her head as she glares at the mirror.

Maud knocks again. "May I come in?"

The door opens and Maud peeks around the edge. She pushes the door wide open and walks in. "What's up?"

Rosa turns from the mirror. "It's the pretending. We pretend we're a couple. We pretend we're not a couple. It depends on the situation. We send a Christmas card to Helen and Nawal and sign both our names. I send one to my mother and sign only my name." She looks at Maud, looks into her eyes. "Why can't we spend Christmas together?"

Maud stares at Rosa for a moment before speaking.

"You think I don't care? I hate leaving you. But what do you want me to do about it? It's a hopeless situation. Why do you have to make it harder?"

Rosa says nothing. Each year she resents spending Christmas away from Maud, resents it more than she knows how to express in words, and this year she is determined to change it. But how? She swallows to stop the tears. She wants to say to Maud, It is connected to our lives as lesbians and that makes our separation feel worse—if that's possible. It's like a betrayal of our very lives. A betrayal of our sexual orientation. No. It is much more than sexual orientation. That's a heterosexual concept, that lesbians are lesbians because of our sexuality. It's not merely who we sleep with. A woman can be celibate and be a lesbian. Being lesbian is not merely sexual, not necessarily sexual at all. It's ...

"Why are you so quiet? Come back to the living room." Maud rests a hand on Rosa's shoulder. "I'll help you string the rest of the cranberries."

Rosa tilts her head and brushes her cheek along Maud's hand. "I feel like I'm denying who I am. I love you. I want the whole world to know. I want everyone to see us as a couple. What's wrong with that?"

"There's nothing wrong with that. It's the most natural thing in this world. But you make yourself sick about it because you take all this too seriously, and it's not worth it. Come on. Wash your face."

Maud watches as Rosa turns on the cold water tap and splashes water on her face. She follows Rosa into the living room and sits on the floor, in front of Rosa's chair, her shoulders between Rosa's knees.

"If you want to know what I think, I think straights get carried away with this togetherness business." Maud turns to look up at Rosa. "They have to do every single thing together. We don't have to imitate them. Why should we?"

Rosa shrugs and reaches for a cigarette and the orange lighter. "Are you saying we spend Christmas apart because we want to? Not because we're lesbians?" She lights the cigarette and inhales.

"No. You know I don't mean that. Spending Christmas together doesn't make us a couple and spending it apart doesn't stop us from being a couple. It's how we feel about each other that matters because that's all that really matters."

Rosa exhales forcefully. "Yeah. But there's something wrong with that logic. But it doesn't matter. Maud, I want to be with you at Christmas. That's all I want."

"Yes and you want to see your mother too. I want to see my family. They live six hundred miles apart. What do you think we can do? It's an impossible situation."

"It's not six hundred miles from Kingston to Kitchener."

"It might as well be. It's too far to spend Christmas together and with both our families because we'd spend all day on the 401. We'd be tired and we wouldn't see anyone. That's no way to spend Christmas."

Rosa reaches out to stroke Maud's hair. "I know."

Maud sighs loudly. "You always want too much. You know that, don't you. You want too much."

"Is it too much to want to spend Christmas with you!"

"Look who's raising her voice now."

Rosa sighs, a small sigh. She bends forward and kisses the top of Maud's head. "The tree is nice, huh."

Maud turns and takes Rosa's hand. "Yeah. Best tree we've ever had. You know there's no way we can do it because we can't be together and with our families. There's no way. Why can't you accept it?"

Rosa nods.

"But I've got an idea." Maud squeezes Rosa's hand and smiles. "We could have our own Christmas together, before we leave. Our own Christmas with a meal, and we'd open our presents. The whole works. What do you think? I like it."

"It wouldn't be the same."

"Damn, Rosa, you drive me cuckoo. Stubborn! You invented the word."

"I want to spend Christmas with you."

"Yes, well, do you have any ideas?"

Rosa shrugs. What are the options? It's an impossible situation with no solution.

"When you figure it out, let me know. I'm out of ideas." Maud stands up and walks toward the tree.

Rosa picks up the bowl and sits it on her lap. Maud is right. We don't have to mimic het couples. She squashes a soft berry when she tries to force it on the needle. I want to be with Maud. Red juice darkens her stained fingers. I want to be with my mother too. And Maud wants to be with me and she wants to be with her parents and sisters.

She looks at Maud. Before we leave we could have a Christmas dinner here with our friends, our family of women. A lesbian Christmas. No, a lesbian Solstice. Yes, that's it. We could invite Helen and Nawal, and Liam, Maryse and Linda. It won't be the same as spending Christmas with Maud, but ... the fist in her stomach relaxes a little. And Ingrid and Eileen, and Giselle. A lesbian winter Solstice celebration.

"What kind of celebration would we have here?"

Maud is winding the first string of cranberries around the tree. She pauses and turns to look at Rosa. "It could just be the two of us or we could invite some friends for a Christmas meal. We could all sit around the tree and sing carols. What do you think? How about the Sunday before Christmas? Next Sunday. We'll invite Helen and her new love, Nawal. And your friend Liam."

Rosa is amazed, and it is not the first time this has happened, that Maud is thinking the very same thing that she is thinking. "Okay, let's do that. And how about we invite Giselle and Maryse and Linda and Ingrid and Eileen?"

Rosa pushes the needle through a hard berry, and then another hard one. The berries slide easily along the wet thread.

"No, not Eileen and Ingrid. I don't want Eileen here."

"Why not?"

"I don't like Eileen. Don't ask me why because I don't know. I just don't like her."

"I didn't know that you didn't like her."

"Do you like her? How can you like her. She's always saying hurtful things to Ingrid. She's got a mean streak in her that pisses me off."

"I know. It bothers me sometimes. But, Maud, I really like Ingrid. We've been friends for years and I want her to be here with us."

"Okay then, invite them if you want to."

"Are you sure?"

"Yes, invite them. But I'm warning you I might say something to Eileen, because if she starts on at Ingrid I'll have to say something to her. I won't be able to stop myself."

"Okay," Rosa agrees, hoping Eileen will be on her best behaviour for a change. She is so encouraged by the change in mood that she decides to tell Maud some of the other ideas she has about Christmas. "Maud, let's make it a different kind of holiday celebration. Like, let's not have turkey. Let's have a vegetarian meal instead. And we won't wrap the presents in paper. We'll use tea towels or cloth napkins or something instead of wrapping paper and spare some trees. And let's go through the cookbooks when we're done. We'll make something special. How does that sound?" Rosa laughs. "How about we ask everyone to bring a dish. A lesbian potluck winter Solstice dinner." The words roll off her tongue.

"That's it. We'll start a new tradition. I'll make the pudding. I've always wanted to try making a Christmas pudding. Do you think Helen would make some bread? There's nothing like her bread."

"Yeah." Rosa remembers the taste of Helen's bread as she hums quietly along with her favourite song on the tape. She feels excited at the thought of having all their friends together for a lesbian Solstice dinner. Next year, she decides to herself, we will do it differently. Next year, I will insist that we spend Christmas Day together. Somehow we'll find a way to do it. I have a year to think of a way around it. Maybe we won't see our families. Maybe we'll stay here, just the two of us. Rosa sighs, without being aware of it. But I've always spent Christmas with Mom.

She slides a cranberry easily along the needle, then another one and another, and sings softly with Peter, Paul and Mary. "O sing our songs and raise the Torah, raise the Torah, right the wrongs and light menorah, light menorah."

Maud is standing back, admiring the tree.

"Why must it be a Scots pine? I can never remember."

"It's the perfect Christmas tree because it's bushy and beautiful. Most people get a spruce. Even those artificial trees are made to look like spruces. But a Scots pine is better." Maud turns to look at Rosa. "Is the next string ready yet?"

Rosa shakes her head. "It's getting there." She uses both hands to lift the gigantic necklace of cranberries from the tin bowl for Maud to see. "Why don't you sit beside me while I finish it."

"This is the last ball," Maud warns. She hangs it on a low branch and then sits beside Rosa. "I love you Rosa."

"Yeah, I know." Rosa squeezes Maud's hand, leaving a faint blush of squashed cranberry juice on Maud's thumb. "What shall we cook for the party? We'll have to plan a menu. Do you want to call Helen and invite her and Nawal while I finish this string? And phone Giselle too. Then I'll phone the others while you're putting the icicles on the tree." She rests her face against Maud's shoulder. "Do you know, sometimes I wonder if I should say anything to Ingrid about the way Eileen talks to her. But I'm afraid she'll hate me if I say anything bad about Eileen."

"Someone needs to say something to Ingrid sooner or later. Maybe I'll take her aside and say something, so you won't have to worry about your friendship with her." Maud takes the bowl of cranberries on to her lap. "Why don't you start phoning everyone while I finish this. We have a lot still to do."

INVERT SUGAR

FLORENCE GRANDVIEW

When I took Mavis down the trail where I hung out as a kid, I was not expecting to have a big revelation. This was in December when the deciduous trees that crowded the way were bare, giving us a scenic view of the ravine. The mud we sank into was the colour of Mr. Flakey's Chocolate Pies, and I was feeling years younger.

"Scenic view," mumbled Mavis, grabbing my shoulder for support. "Look at those rubber tires floating in the creek. And someone's orange panties are hanging on the limb of that tree. Guess what we'll find next."

"Those aren't someone's panties," I patiently explained, "it's a trail-marker. The people here can't afford fancy fluorescent ones." I hadn't been on that trail in almost twenty-five years, and was surprised to see it looked exactly as I'd remembered. The path itself was still visible, and the woods had not been bulldozed in favour of boring developments.

"You said the ground would be frozen this time of year and here we are sinking in the muck," Mavis continued. "What's the big idea?"

Well, the big idea, as if Mavis didn't know, was that I wanted to do a little communing with nature—something Mavis and I could not do in the city. Her grumpiness was due to her bad back. Mavis wrecked her back by lifting too many heavy objects over the years. I thought a little exercise like this might do her good, but I was mistaken.

Also these woods, scanty as they were, held a lot of nostalgia for me. They were only an hour's drive from the city, yet I seldom came out this way anymore. I was having a specific hankering to see the old tree-swing that my friends and I made so long ago.

"Hang on, Mavis," I said, "this place is giving me a flood of memories."

"The creek smells like they dump the sewer in there," Mavis observed, but I ignored it. I was thinking about the last time I'd been down that trail, when I was no more than twelve.

The last time I'd been there was the day I had a falling out with my best friend Henry. I was a tomboy and hung out mostly with boys. I had one girlfriend, Donna Haygreen, but I'd had a falling out with her too, just before the one with Henry. It was late summer, almost time for the new school year to begin.

Henry was starting to associate with a gang of boys much older than us. I don't expect anyone to remember all these names but there was Bruce Haygreen (Donna's older brother), Victor Vox and his brother Butch. That's right, Butch. Sometimes my older brother Lester used to run with that crowd.

These older guys took to hanging around our tree-swing all of a sudden. We couldn't really claim it as our own—they didn't respect squatters' rights, and they were bigger than us.

Mavis let go of my shoulder and interrupted these memories. "Look here," she said, "you go on and meditate and do whatever you want to do. I'm gonna stay right here."

I turned around to look. Mavis plopped herself on a big stump just off the beaten path. It was green with moss and most likely very damp. "I don't like sinking in the muck, but I know this means a lot to you." Mavis gestured to the trees and the lazily flowing creek. "Go ahead without me. I'll wait."

This was the closest thing to good-natured that I'd ever seen Mavis, so I thanked her and carried on. I knew I was out of her sight by the time I hit the bottom of the trail, so Mavis did not see me trip over an exposed root and fall against the familiar tree that used to hold our tree-swing. I knew right away that this was my tree, even before I got such a close look. The swing itself was gone—not even a rotting shred remained.

It was then, as I held onto the scratchy trunk for support, that I had a flash of belated insight into my memories. It was to do with Henry and our falling out. "Mavis," I called in a panic, as I was having an uncanny recollection of Henry and me. The fall I took must have given me quite a jolt. Perhaps I didn't even call out loud—in any case, Mavis was too far to hear.

I saw myself, in my mind's eye, coming down the trail as a twelve-year-old kid, looking for Henry. I'd just been to his house, and his mum said, "No, he ain't here, he must be in that son-of-a-bitchin' bush," so that's where I headed.

That summer had been so hot and dry, there was no mud along the trail—only the occasional orange-coloured leaf that had fallen early from a tree. Visibility was poor because of all the foliage.

I was preceded by a cloud of brown dust as I hit the bottom of the trail. Henry and a couple of other boys our age were hanging around at the tree, but so were these older guys I've mentioned. They were standing in a close circle, and Victor Vox spun around when he heard me coming. "Bugger off," he said.

Victor Vox was the toughest of the lot, and this was the first time he saw fit to speak to me. My brother Lester was not amongst them; this was a good thing because he would have pounded me if Victor told him to. Donna's brother Bruce was there, and Victor's brother Butch. One of them hissed at Henry, "You're her friend—take her outta here."

Henry didn't say anything. With a sulky look on his face he dutifully climbed the trail. Having no choice, and having no idea what all the hoopla was about, I followed.

At first I figured the guys were smoking and drinking down there, but Victor, Bruce and Butch were too old and arrogant to have to hide anymore. They did such things any place they pleased—in the balcony of the New Century theatre, in front of their parents, in the schoolyard—and no one dared stop them. It was just us younger kids who still had to hide out in order to smoke and drink, and then we'd get caught anyway.

Henry didn't speak to me the whole way back to his place—he just mumbled goodbye as he turned towards his driveway. I continued on home with the idea of making amends with Henry for whatever he was ticked off about. Tomorrow was another day.

The next evening after supper I went to Henry's place and found him sitting on the front steps, listening to records. His portable record player was out there with an extension cord. "Oh hi," he called above the music, so I knew we were on speaking terms.

He had a new record, *Easier Said Than Done,* by the Essex. We always used to crank up the radio whenever it came on, so I was excited to see that Henry had his own copy, from one day to the next. "How did you get that?" I wanted to know. "Your old man gave you some money, I bet."

"It's Victor's record. He lent it to me," Henry answered. He always had a serious face, and it got more serious as he added, "I have to tell you something. Bruce and Butch and Victor said I couldn't hang around with them anymore—unless I quit seeing you."

I had to sit a moment and think about what to say. I wanted to blurt out, "How come big tough Victor and his gang are your best friends, just like that? Only last week they were calling us sick names and saying you were stupid and everything else."

I didn't end up saying this, but it's true they thought Henry was stupid—they called him the big and dumb type. Well, he was big, as in big for his age, but not dumb. He did flunk grade two but that doesn't mean anything. If people thought he was dumb, it's because he had a few stubborn ideas, that's all.

For example, we used to crank up the radio for Peter, Paul and Mary songs, and Henry thought that Peter, Paul and Mary were only two people—the guy's name was Peter Paul and the woman's name was Mary. I knew otherwise, especially because they'd been on the television so many times. Henry believed he was hearing not three voices, but two—like Dick and DeeDee, or Dale and Grace—and didn't people laugh.

Not me, I didn't laugh, because I made the same kinds of mistakes. Like one time, I was in the New Century theatre and saw the preview for the next week's attraction. It said: "See how life must go on in a city of faceless people."

I got all my friends to come and see—I thought it would be an exquisite horror movie like Arthur Crabtree's *Fiend Without a Face*. Instead, all we got was a complicated soap opera. Everyone thought I was small and dumb—everyone but Henry, who understood.

These honest mistakes had not been recent, but they seemed to strengthen the friendship between Henry and me—and here he was telling me to disappear. "What are you talking about?" I finally asked.

Henry just sat there, and then he flipped his new record over to the "B" side. It was *Are You Going My Way*, a song about somewhere where the stars always shone and the nights were full of joy, and if you decided you didn't want to go, you'd be sorry—think it over. This reflected my frame of mind on Henry's concrete steps.

Eventually he answered me. "It's hard to explain because I think you won't understand. Like, I'll ask you something: do you know what cum is?"

"No."

"Well, it's white. Now, do you know what an invert sugar is?"

I had a feeling I should have known the answer, but I just said, "No."

"Okay. An invert sugar is a guy who loves other guys."

"Can it be a girl who loves other girls, too?"

"I don't know. I guess so. I never thought about it." After some silence, Henry added, "I'm taking my records in now, and I'm heading for the tree-swing before it gets too dark. I'm sorry, but you can't go with me."

Since it was clear I wasn't wanted at our tree-swing anymore, I just went home—but I certainly knew what an invert sugar was. I just didn't know what it was called.

It so happened that Donna Haygreen and I had had some experience in that vein, not long before. In fact, it had to do with our falling out, which I've already mentioned.

She'd been over at my place and we were watching this sick movie on the television—a soap opera. It was a bit like the city of faceless people, but the love scenes were more frequent.

No one else was home and I was taken with a new idea. "Donna, let's you and me try that out."

"You're mental," she replied in her husky voice, but later she reconsidered and we ended up having our own love scene. This happened the following night as well, without a movie to prompt us.

Late the next afternoon, I saw Donna talking with the toughest girl we knew—Stormy Paylin. When they saw me coming, the two of them lowered their voices to a whisper.

Then Donna kind of swaggered over to where I was walking. "Hey," she called. "I don't want you hanging around with me anymore. Otherwise I'll have to pound you."

Stormy Paylin stayed at a distance, staring at me with her fierce brown eyes. I knew this was serious, but I giggled and said, "Donna, I'm not afraid of you."

"Looks like I'll have to start pounding you now," she said, and pushed me twice in the chest. That's how you started out pounding someone in our neighbourhood—pushing them in the chest.

It didn't really hurt but this was before our road was paved. I didn't want to fall and get cut on the gravel. "Stop it, Donna."

"You'd better not say what happened last night," she whispered so softly I could barely make it out, and then she pushed me again.

"I said stop it." Then I took off running and could feel Stormy Paylin's frozen look from behind. I knew that running away from a fight would brand me a chicken for life, with nothing but scorn from Donna, but I didn't know what else to do. My summer was ruined.

Since I didn't dare tell anyone about Donna and me, I certainly couldn't mention it to Henry on his front steps. I didn't have a clue what he'd been trying to tell me then, anyway.

That was my big revelation—I finally figured out what Victor and his gang were doing at the tree-swing. They were—as Mavis would put it—having themselves a relationship. The unbelievable thing is that it took me almost twenty-five years to realize this: Henry and I had been in the same boat, you might say, and we didn't even know it. The tree I was resting against was like an old relative, telling a secret of souls long gone.

The souls long gone in this case were Bruce and Donna, who moved up north and both married young, at seventeen years old; Victor and Butch, who stayed around and got married and divorced at least twice before I lost track; Henry, who joined some macho motorcycle gang and never did talk to me again, or at least not in any close way. In other words, I'm certain I'm the only one who remained an invert sugar after all these years.

I stood and listened to the woods for a moment. The only sounds were the rippling creek below and the screeching crows overhead. Then I heard Mavis.

"I hope you've had enough because I got tired of waiting—this cold and dampness makes my back fifty times worse." She was cautiously coming down the rest of the trail.

"Wait right there, Mavis. I'm coming up to meet you." I began the rather challenging uphill climb.

"It's about time, you silly thing. I was beginning to think you didn't care two figs about me."

"Of course I do, Mavis, you know I do," I kept repeating as I slid through the muck and past the trees like brown skeletons, reaching for me.

RITA

KAREN BOEGH

The first thing Rita notices, driving through the dry valley, is the orchards stretching down from the roads, miles of them in the heat. The monotony of them is broken occasionally by lone, scattered houses—here, a white square house set off in the distance, with a dry patch of dirt in front of it; there, a timber-framed house closer to the road's edge, a clothesline roped across its back lawn and a bicycle dropped onto its driveway. Outside the front doors of these houses people sit in lawn chairs, oblivious to the highway that bares them, bathrobes and crying babies and bottles of beer, to the view of motorists who wind slowly around the valley.

But it is the orchards that amaze Rita. She can't bring herself, at first, to think of them as trees. They barely seem alive. Merely squat, gnarled pieces of old sculpture tagged with dusty rope and encircled by barbed wire. Men and women leaning against them on ladders, shaking their branches as though confident that something living, life-giving, will drop from them. Gloved hands snapping off cherries, apples and grapes as though they were wax. To Rita these vital plots of farmland are no more than dead, geometric rows of irrigated, cultivated, sheared—things. She has come from the cold winds and forests of northern Ontario, the Canadian Shield. Has never seen such precision grafted onto the landscape, like canvas stretched over wood. She gapes at it through her windshield.

This is the part of Canada she has chosen, sight unseen, to transfer to from her old job. A not-unprecedented attempt to escape her own life. She drives around the valley to acquaint herself with the area, then finally rents a house in a small town an hour's drive from her new job. It is a quiet spot, near a lake. After moving in, she occasionally takes long drives down the back roads, around the orchards. Warning signs hang at regular intervals on fences facing the road: *These apples have been treated with pesticides.* Tractors slowly grind their way like ants up the hills. Water hoses whip out spray in mechanical circular motions. Now and then the snap of a pistol shot soars over the orchards to frighten birds away.

As she begins talking to people, she discovers that there are no mosquitoes in the nearby towns and countryside of the valley; their breeding grounds have been treated with pesticides for so many years that they have been eradicated. This horrifies her at first—the sterility of it—but soon, like the others, she takes their absence for granted and appreciates life without them.

She grows used to this dry unfamiliar country, and is content.

Early one evening, making the long drive home from work down her favourite stretch of highway, she approaches a small band of hitch-hikers standing on the gravel shoulder. Three of them—unusual among the throngs that clog the shoulders in summer, because they are women. A tall woman stands in front of the others, her long dark hair blowing across the breast of a deeply muscular woman wearing a bright pink scarf round her short hair. Behind them squats a blond-haired girl, putting something into a bag.

Rita makes her decision to pick them up long before she reaches them. She remembers the pledge she made to herself, never again to pick up hitch-hikers. It was while living in Ontario that she picked up Anne-Marie as a hitch-hiker. They made a horribly mismatched pair—both of them serious and insecure, so dependent on each other that they could never have lived reasonably together. The result was a turbulent mess: fights, jealousy, short bursts of I'll-show-you infidelity followed by long bouts of monogamous passion. Two years of her life. She is still recuperating from the stress of Anne-Marie's bent for drawn-out analyses of their relationship's problems, followed by melodramatic showdowns when Rita wasn't quite able to admit the problems were mostly her fault.

But already, even though Rita is lonelier here in this new place, she feels stronger than in those long-ago days, more solid. Her post-breakup indictment of all wayfarers and hitch-hikers as unstable fanatics seems a silly one. *This is a new stage for me*, she thinks. *A new beginning.*

She pulls smoothly over to the gravel just in front of the women, then slides over and pushes open her passenger door. As the women pile in with their gear, exchanging hurried hellos and ensuring mutual destinations, Rita realizes this is going to be merely a pleasant trip, a friendly one. She will drive them a few miles up the road, then go on her way. A good Samaritan. The thought makes her feel good. Kind-hearted, open to new people, yet at the same time secure, centred in herself. She smiles at the tall dark-haired woman sitting next to her, who identifies herself as Louise.

"Do you know French?" Louise asks.

"No, I'm sorry." For two years she lived in Ottawa, always intending to learn.

"That's alright." Louise says, unconcerned. "Our friends warned us not to expect it out here. Anyway, I can speak good English. Lise here is not too bad, but she's shy about it, and Micheline—nothing. So I translate for everybody. Vancouver's pretty far from here, huh?"

"Pretty far," Rita says. "Over two hundred miles. I can only take you to Peachland, though." They are still in the heart of British Columbia.

"That's kind enough." Louise says something in French to the others, and they laugh. She introduces them to Rita; they wave at her in the rear-view mirror.

Louise explains that they are all from Quebec, spending the summer picking fruit and hitching around. They've heard a lot about Vancouver and the Island and want to see it before they go back home.

"Where are you from?" Louise asks Rita.

"Thunder Bay."

Louise laughs, says something again to the other women. "Tundra Bay!" she snorts. "We know it well. Nothing but bars and hockey rinks. But you managed to escape, eh?"

Rita shrugs, smiles shyly. "It wasn't so bad, but I like to travel around. Live in a new place every few years."

"Very good!" nods Louise emphatically. This confident air of endorsement amuses Rita. "Very open-minded," Louise goes on, running her hand through her dark hair. "I am like that too, you know? I want to see the whole big country!" She stretches out her arms as if to embrace the highway.

As they drive on through miles of brush and sandy rock-cliffs Rita discovers that this woman is a non-stop talker. She exclaims at the scenery, the houses they pass, other hitch-hikers. Yet her comments are intelligent and thoughtful—she is not simple-minded, a trait Rita often associates with perky or talkative people. She is also funny, with a sarcastic humour Rita likes when she's not too often the target of it. Rita rarely meets such confident, happy women without some trace of phoniness or self-consciousness about them. It is how she would like to be herself.

"Do you care if I smoke?" says Louise, pulling out a pack of cigarettes.

"Not at all," says Rita, and offers a lighter from her front shirt pocket.

"You smoke too?" Louise asks, as though amazed, then impulsively grabs Rita round the shoulders and squeezes her. "A partner in crime!" she cries. In explanation, she points her thumb towards the back seat. "These two never leave me alone about my smoking. Of course, *they're* perfect!"

The damp cloth sticks to Rita's skin where Louise's arm rested on her. She drew back instinctively when touched, but the sensation was unexpectedly warm, non-threatening, welcoming. She feels a slight pull of attraction to this woman, but immediately shrugs it off. She has always fallen in love far too easily. From now on she intends to recognize it early and avoid it for what it is.

But as they drive on, she is forced to respond to Louise's incessant, questioning curiosity. It is unusual for Rita to talk about herself—as a matter of fact, she hates it—but she is tempted to reveal herself to this woman. Louise's face is open, devoid of all expression of distaste or disapproval, her body relaxed, even her palms spread open like leaves on her lap. Her interest in Rita seems innocent, yet the questions she asks are sophisticated and probing, as though she is aware of the intensity behind Rita's story and is looking for it. Rita is drawn in deeper than she wants to be. She wants to talk, but also resists it. Louise doesn't seem to sense her hesitation or to care about it. She fills in the awkward gaps in conversation with understanding words and diverting, self-deprecating jokes. Rita feels another pang of attraction, but fights it stoically. She steals secret glances at Louise, determined to find flaws. Louise is not her type, physically—she is conventionally pretty, too femme, too fluttery. And too young. But Rita is not old herself, just tired. She feels older than her years, although she is not yet thirty.

As a comfortable silence settles over the women in the car, Rita thinks about her past relationships. All she can remember is the failed chemistry of them, the complexity of them. They always seemed such a struggle—the endless cycle of searching out women on the street or at work, of confirming whether some measure of attention or desire lurked there, then, once a relationship was begun (if she was lucky enough to get that far), the task of grounding it, stabilizing it in the face of unending obstacles. And for her, at one stage or another, the bond ultimately faltered, fell apart. She cannot believe this was always her fault. It is why she is so tired, why she has decided to put up defences to protect herself (against Anne-Marie and all the other mixed-up, defenceless women in the world). Suddenly, the thought of falling in love all over again with someone like this pretty, flighty stranger sitting next to her, who is probably not even a dyke anyway, dismays her so much that she willingly puts all her attention back towards the road and towards getting home.

~

Even in this early evening air, the heat is strong. As they approach one of the many small towns dissected by the highway, the traffic builds and the car slows to a crawl. Louise rolls down her window and rests her arm on the door. As they pass the town and speed up again, her long hair vanishes out the window and slaps against the roof.

A sense of gloom builds on Rita. She is proud of herself for having shut the door on what was probably only another failed infatuation, but she is left feeling disappointed and frustrated. It is an unusual form of frustration for her, who usually pursues every attraction on the chance it may lead to love or even just friendship. These feelings are made worse by having dwelled on other old memories, the first time she's thought of them much since she came here. She suddenly wishes she hadn't picked these women up.

"Ah, this breeze!" Louise suddenly says, breaking Rita's reverie. She seems unaware of, or unconcerned about, the change in Rita's mood. "Why don't you step on the gas?" she asks. Her tone is half-playful. "Your car is very hot."

And why not? With a touch of savage vengeance, Rita squeezes the pedal, feels the engine gun, the car surge forward. Her car is a used 1982 Datsun, not powerful, and she doesn't test it much. But now it responds well, and she is somehow pleased.

The other three women laugh and clap their hands. In the back they roll down their windows. "We'll get to Vancouver tonight at this rate!" yells Louise. Again she speaks to the others, then turns back to Rita, forcing Rita, by a tap on her wrist, to meet her eyes. "I told them," she says, "that you've decided to take us to Vancouver yourself."

Rita looks at her, startled. All the attraction she felt earlier, that she had banished with such austere, careful self-discipline, rushes back like an old friend. *Watch it, Rita.* Louise smiles coyly, as if aware of the agitation she has caused and of her power to dispel it. "Don't worry, I'm just putting you on a little bit. We're not going to hijack you."

"Look!" she suddenly says, pointing across Rita's field of vision. They have travelled onto a straight stretch of highway, where buildings and houses crowd the shoulder. "A bar, right on the side of the road!" She lightly taps Rita's forearm. "Let's pull in and have a drink. I'm very thirsty."

Rita hesitates. She wants to go, but doesn't want to show any desire. She is uncomfortable with Louise's familiarity, can't tell if she is making fun of her, trying to cheer her up or, worse, taking advantage of her. But it also seems possible to her, for the first time, that Louise is attracted to her. She has seen worse methods of testing the waters of attraction. Even so, she isn't Rita's kind. But it is somehow this very difference, its lure of the unexpected, the easy flirtation of it, that intrigues Rita. Louise's light-heartedness, her self-assured laughter, is a change from any woman Rita has allowed herself to know—certainly a change from Anne-Marie—and she can't help liking it. She suddenly understands that she needn't take it seriously, needn't take it any further than an easy flirtation. She too can be this careless and simple.

Just as they are gliding past the building, Rita pulls in at the last minute, squealing the tires and cutting across the path of an oncoming car. They bullet onto the gravel driveway, kicking up rocks and dust. The car they nearly cut off peals its horn in anger as it screams by. Louise laughs loudly, clutching her stomach with one hand and the dashboard for support with the other.

"You're a wild woman!" she cries to Rita as they coast to a stop in front of the pub, and Rita feels ridiculously pleased. Like a reckless teenager. She looks back to be sure the others are alright. They're smiling happily.

"Now we *really* need a drink!" Louise says, and jumps out.

The pub they go into has an Irish name. It stands on a large patch of gravel, a brown brick and wood building with a few tufts of grass sprouting from its foundation. Rita passes it every day on her way home from work but has never gone in. She has been lonely for friendship since she moved.

The transition from glaring sun and heat to the darkness and coolness of the pub makes Rita almost dizzy. The other women quibble about where to sit; Rita wants only to be with her back to the wall so that she can look around her. The pub is half-empty. A few men huddle on bar stools, two or three groups of men and women, mostly middle-aged, are scattered at tables.

When they finally decide on a table, Louise sits next to her. The other two women, whose names Rita can no longer properly recall, sit facing them with their backs to the room. Rita is sure that Louise manipulated the situation to get next to her, but she doesn't allow herself to indulge the fantasy. She is becoming carried away with childishness. An aging, love-starved woman, she thinks of herself, not unkindly.

As they drink pints of cold beer, the three women talk to each other in French. Louise occasionally translates for Rita. She doesn't feel left out. She likes to listen to their rhythmic voices, see them argue and point around the room, their silver bracelets sliding down their arms. Louise touches Rita's arm to punctuate her sentences—this causes Rita to miss most of what she is saying. She nods and injects unintelligible comments, but Louise doesn't seem to need or demand much feedback. She likes to talk. And Rita likes to listen. She sits back against her chair, listening to Louise's voice, which is hoarse and deep and heavily accented. She herself is only drinking Coke, but feels so relaxed that she might as well be drunk. She knows that this is what she has been looking for since she came here, this feeling of peace, of just being comfortable with somebody. And she doesn't want it to end.

They spend over an hour in the pub. Louise becomes increasingly attentive to her. Her touch lingers. She smiles, an honest smile that crinkles the tanned lines at the corners of her eyes, and Rita allows herself to smile back openly. *Can it be?* Her conviction that she needn't take the attraction seriously dies like any new conviction that hasn't been deepened by reflection and experience. Louise guzzles down the last of her beer and lays the bottle solidly on the table. "Are we girls all ready to go?" She throws some bills on the table as she rises, then pulls out her chair so that Rita can get out from behind the table more easily.

Everything Louise does convinces Rita that Louise cares for her. But Rita is still wary. Louise's attention is a mysterious, flowing kind, extended to her other two friends as easily as to Rita. Rita cannot be sure that it means anything at all. The four of them walk slowly out to the car. They rearrange their gear more comfortably, then Rita starts the car and drives away.

Back on the highway, her mind begins to work quickly. She has almost reached her turnoff, the road which she takes to get home. She is torn between keeping to her vow not to get involved and dropping these women off as she had planned, and trying to think of a way to keep Louise with her, to make the contact last longer so that they can figure out each other's intentions. She could, she thinks, invite the three of them to stay the night at her place, for the sake of safety. That would sound convincing. Already the deepening shadows of trees and buildings lie thin as knives across the highway.

Everyone has grown silent. Louise stares out the window, her arm draped along the door. The engine drones. Several times Rita opens her mouth to speak, but the timing seems wrong. She waits. She tries out different lines, different approaches to the question. But as the silence grows longer, a fear of Louise's laughter stops her. What if she finds Rita's offer strange, overdone? Rita has in the past built up fantasies which turn out to have no basis in reality. She tries to see herself, ruthlessly and honestly, through Louise's eyes; sees herself a reserved but friendly stranger who has given three kindred women a ride and is obligated to do nothing more. In this light, Louise's openness and friendliness suddenly strike Rita as mundane and indiscriminate, a trait she probably exhibits with every driver she accepts a ride from—every man and every woman. It is just her way.

And now Louise seems preoccupied, sullen. Perhaps she is the moody type. Rita has had enough experience with that kind of woman to recognize the signs.

As though sensing Rita's thoughts, Louise suddenly turns her head and says laconically, "Whenever you reach your exit, of course, just let us know." She straightens the gear at her feet, shifts about in her seat. She seems restless.

Rita feels defeated. They are, of course, expecting to go; to invite them to stay with her now would seem strange and unnecessary. She says nothing, then suddenly pulls over to the dirt shoulder. The mud flaps scrape the rocks as the car glides to a stop. "The turnoff up ahead is mine," she says.

Louise glances at her sharply. "Okay," she says, then hesitates, staring ahead as though searching for the right parting words. "Thank you very much for your kindness." She climbs out without another word. The two women in back sit for a moment, confused perhaps at the abruptness of the goodbye, then climb out too. Louise recklessly slams the door; the rolled-down window rattles inside with the force of it. At this, Rita guns the engine and pulls away, the wheels sliding on the stones.

As she accelerates down the highway she glances once in her mirror and sees the other two women dumping their gear on the ground. Louise has already stuck out her thumb.

~

She takes her turnoff and heads down toward the lake. She condemns herself immediately, harshly. Once again, she thinks, she took someone's attention too seriously, too personally. She fears that she revealed this somehow, is sure that she displayed too much and so embarrassed herself, and Louise. She passes houses without seeing them—their ugly wire fences and dusty mailboxes with peeling paint. She passes the township dump, then takes a steep right turn down a heavy gravel road, one that rattles her bones and teeth and jostles her car. As she reaches the end of the road, she slows down. At the edge of an orchard is her driveway, the driveway of the house she is renting. A blue square house, a willow tree in front, a dry strip of grass near the road for a lawn.

She stops the car in front of the house. She sits behind the wheel and watches the owner of the orchard, Mr. Martin, pruning an apple tree from a ladder. He works diligently around his orchard, dawn to dusk.

He glances over at her and smiles. "You're home late today!" he calls, making conversation. She doesn't know him really, him or his wife, but they are friendly and have tried to make her feel comfortable in their old house. They live in a newer, nicer house on the hill.

But she's in no mood for the chatter of acquaintances. How absurd, she thinks crabbily, that because this man knows her routine—when she leaves for work and arrives again at night—that he presumes to know anything about her! He has probably already pegged her as the solid, predictable type, has come to his conclusion about her just as she has reached hers about him. She sits in her car and says nothing in response, disliking him. The thought of going into the house, into the silence, and listening to the snip, snip of his shears from her kitchen window while she makes dinner, is unbearable.

She starts up her car again and heads toward the main road. The thought of Louise's arm stretched possessively on her door again makes her feel ill with excitement. But still she fears that in going back, she will be grovelling for something that doesn't exist. Yet she drives on, worried only that another car may pick them up before she gets there. Suddenly she just wants the thing settled. She'll let Louise make the decision. Reject or accept her. This abdication of responsibility makes her feel happy and light-headed.

By the time she reaches the main turnoff road, twilight has settled over the valley. The air is cooler. Squares of light glow weakly from windows. She flicks her headlights on even though she can see without them. Her fears of humiliation seem childish and absurd when in her mind she remembers Louise's face, and the friendly faces of the other two women. *Just let them be there*, she thinks.

She turns quickly onto the main highway. As she approaches the spot where she left them, her hopes plummet. They are gone. An indentation in the sand is all that remains of their gear. But as she drives right by the spot, peering into the dusk to be sure, she sees them sitting together off the road, a map spread out across their knees. Her heart leaps. As she slows down, Louise's head lifts from the map; she glances at Rita for a moment, then drops her head again. Was it a dismissal, or did she simply not see? It is getting dark now. Rita veers off into the shoulder, then makes another U-turn onto the other side of the highway. As she approaches them her hands shake on the wheel.

They sit hunched over the map, absorbed in it. At the last minute she almost drives right by them, but Louise's head lifts again, so she stops. The three of them stand slowly, stretching their arms and legs, and by the hesitant way Louise walks toward the car, Rita can tell that she doesn't recognize her. She leans forward so that her face is framed in the passenger window. Louise opens the door.

Louise shows no surprise when their eyes meet, but smiles. "Have you come to save me?" she asks, with none of the mockery Rita expects.

Rita mumbles something about the darkness, about the dangers waiting for women travellers on the road.

"Don't I know it," says Louise. Her head vanishes from the window and she walks back to the road edge to her friends. Rita hears their companionate voices in the darkness as they pick up their gear.

The drive back is a silent one, but Rita relaxes in the cocoon of darkness. Crickets sing along the road. Groups of them hop out randomly from the dark invisible grass, their bodies glowing momentarily in the glare of the headlights. From the dashboard a dim green light spills onto Rita's lap. In the back seat the two women talk to each other in French.

As they bear down the gravel road, Rita hears rather than sees Louise pull a cigarette from her shoulder bag. She passes along her lighter, her hand slightly trembling. She is ashamed of her nervousness, ashamed that the source of that nervousness should sense it. The fragile vulnerability of it. But when she reaches out to get the lighter back, Louise instead snares her hand, entwines their fingers, then holds the hand beside her on the seat. Rita is surprised although she knows she shouldn't be. At the same time she is infused with a strange, almost giddy sense of self-confidence: she did not, after all, imagine anything. Louise's hand in hers feels small and firm, encrusted with dirt from the road.

With her other hand, Louise holds her cigarette firmly. The fragrance of its smoke drifts to the car ceiling. She looks out into the cool night, at the mounds of the hills curled like sleeping cats against the darker sky. "This is a *beautiful* place," she says. And there is such confidence in her voice that Rita finally believes it too.

THE MILKY WAY

ANN DECTER

Between ending and beginning, there are galaxies. Light years where existence cannot be supported without establishing a new relationship between space, time and energy. That was it, for Jerry, young and not so young, late and early at the same time. That was it, to go somewhere, find somewhere, be somewhere else, without looking, without knowing where, without even knowing she was looking. She ignored the moments when her attention drifted to a smile on the subway or a certain turn of a head and dangling earring. She did not realize, in her mind, that she had stared when she saw two women kissing an everyday lovers' goodbye kiss, a domestic kiss, before parting outside a repertory cinema. She recognized, instead, a little shock now and then, subtle jolts that reminded her body of plugging in the block heater on her mother's car when the cord was damp. An electric current that would skip up her arm, making her nerves sizzle and squirm. Even that light rush was almost too much.

~

"I'm not a dyke, I'm just a tomboy," Jerry used to say, when people would ask. When lesbians or gay men would ask, really, because the mistake that straight people made was to think that she was a guy, their world being a choice of only two options: Sex M☐ F☐ Pick one. Not the one you want, the one you are. Forms aren't about what you want, they're about characteristics. Sexual preference is not included in the census forms, like real characteristics. So straight people had never assumed Jerry was a lesbian, or not very often at least.

~

Of course, there came a time when Jerry stopped claiming tomboy status, or rather, could no longer bring herself to deny lesbianism and claim heterosexuality, even though it was misleading, given that her lover at the time was a man. It all connected to the author, to words and sentences and a book that re-configured the space between Jerry and herself.

~

If Jerry turned, if she pivoted at any one point, so that the edge of her vision shifted toward the centre, it may have been when she first read the words: "An unique identical woman. The difference with her and me is that we know the road backwards, from object to subject." That simple translation translated Jerry. She twisted and flipped inside herself, uncramped and loosened, surreptitiously released from a strait jacket. Jerry was no longer looking at herself from the outside and the inside, she was suddenly whole and unique, gazing out onto the back of the world, looking at the skyline from behind the city, where you see all the old buildings first, Toronto from east of downtown, or New York City from Brooklyn or the Tappan Zee Bridge, views that no one ever uses for the opening shots of a movie. The back door of the world was ajar, Jerry stared forward, then picked up the book and bolted down two flights of stairs from her attic bedroom to Sharon's apartment, knocked perfunctorily and entered. Sharon stood at the sink washing her dishes, watching a re-run of *Hart to Hart* on television.

"Look at this sentence," Jerry shoved the book between Sharon and the dishwater.

"My hands," Sharon objected.

"Never mind your hands, just read this part." Sharon hated when anyone got bossy.

"Which part then?"

"Here."

"Where?"

"Here. 'An unique identical woman,' you read it ... I don't want to read it to—look just read it, it's only a sentence."

"Okay already, I'm reading, 'An unique identical woman' sounds better 'a' than 'an,' even though it's right."

"I know, I know, go on."

" ... 'The difference with her and me is that we know the road backwards, from object to subject.' ... yes. Exactly."

"Exactly."

"What is this stuff?"

"A book, it's a novel, sort of, except, well, you can't, at least I can't, really tell if there's any characters or not, except the mother and of course she doesn't get to say anything really anyway. It's like the writer is the narrator and she's speaking, just thinking and speaking and pulling everything together and sometimes it's just so, so, succinct, and then sometimes I don't understand at all but I don't feel like that matters. Should I read and you listen?"

"Yeah, I'll finish the dishes. I like when you read." Sharon turned down the sound on the television and they poured the book over themselves, reading lines aloud, reading lines and not between lines, explaining themselves to themselves. So many years of conversations summed up in that simple phrase, *the road backwards, from object to subject*. And even though the book declared, "If it weren't lesbian, this text would make no sense at all," Jerry was only aware of making sense of herself, not of gaps or a galaxy or what might come open unexpectedly. She was oblivious, still, to the little shocks and even to the way she had stared at a young woman in the subway at Yonge and Bloor the morning before.

~

Jerry found the big gap, the gap of prejudice, when she did a presentation on the author's writing in her evening class a few months later. Jerry had questioned why the course, "Women and Literature" covered only one book by a Canadian writer, asking if Canadian writers could be substituted for those on the course list. When Professor Della Arkin answered nervously and defensively "Do you have any suggestions?" all Jerry could think of was the author, and the road that no longer ran backwards.

~

So Jerry came to sit, one cold Wednesday evening in late February, in a room with twenty-seven women and one man, and explain about the road from object to subject, and speak from the outside to the inside, without having arrived anywhere yet. When Jerry finished, Della Arkin adjusted her tortoise-shell glasses just a touch, fluffed her perm abruptly and then began to talk distractedly. "My father," she said quietly, "is dying. I was sitting with him, when? Oh, just the other night, and we were talking, and all I could think about was how far away he'd been, all my life, how far away I was now, and I love my father, very, very much. It's that distance, we never can bridge." She looked up and around the room. The room heaved a sigh of relief and a chorus of voices began anecdotes about fathers and relationships with fathers, dead, living and in between. Jerry cringed. Having already watched her father die she was not lured by the discussion. She searched Della's face for some recognition that she had intentionally forced the theoretical content of the presentation into the literal. It did not appear. Patriarchy was simply dying in the form of Della Arkin's father. Just as Jerry began to feel herself becoming completely invisible, a gracious voice interrupted.

"I object," said Jeni Carruthers, an outspoken and studious lesbian. "Tonight's writers are the only lesbian writers on this course and we are not talking about them. What are you all avoiding? Della," she gave an imperious nod of her well-groomed and nearly hairless head, " I think we should be discussing the content of Jerry's presentation."

~

And then they did talk about the author's work, about her continent of writers and her imperative to re-invent the world. Jerry was gratified, because the middle-aged women from the suburbs tried not to worry about the dinners that may or may not have been provided while they listened to talk of roads that ran backwards, and the need to murder the womb. Gratified, because they had listened. She could hear in their words that they had struggled and reached and brought their attention to that room and those words, to the writing and the author whose ideas could have just run up hard against them.

"So you want us," said Marg, a retired school principal, slowly, the words struggling out, "you want us to re-examine everything, and begin again, from, from ourselves, kind of, well, outward, into the world, instead of the other way around, like we're used to."

"Yeah," "Right," "Yes," "That's it," came the chorus from Jeni and from Claire beside her, from Donna who went for coffee with them after class and finally from Jerry.

As they all rose from their seats Jerry heard Jeni and Claire muttering about homophobia, heard the woman next to her saying "Well, I don't know if I buy it, but she did a good job, I mean it's so different."

As she collected her notes and books, John, the only man in the class, stopped and said how much he liked the lecture. She looked into his eyes and saw that he was gay, and saw her as gay. Then Jerry finally realized that she, herself, was the only person in the classroom who didn't think Jerry was a lesbian. Outside the inside.

When Jeni invited her for coffee, Jerry said yes, still staring into the gap she had just found.

"I'm so angry at Della," Jeni dropped the words theatrically as they walked along Bloor Street, "she's so homophobic."

"We can't let her get away with that stuff," said Claire. "She's just afraid of us as lesbians, eh, Jerry?"

I'm not, I'm not, I'm not, "Uh, yeah well, uh, she's certainly afraid of something, I mean, you bring up women seeing the world from their own point of view and she starts talking about her father dying and she doesn't even know why she's talking about her father dying. The whole social order shrivelling up in one man. Well, it's like her saying that for Kate Chopin drowning was a form of sexual freedom."

"Hey," said Claire, " you didn't say anything in that discussion—suicide as freedom in *The Awakening*—how come you didn't help me out there?"

"I hadn't read the book, yet," Jerry laughed as she answered and Claire jostled her with a tattered gym bag.

"What does a lesbian with a six-inch labia have for breakfast?" said Jeni, in a loud voice as she opened the door to the Last Granola Café.

"If I didn't know you so well ... " Claire held the door for Jerry, who averted her eyes and followed them in, nervous that she wasn't going to understand the joke. Re-inventing the world was one thing. Saying labia in a restaurant, even the Last Chance Granola Café, was entirely different. Her cheeks were reddening—she hoped she could pass it off as due to the cold weather.

"Toast," Jerry heard Jeni say, amid peels of laughter.

~

As they sipped their herbal teas Jerry thought about how everyone—the straight women, the gay man, the lesbians—everyone, assumed she was a lesbian, because she could, or maybe just because she would, study and lecture on a lesbian text. She learned about how narrow vision creates a narrow world with very sharp boundaries. Later, she asked Linda, a straight friend, about limited vision. Linda worked at the provincial legislature and wrote occasionally for the feminist monthly. Jerry remembered Linda complaining about something similar when she had publicised the hate literature that was being distributed to MPPs while the legislature was debating a bill to extend the provincial human rights act to cover sexual orientation.

"Oh, yeah," Linda nodded knowingly, " I've come to the conclusion that it's because society is so homophobic. No one believes anyone would bother unless you were lesbian yourself."

When Jerry got home from the Granola Café she told Sharon about being unable to say she wasn't a lesbian. About the denial getting stuck in her throat.

"Uh-oh," Sharon answered, and then laughed.

Jerry still had her male lover.

A few weeks later, on the first sunny and warm International Women's Day march in years, as it wove excitedly through downtown Toronto, there was Jerry, near the front of the long crowd, where the hollering and whooping was loudest. Where a lesbian was leading the crowd in chanting, "We are the D Y K-E-S, we are the D-D-Y K-E-S." Jerry looked up at the overpass between Eaton's and Simpson's, to see two men in suits watching intently. As the women's voices reached them they leaned back and laughed, shaking their heads at the audacity. Jerry, of course, wasn't chanting, because she wasn't really a dyke, and Jerry had a need for clarity and control.

Jerry went to the women's dance that night with Sharon and ran into Linda and her friend Libby. By midnight Sharon and Libby had gone home. Jerry and Linda, who billed themselves as non-homophobic straight women, stayed until the dance closed down. Just soaking it in.

"Labia," Jerry said to herself as they danced, several feet apart.

"What?" Linda hollered over the driving disco beat.

"Nothing," Jerry smiled.

"What?"

"Noth-ing," Jerry hollered, then, realizing that no one could hear her she repeated, "Labia labia labia labia labia labia," as the strobe flashed overhead.

~

Not long after International Women's Day Jerry learned that the author would be conducting a ten-day workshop. Sharon convinced her to go, and she went, out to the city on the lake, wondering what an intensive workshop on feminism and writing would be like, not thinking at all about anything physical or sexual or even emotional. Her literature class had ended while Jerry was still practising saying labia in a dark room filled with loud music. She still had her male lover. He was what lesbians call a "nice man." "Nice" men are straight men who believe in feminism, who don't develop a need to hurt a woman once they have had sex together, men who are aware of their ability to dominate physically and take pains to avoid it, men who get lonely, who do their own dishes and laundry and mind their own homes, and who have friendships with women. But, of course, they are still men.

~

Jerry arrived at the workshop careful and awkward, unsure of her writing and sure that writing was the subject of her journey. When students and teachers met on the first night to go around the circle, as feminists do, and say who they were, Jerry noticed Lise. Lise had a careless manner and a tidy appearance, she had small hands, and big eyes. As the days progressed Jerry also discovered that Lise had a laugh that burst forth regardless of circumstances.

~

Lise had a phrase, "Une femme hors de contexte" that had followed her to the workshop, that ate and slept with her, that swam with her when she and Jerry took a break and walked across the big field over to the pool. A woman out of context could mean and do a lot of things. A woman out of context looks at the moon. A woman out of context reads Foucault. A woman out of context walks when she means to take the bus, takes the bus when she means to walk, makes porridge for supper, chicken soup for breakfast and skips lunch because she's allergic to cats. Context is the sense we make of the world. The way we make sense of the world. Day after day Jerry wrote, talked with Lise and other women, swam, wrote, laughed with Lise and other women. Smoked, slept, dreamt of Lise, and then her mother, and did not remember the dreams. Laughed and laughed with Lise when they were too restless to work. Met Lise's lover when she came from Montreal for a reading by the instructors. Waited for Lise when it was time for a meal, looked for Lise when she wanted to swim. Some say the essence of love is waiting.

~

By the end of a week, they had all settled into the safety of the environment, and the pressure to create had built to a crescendo of energy. Jerry could hardly sleep for wanting to finish her piece for the author to read before the time was up, to finish the piece while still in context, this context. Early one evening Jerry heard music at the end of the hall. The sound of beer bottles clinking became clear as she drew closer to the impromptu party. A few beer had been drunk, someone had put on music. The author asked Jerry, who had just left her characters alone on a precipice in her room, "Would you like to dance?" and then she hesitated, and smiled and put the beer in her hand down on a side table. While the whole room stopped to hear her, she added, "Oh, wait, first, I should ask you, are you a lesbian?"

"I don't know," Jerry managed, starting to laugh. Laughter and honesty were as far as she could get anyway, because how can you lie to someone whose writing has opened the back door to the world? How could she dance and laugh at nothing, holding a woman who had showed her where a whole continent existed to be explored?

"Well, you have to ask," the author laughed, and then everyone laughed, and in the laughing room she waltzed off with a young lesbian who was not shy of arms that knew so much.

Jerry was still sure that "I don't know" was better than to have claimed that she knew what she no longer knew, for Jerry recognized her own need for clarity. Or so she thought, as she watched the author dance away and the gap widen again.

Jerry slipped into a large chair and thought about the exercise they had done on the first day of the workshop. They were asked to make two lists, one beginning "Women, we are," and the other "Women, they are." One list of words described the characteristics of women they identified with, women who were themselves. The second list contained adjectives and descriptions of women, that they did not identify with. It was a way of seeing quickly where all the students were at, a way of separating subject from object. Quick, clear, clean. Jerry thought about Lise, and how she had written heterosexual on the second list. "Women, they are ... 'eterosexual," Lise read aloud, dropping the "h," her voice and her face to the floor. And before she felt the jealousy, Jerry felt her anger rise, that a lesbian would feel that even this was not a safe place. When Lise came and perched adroitly on the overstuffed arm of her chair, Jerry did not think about whether she had been in the room or not when Jerry said "I don't know." Even though she still "had" her male lover, Jerry was beginning to know the distance from here to there and beginning to find that she did not want to go back across.

~

They talked and drank, and then danced, and Lise felt small and strong and sure, and it wasn't hard to hold her. And while they were dancing close together Jerry said "Labia" very plainly, and Lise said "What?"

And Jerry said "Labia, it's from a joke."

And Lise said, "En français?"

And Jerry said, "*Sais pas*. I'm not even sure that I'm sure what it means in English. Let's look it up."

They went down the hall to Jerry's room and looked it up in the French-English dictionary Jerry had bought at the campus bookstore to try to make it possible for her to read Lise's writing.

"Lèvres," Lise said.

"Lips," said Jerry.

"But also, la-bee-yah," said Lise, looking inquiringly at Jerry. Jerry was not comfortable. Her cheeks reddened quickly. Lise stifled laughter.

"No, it's just a joke, " Jerry said quickly, suddenly realizing what a gaffe she had made. Words of love and all that.

Lise still looked very dubious. "So, what is the joke then?"

"Never mind. It's a bad joke."

"What is it?"

"I can't tell it."

"So why were you thinking of it?"

"I wasn't thinking of the joke, just the word, well the word and the circumstances of the joke but, look, never mind, really, it has to do with a lot of things, never mind."

Lise still appeared dubious, but she was very amused by Jerry's obvious nervousness.

"It's just a word I couldn't say, and now I can say it. That's all. A woman out of context practices a word."

"Okay, but watch where you say it now that it's yours."

"Okay. Honest, I didn't mean anything." Or did I? Jerry thought. Well sort of. "Context," she repeated to Lise. "It's just about context." And they went back to the little party, and danced with each other and other women, and retired for the night, to their rooms side by side, where Jerry dreamt of Lise and Lise dreamt of falling into water and both of them remembered their dreaming.

~

On the last night there was a planned party after the students had read from their work. They were calm now, and orderly. The author danced with each of her students, and Jerry could dance with her as a daughter might dance with her mother, loving and reverent, and with no questions open. Jerry danced with Lise, too, and as the party wound down, they went out to walk by the lakeside, to talk about how to say goodbye before they returned to the rest of their lives. Jerry was still thinking about Lise's list, "Women, they are heterosexual," about the gap and their friendship, about the dream she had had which was not asexual or heterosexual but lustful and clear and controlled. The stars were high above the lakeshore. The night was dark and thin, the moon was starting to rise, and before it dimmed the rest of the sky, Jerry leaned back on the grass and drank in the Milky Way.

"Do you think we would have become as close if you knew I was heterosexual?" she asked Lise quietly.

Lise began to laugh, and as laughter had been infectious through their short, intense friendship, Jerry, too, began to laugh.

"You're not angry?" Jerry said finally. " I mean that I didn't say anything. I didn't even want to say anything now, but I knew I'd have to tell you sometime and I didn't want to do it in a letter. Well, actually I did want to do it in a letter, but then I'd wonder how you really took it, so I thought I'd better tell you before I go home."

"Okay, okay," Lise said quietly. Then laughed again. "I often fall for heterosexual women. I dreamt about falling last night, you know, but when I fell I landed in water. I often dream about falling."

"I dreamt about you last night. About holding you and how it felt."

"That's not very 'eterosexual."

"No, it isn't." And they both laughed.

"So you have a lover? A man?"

"Yeah. Well, I did, I guess."

"Poor guy."

"Yeah."

Lise wanted to laugh but thought better of it.

"So I come here for ten days to write and presto I'm a radical feminist," Jerry reflected.

"Is that all?"

"Can't get the word out."

"Like that other one."

"Yeah, but don't say it. I'll just get embarrassed again. Maybe I'll practice."

"That must have been some joke."

"No, it was a very bad joke. It just brings back a lot of confusion, and I like clarity."

"So I see."

"Okay, well, now you see why I have to work at it."

And the moon rose, and they lay beneath the stars by the lake, and the moonlight danced across the water, and in the shadows they saw a movement. A dark figure danced across the water, her arms outstretched, her body flowing and ballooning.

"Look there," Lise pointed.

"I see her."

"Peut-être c'est la femme hors de contexte."

"*Une femme hors de contexte danse avec les étoiles et la lune.* At least," said Jerry slowly, coming to a conclusion, "at least it's not me anymore."

And when they wanted to sleep, they went indoors, because they were not quite sure that two women could sleep outside safely, in a small university town on the shores of a great lake, even if both of them would probably have been mistaken for guys by most of the population.

~

In the morning, after parting and promises—yes she would visit Montreal before Lise and her lover moved west—Jerry chose a seat on the train and began the journey to Toronto. She relaxed in her seat, elated, tired, nervous. She closed her eyes and saw the Milky Way, and the author and Lise, up there in the Milky Way, standing on a cloud of stars, and suddenly, Jerry too was there. Sitting, with a typewriter on her lap, her feet dangling over the edge of the cloud, typing page after page that floated down to the earth. Lise and the author argued and laughed, and walked easily around on the thin cloud of stars. Jerry sat firm, listening, with the typewriter on her lap, explaining what they were saying to the rest of the world. Writing, from the very edge of the inside of the outside, back across that gap in which she had so recently dwelled, back across the difference between we and they, across the outside to the inside, to anyone who would read and listen, to everyone who would read and listen, so that someday the centre would move. The train rode easily to Toronto while Jerry closed her eyes and sat on the Milky Way.

INSIDE OUTSIDE

SARAH LOUISE

Rosemary hung her redwood shingle outside her office door and waited for her first client to arrive. Her life had changed since things with the bass player, despite many reconciliations, refused to work out. His failure to make it in the pizza business was the last straw—all those hours Rosemary spent sweating in front of hot ovens, and oiling pizza pans, had come to naught. The day he declared bankruptcy she changed the locks on their apartment. She put his clothes and black bass out in the hall and the next day when she opened the door, there was a ceramic pizza pin dangling by a steel string from the doorknob. If this is supposed to make me cry, she thought, you can forget it. And went right out to enrol at UCLA as a psychology student.

Psychology was hard, especially in California. Los Angeles is hot in the summer, as bad as a pizza oven almost, and there are as many schools of human behaviour as there are record companies and movie studios. Staying on top of all this, and having to work in restaurants besides, can be a daunting experience, but Rosemary survived. In six years, she earned her M.A. and the right to provide professional advice. She also altered her name and acquired a new identity, for use in her personal life only. Her stint with the bass player had given her a new appreciation for the name Delilah, which she called herself at night when she sat in bars and looked for women who resembled her sister Lucille.

As a psychologist, Rosemary knew that being in love with your sister was bad news, but as cruising Delilah, she wasn't so sure. And somewhere near the intersection of her two identities, Rosemary-Delilah remembered that human adults tend to mate with people who remind them of their parents. If that sort of unimaginative behaviour was okay, or at least too prevalent to be advised against, then it must be okay to prefer women who look like your sister. Or so Rosemary-Delilah reasoned between glasses of sweet white wine at the San Clemente Inn, where she used to work. Of course, had she been more experienced at either of her new pursuits, she wouldn't have been looking for women to take home in such a mainstream, middle-class establishment. She wouldn't have thought it so easy to make an analogy that would stick between large numbers of normal people confusing parents and lovers, and a lone woman in love with her own sister.

Now right here is where I have to stop telling this story as though I were a disinterested outsider and fess up to the fact that I'm Lucille. God only knows why my sister's former male lover found it necessary to tell me she's been searching for my twin in het bars during happy hour, but now that I know, there are several things I have to wonder, and several more I don't need to wonder about at all. First off, our already strained relations became much worse once Rosemary learned to talk some thirty years ago, so I'm not surprised that even though I'm a real lesbian, she didn't consult me about technique and promising locations before she switched from men to women. Assuming, of course, that she actually intends to realign herself. My source wasn't exactly unbiased, and Rosemary has often emphasized her lack of female friends, supposedly due to her success with men. I can believe it though. It makes sense that intense dislike of whomever or whatever is symptomatic of intense but stifled attraction to the same whomever or whatever. And more than any other woman, I've been the object of my sister's distaste, so it makes both flattering and frustrating sense that she won't settle for anyone less than my double. What I'm wondering is how all this will affect the relationship between Rosemary and the real me. Will we finally have something to talk about, something to agree on, or will she feel less inclined than usual to get to know me? On the other hand, what's she going to do if and when she finds my spitting image? Right here I'm into fear and trembling. She could unconsciously transfer the whole load of sibling rivalry to her. Worse, she could be having major power and control fantasies that she could never act out with me. Worse still, at least for me, is that I might know the poor woman, in which case I'd be in a position too Freudian to contemplate. I can't tell whether my occasional wish that Rosemary would just come directly to me is cowardly, foolhardy, or titillating, but there it is.

This might be a good time for someone with more facts to take over this story, but not before I relate two events that could be especially relevant. Once, when Rosemary was four and I was eight, we decided to find out what tongues tasted like, so we stuck ours out and lunged at each other, meeting tip to tip. This represented an extraordinary leap over mutual repulsion, though it lasted only a second and we gagged on the metallic taste. Years later, when she was twelve and I was sixteen, our parents went out for the evening, another unusual occurrence. We were sitting on opposite ends of the couch, in the living room nobody ever used, our legs stretched out on the cushions, toes touching. Lights low. Two scared kids sharing a little piece of warm and unexpected togetherness. That was short-lived too, but the point is, Rosemary and I got close, however briefly, and maybe she made more of that than I ever imagined.

As anyone with insight can see, Lucille—who is a lawyer as well as a real lesbian—has an unresolved need to be admired and emulated by her sister, and has been using her lawyerly ability to argue in favour of anything under the sun to get her wish. It's my pleasure to tell you that Delilah did eventually find the woman of her dreams, me, while sipping margaritas on the terrace of a Laguna Beach hotel. I was a lifeguard working my way through counselling psych and I do look a lot like Lucille, which is not to say that I'm a mere substitute. We all need a way to orient ourselves in new situations and Delilah was no exception. Since we became friends and lovers, Delilah has put her relationship with Lucille into perspective. She still doesn't like her very much but at least she knows it's all because of her parents. Everything has to be somebody's fault, even if they don't do it on purpose, and it helps to know when you're in the clear. Someday, though it's not at the top of her priority list, Delilah will try to get to know her sister as if she were just another woman on the street. They'll meet for spinach omelets in an L.A. restaurant and take turns talking. Afterwards, they might shake hands. They could decide to hug on some occasion further down the road, or they could decide to call it quits without ever making physical contact. Delilah is very careful about who she touches and why. It had something to do with her Catholic upbringing, rife with confusing taboos. I mean, ritual touching, as in baptism and confirmation, is very solemn and can only be done by priests—total strangers in control of your fate. Girls and boys touching is a no-no because it leads to temptation, allowed only between married people who make amends by having babies. Touching between people of the same sex is biblically unnatural, while adults hitting kids can be justified under almost any circumstances. All in all, it's a wonder of the world that Delilah and I are non-violently tactile, wouldn't you say.

One last thing about Lucille and Delilah. Honestly, from my point of view they should call it quits without further ado. That way, I could be as sure as it's possible to be, without our moving to another planet, of my unique place in Delilah's universe. Who knows how long it will take Delilah to deal with Lucille. Meanwhile I've studied enough psychology to know that family dynamics are often impervious to change, even with the best intentions. In the present context, that means these two could obsess over each other indefinitely and without ever admitting it, the fallout descending on interested bystanders like myself. This may not be very even-handed of me, but I'm all for eliminating sources of anxiety. Simplicity is best, or things are cleaner in the stratosphere, or something like that. This is also a conviction I keep under wraps for obvious personal and professional reasons. Life isn't easy.

Once in a while, though, it's fun. Take the first time Delilah and I went to her big white apartment. Thick white carpets, white upholstery, white drapes, white jasmine blossoms outside the kitchen window that filled with hummingbirds in the morning. She was nervous because she'd never been with a woman before. She thought we should have some wine, so we did. I told her not to worry, but being Delilah, she wanted some definite verbal clues. Just relax, I said. Nothing holds a candle to beard-free, ball-free sex between two women flashing like neon signs. I was already aware of Delilah's need for people to be right up front, and my advice reassured her to an amazing extent. We stayed up all night in her big white bed, touching like feathers—like opening presents on birthdays, like incantations delivered by fluent fingers and summer skin. We experienced a shift in dimension, molecular exchange, true intersection. We had no regrets.

For breakfast we had a giant artichoke dipped in lemon-and-butter sauce, which was a bit hard to take. In fact I've never seen Delilah eat anything else before dark. She says that the long process of peeling off the leaves until you get to the heart helps put her in a professional frame of mind. Even on her worst days, she swears by her artichoke to keep from short changing her clients.

As you might expect, things haven't been a hundred percent uphill since that first night at Delilah's. It's hard for a woman to leave a lifetime of heterosexuality behind. Sometimes when we're out for dinner, Delilah's attention wanders to the man at the next table and she loses track of our conversation. She has a poster of Prince in the nude on the back of her bedroom door and her own copy of *Purple Rain*. Now and then she wonders if she should go to bed with a man just to refresh her memory. I wouldn't be human if I didn't admit that I'm bothered by Delilah's foot in the other camp. If I'm not careful I could get downright depressed and give Delilah ultimatums which, as we all know, only make things worse. I could lose my status as woman of her dreams, even without Lucille in the picture. Now as a professional, and a self-confident lesbian, I know this would not be the end of the wider world, but as a woman in love I'd rather keep Delilah close. So whenever I find myself on the verge of stifling her, I try to remember things like our night of no regrets, and what a promising step in the right direction that was. Sometimes it works amazingly well.

Not far from Lucille's rather seedy law office is an old neon sign in the shape of a fish, hanging outside a white church. The sign is blue along its perimeter and the letters that spell "Jesus Saves" are multicoloured. When she drives by the church late at night, something about the vivid colours above the deserted street gives Lucille the feeling she's in another era, her idea of the forties when Bogart sent Mary Astor up the river in *The Maltese Falcon* and Rosie the Riveter served her country in greasy overalls. It's not just the sign, it's the neighbourhood too, like the one her parents grew up in. Lots of Italian families with a grandmother who still makes her own pasta and a grandson who makes passable wine. The wooden post-war houses are well seasoned, inside and out, and always dark by 11 p.m. Sometimes a nostalgia that's not quite hers comes over Lucille. She wants to go back to a place that never was, where she can call her mother when she's lonely or scared, where friends and lovers never disappear, where people start over as often as it takes to get things right. She wants a home she can take for granted.

Once in awhile, after she's been through the neighbourhood and past the sign, Lucille has a strong urge to phone her sister Rosemary just to see what they could manage if they really put their minds to it. They are, she tells herself, two intelligent women who think a lot about other people's problems. What if they gave serious regard to their own long neglected sisterhood? They might never figure out, to their mutual satisfaction, whose fault everything is, but years from now they could be sitting on their back porch sipping sweet white wine and Scotch on the rocks. It could be October or November, right around their birthdays. They would regard each other warmly and with a touch of good-natured antagonism. Lucille might brush a stray hair from her sister's cheek. Rosemary would smile, her fingers moving slowly up and down the stem of her glass. Anything could happen.

CASS, GOOBERS AND GIRLIES

JAYNE HOLOWACHUK

Erin went directly to the kitchen. She took a small paring knife from the drawer, slipped it into her coat pocket and went out the back door. She walked slowly down the hill to the treehouse, hoisted herself up the rope, and sat cross-legged on the floor.

I know I'll never be able to say what people want to hear or do as they expect or be as they want me to be, she thought. Aloud she said, "I'm lousy at faking."

She leaned back against one of the benches, reached for the knife in her pocket and began to whittle away at the tree trunk. She thought back to nine years ago, to her first day of school.

Back then, Erin hated firsts. She had survived her brother's first birthday, first words, first steps and first performance on the grown-up potty. She had even survived the adult exaggeration of these common affairs.

The first day of kindergarten was no exception. Her mother painstakingly pressed Erin's dress, brushed and braided Erin's fine, blond hair, polished Erin's shoes and packed Erin's schoolbag. The finished product stood at the junction of Pinegrove and Stanton Roads, attempting calm. The thought of fourteen years of similar mornings was horrifying.

As mother and daughter waited for the schoolbus, Mrs. Marsdale embarked on a futile lecture about decorum: "You really must remember to behave like a proper young lady."

Erin's response was sullen: "I'm no lady and don't ever mean to be." She was spared reproach when another girl and mother appeared.

"Yeah, hi. I'm Cassandra. Call me Cass," the girl announced, leaning against a large elm and tapping her foot impatiently, as if waiting for the bus was keeping her from a multitude of important functions.

"I'm Erin Marsdale. I live just down there," Erin said, shyly, gesturing towards a three-storey white house on a huge lot. "You new here?"

"Just moved a couple days ago."

"Oh."

The two stood a safe distance apart, looking down at four white shoes. "Goofy, aren't they?" commented Cass.

"Yeah—to match our dresses." Erin kicked at blades of grass, wondering what to say, while the mothers chatted amicably. Suddenly a large toad hopped past. The girls set out in pursuit, oblivious to frantic parental warnings.

"You're not afraid of toads?" Cass asked.

"Of course not—I'm used to frog guts. My father chases them with the lawn mower."

"Wow! Neat-O!" said Cass, as the yellow bus finally arrived to carry them into their first year of school.

Erin and Cass did their best to initiate spirit into all activities. They presented their teacher with apples, glued to her desk. In art class they fingerpainted a three-dimensional mural on the wall, the floor, a few classmates and themselves. During nap time they dropped a paper ball into the nostril of a snoring boy to see if it would come out his mouth, and then watched in awe as the teacher dug it out with a fuchsia-enamelled fingernail.

Despite these escapades, at the end of the year the two were promoted into grade one at a small school near their homes. Most girls in the lower grades seemed to think of themselves as sophisticated young ladies. Pastel dresses with frills, coordinating hair ribbons, white patent leather shoes and fluffy ankle socks was the only acceptable attire.

Costumes like this were of no use to Erin and Cass, who wrestled and played baseball with the boys, and climbed willow trees to swing ape-like across the school's creek. To the horror of their pristine peers, the two insisted on wearing trousers and behaving in a manner that closely resembled that of their male counterparts. Thus, their status was lowered to that of boys, at an age when the appropriate attitude to the opposite sex ranged from indifference to hostility. "The Girlies," as Erin and Cass called the other girls, were not subtle in their disapproval. In response, the two tormented the enemy at every opportunity.

By grade two, Erin felt the need for more variety in their lives, and proposed to Cass that they find another companion. Cass consented, and even suggested a possible candidate in the girl who lived across the street from her. So the two spent a week camouflaging themselves behind bushes, secretly observing the candidate's behaviour.

It was necessary, before final convocation into the twosome, to examine the candidate's reaction under pressure. The Goober Test was devised for this purpose. After school, Erin and Cass hid in Mr. Ditweiler's forsythia hedge. Before long, they detected their red-headed target sauntering toward them. As she rounded the hedge, they pounced, grabbed her, and wrestled her to the ground. Cass rolled her face-up and sat on her legs. Erin straddled her stomach, pinning her wrists above her head. As the girl began to wail—full-bodied, guttural hollering—Erin summoned the world's largest gob of saliva and let it dangle, mere inches from the girl's face. Their victim had a choice: she could attempt to wriggle free, at the risk of dislodging the goober; or she could remain motionless and hope her attacker was not so disgusting as to drop the blob.

The candidate was a woman of steel, refusing to break eye contact with Erin. Her intense glare proved that she was worthy of their company. The goober was sucked safely back into Erin's mouth and the stocky girl sprang to her feet, slugging both predators in the stomach. "Whaddaya think you're doin'" she demanded, one hand on her hip.

"We've been observing you," grunted Erin.

"So?"

"Wanna be friends?" asked Cass.

"You're weird," the girl proclaimed, and walked away. Cass and Erin shrugged and ran off to play ball.

An hour into their game, the girl wandered into Erin's yard. "Hey!" Cass and Erin greeted her in unison.

"Been watching you back," she said coolly.

"Changed your mind?" Cass was equally cool.

"Only if you promise not to try the spit stuff again."

"Deal!" said Erin, shaking hands.

"But you're still weird!" the girl laughed, running off to fetch her glove. It was then that Cass and Erin realized they didn't know the girl's name. They resolved to call her Ball—the name burned into a wooden plaque at the entrance to her driveway.

With the help of Mr. Marsdale, the three constructed a treehouse in a grand old oak behind Erin's house. They camped out in it, and secreted themselves there to spy on neighbours through binoculars. When winter came, they huddled together high in the barren branches, trading hockey cards and ghost stories, and star-gazing through Cass' telescope. They imagined martians and stellar civilizations.

But Erin's restlessness remained, and in the spring of grade three the trio decided to bestow the great honour of their company upon yet another school misfit. A meeting was called for a Saturday to select a suitable candidate.

On that day, Erin ran out her back door, turned somersaults down the hill in her yard and hoisted herself up the treehouse rope. Ball and Cass greeted her, but their smiles faded as they watched Erin's eyes bulge and her face flush scarlet. There sat an intruder.

"You better wait outside, Kelly," Cass addressed the girl.

"If you value any of your vital organs, you'll leave and you'll do it quickly." Erin's eyes were ablaze. The girl obeyed.

"What's she doing here!"

Ball began, "Well, we kinda thought that ... "

"No! No one's allowed up here unless they're one of us!"

"But she is one of us," Cass tried to explain.

"She's what! Since when?"

"We ... yesterday ... got a perfect chance ... jumped her. Did the Goober Test," explained Ball.

"Without me? I thought we do stuff together?" Erin was suddenly more hurt than enraged.

"Well, she did pass," rationalized Cass.

"Oh, just go pass wind if you'd rather have her in the gang than me!" Erin strode to the door, whirled around and hurled another insult, "I hope you all drown in a pile of poop!" Then she slid down the rope and ran home, where she slammed all doors in her way. In her room, she sat in silence, watching blood drip slowly from her rope-burned hands.

Over the next few weeks, Erin spent much of her time sulking alone and managed to avoid the enemy until school let out. But one afternoon soon after, she heard an annoying racket in the backyard. It sounded too much like her dog dismembering the neighbour's cat, so she peered outside. Beneath the bedroom window stood the traitors, in the frilliest of dresses and holding large bouquets of daisies. Accompanied by disturbing noises from Cass' banjo, all three sang "Bring Back my Bonnie" in stomach-churning falsettos. Erin fought a smile, but the sight of these ardent tomboys serenading her like love-sick teenagers was unbearable.

"Don't you look pretty!" she yelled out the window, knowing this was the most profane insult. Cass, Ball and Kelly wiped imaginary tears from their cheeks and pleaded with their pal to return, to save them from becoming girlies. Erin ran out of the house and planted a welcoming punch in Kelly's stomach.

And Kelly was not a bad choice after all: she had no use for dresses or skipping-rope games. She was slow at times, so they fondly called her "Bonehead" or "Boner." Together, the four misfits were rebels.

Their favourite Saturday afternoon pastime became an activity remembered for years by local children and motorists. The four met on Stanton Road, which dropped steeply to cross the town's main street. At the peak, one girl hopped on her bike and wrapped a rubber skipping-rope around her waist, leaving a trailing end on each side. Two others mounted their skateboards and held the rope handles, while a fourth acted as spotter at the bottom of the hill. Gravity, and the driver's frenzied pedalling, brought the "skiers" to near-flight as they approached the crossroads.

Seconds before they reached the highway, the spotter yelled "GO!" and frantically waved her arms, indicating a safe passage; or, she screamed "MAYDAY!" The latter complicated things considerably. At the precise moment the mayday cry reached their ears, the two skiers released the rope and veered onto their respective sides of the road. Completing a minimum of three rolls, they landed dramatically in four-foot ditches. The cyclist, sensing the rope's slackness, executed a ninety-degree turn onto the shoulder of the highway, spun a couple of three-sixties, and skidded to a stop on the gravel.

At times, a large crowd of spectators gathered. On one tense occasion, Boner gave the mayday call an instant too late. Erin, speeding out of control, could only close her eyes and hope very hard to happen upon a break in traffic. Racing toward a thick stream of cars, she pitched herself off her bicycle at the last second and landed inches from the road. There she watched in horror as her bike continued into traffic and was flattened beneath a transport truck.

The foursome rarely spoke about this activity. Erin knew, as she soared down the hill with her heart pounding hard enough to crush her ribs, that it was something that had to be done. Each time she survived, she stood reassured that she could indeed be trusted, and had someone to depend upon when it most mattered. Afterwards, as their hearts resumed beating, the girls walked—in silence, on ground which seemed to Erin more solid, warm and alive. To grab life by the neck and shake it up as much as it shook her, made Erin feel a little more in control.

~ PART TWO ~

The four arrived intact for their first day of grade five.

Their new teacher used alphabetic seating plans, and Erin was now situated directly in front of Boner. Students in this class were required to grade one another's tests, by passing papers to the child seated behind. Because the four rarely spoke of such mundane things, Boner had been unaware of Erin's academic ability. Now, for three months, each of Erin's tests were returned bearing the word "BROWNER" in black lettering across the top. Erin assumed this to be an insult, but, unaware of its exact meaning, was not unduly offended.

One day, when Erin was in a particularly foul mood, Boner wrote "ASS KISSER" in large, blood-red letters. Erin was indeed familiar with the implications of this phrase, and the attacks had occurred too often for her to continue to ignore them. She scribbled "WAR—4:00 p.m., out back" on her test and returned it. This was not to be one of their friendly skirmishes.

Erin counted the seconds until four o'clock. It would be inadequate to state that she possessed fear. She was small, and Boner towered over most boys two years older than she. Spitting straight in a wind storm would be easier than winning this fight. Leaving town was out of the question—news of a scrag-fight had spread rapidly through the small school. Besides, it was imperative that she restore both her minced ego and her honour.

Forty-five students watched as Erin danced around Boner, attempting to tire her. This failing, she dove for Boner's legs, which seemed set in concrete.

Summoning her courage, Erin threw the first punch solidly in Boner's diaphragm. Boner paused for a moment, looking very much like an enraged bull.

"Holy buffalo balls! Perhaps I should've suggested we discuss this?" thought Erin, as the bull charged, grabbed her waist and flung her to the ground. She landed with a hollow thud and Boner slammed punches into her stomach and head.

"Okay—okay—enough already," Erin grunted, gasping for air. The barrage did not stop and Erin passed out.

Later, doubled over in Cass' kitchen with a frozen steak on her face, Erin listened to Ball and Cass recount every gory detail. They were surprised, if elated, that their pal was once again living and breathing.

The following day at school, Boner refused to look anyone in the eye and she sat alone under a tree at lunch and recess. Ball cornered her in the hallway just to say "Hi," but Boner shrugged sheepishly and walked away.

After school, Erin, Cass and Ball met in the treehouse. "When I saw her, she wasn't mad anymore—just real sad," said Ball, who felt guilty. They all realized that Boner's punches had vented an accumulated frustration and anger over being teased through the years. They had failed to realize that each time they called her Bonehead or Boner, they had been inflicting torture.

Erin was more bruised and swollen than guilty. "There's something I think is important," she said quietly. Cass looked up with interest. Sometimes, Erin found the right words for things. "I think," she continued, " if someone wants to survive they have to speak themselves—to be honest about everything they can so that people can understand each other and get along."

"Yeah, you're right," said Cass. "Boner could have told us what was bugging her and we would've stopped."

The exile of Boner from the group triggered something in the other three. They felt less secure. They wondered who would become a different person than they at first appeared to be—who would wander over the edge of self-control. Over time, they installed protective armour, even amongst themselves. They began to speak about past times using phrases like "Remember the time we ... " and "Things sure aren't like they used to be ... "

And indeed things were changing. Unable to repair their failing marriage, Ball's parents finally divorced, and the custody agreement required her to spend weekends and summers with her hippie father. He was attempting to become one with nature on a farm eighty miles away. As grade six ended, Ball packed her bags, bound for the country.

Erin and Cass looked forward to the threesome's reunion in the fall but, come September, they were confronted with an imposter.

"Damn!" said Cass, watching Ball flit about the schoolyard. "She's become a girly—grew some tits, too."

"How nauseating," commented Erin. "Her father probably convinced her to commune with her soul or something." But their laughter was strained. A seriousness washed across Cass' face and she turned to Erin: "Hey, are you going to take off on me too?"

"Of course not. You're stuck with me." Erin punched Cass and soon a full-blown wrestling match erupted. As they rolled in the grass, two classmates walked by.

"Lezzies, lezzies," the boys taunted. Cass and Erin sprang to their feet and gave chase. Finally, winded, they gave up and sat down. "What's a lezzie?" Cass asked, still breathless.

"How should I know? Nothing I'd want to be."

"Naw, me neither."

~ PART THREE ~

In grade seven Erin and Cass became eligible for school teams, and both were selected for baseball, soccer and track. When winter came, Erin joined the Banbury boys' hockey team, to the town's horror. Cass was her trainer. In the summer they kept busy running a lawn-mowing and pool-cleaning business.

Before they knew it, the final year of elementary school was upon them. But a few weeks into the term, Cass changed. She threw evil glares at Erin during class and disappeared immediately after school. She seemed to hate everyone. Erin, confused, allowed her the distance she needed, and hoped the phase would soon pass.

After two weeks of being snubbed, Erin was worried and angry. She cornered Cass. "So, what's your problem? You'd think I have the cooties or something."

"No," Cass muttered, looking at her feet.

"Well, what is it then?" Erin studied her own feet, recalling how she and Cass had stood like this, awkwardly waiting for the bus, on their first day of kindergarten.

Refusing to look up, Cass explained. "My father bought an old school in Grangeville. He's converting it into a studio and art gallery for his artwork."

"Yeah, so?"

"Well, part of it will be our house. Don't you get it? We're moving." Cass raised her head and a huge tear fell down her freckled cheek. Erin's heart turned somersaults, but she wouldn't cry—not when Cass needed her.

"Hey, goof, Grangeville's only two towns away. We'll still be best friends and see each other all the time. It'll be the same as always." Erin heard her own words, as if they weren't her own. She couldn't really believe them. Something had already changed. Now, Erin surprised herself by giving Cass a quick, awkward hug that felt strange, but wonderful. More effective than a traditional slap or punch, it dispelled for a moment the frustration they felt. Once again, it seemed they had no control over their own fates.

Until the move, the two were inseparable. Afterwards, they visited one another on weekends, and spent more time thinking and talking than ever before. Something, more than the move, had already changed. Now, half-child and half-adult, they were unsure how to behave, unsure of themselves. Erin felt the void inside becoming more insistent.

When Erin visited Cass in the old school, they slept on a futon thrown on one of the gallery floors. One night, the two lay side by side with their arms tucked behind their heads, looking up at stars through the skylight. The world seemed so vast and dark, and Erin felt small and isolated. She turned to Cass and found her staring back. So she did then what her body and spirit dictated, rolling over to lay half on top of Cass. In the darkness, she found Cass' lips. Cass moved her hand beneath Erin's tee-shirt and gently trailed her fingers across the smooth skin. Frightened, Erin suddenly rolled off and sat up to look at Cass straight on. She searched her face for a signal, pleading to both stop and continue. Cass' green eyes gleamed, drawing Erin back to her strong body.

As the two bridged the sad emptiness that had separated them for months, Erin wondered how long the urge to reach out to Cass had been dormant within her. They clung desperately to their feelings, and the world no longer seemed so vast and imposing.

As always, the visit came to an end. They hugged goodbye, and Cass whispered in Erin's ear: "I still remember what you said that day—about surviving and speaking yourself. I'm scared, really scared." Erin had squeezed her, hard.

Now, as Erin sat in the treehouse, the familiar ache of the emptiness was, for the first time, silent.

After a long time, Erin brushed wood chips from her clothes. She stood to admire her work. Carved deep into the oak tree and enclosed by a heart were her and Cass' initials. "I've spoken myself," she said. And she was no longer afraid.

MAINTAINING THE PEACE

(and silence)

BRENDA BARNES

Michelle and Amy climbed the stairs to Adam's flat, careful not to slip on the bare board's ice. It was a Saturday night—the night when Amy and Adam usually jammed. Adam and Amy had played music with each other for years and Saturday night was something of a ritual. They would usually play anything from bluegrass banjo to spoons, but tonight was going to be mostly guitar because Michelle was joining them.

Michelle felt a little bit nervous about the whole thing. She felt she had a credible voice and even though she was more than an average "by ear" guitar player, she felt shy about playing in front of people, especially for the first time. She also felt a bit trapped because she and Amy had come together in Amy's car. If only she had her own car. She could leave if she felt uncomfortable. But now she was dependent on Amy, who had suggested they come together. Amy had said there was more room for the cases in Amy's station wagon.

I should never have agreed to this, she thought, remembering the first time she had played alone to Amy. That was only about a month ago, when they had just started seeing each other. Michelle had tried not to let her perceptions of Amy's superior skill intimidate her. She felt then, and still sometimes felt, that she couldn't really let herself go. Amy always seemed so controlled.

"Oh well, perhaps tonight will be okay with Adam," she reassured herself, looking forward to the first beer, something to calm her down. She reached up to the top of the fridge to pet the resident feline.

"That's Norman," Amy offered. "And this is Adam."

"Hi. Pleased to meet you, finally. Nice place." Michelle tried to absorb everything in one glance. The wood stove in the kitchen, all the wooden upright chairs—the only furniture—in varying states of disrepair. Open shelves with mismatching cups and mugs. Papers and pictures haphazardly stuck about—the memorabilia of this person's life. Needs a lot of paint, she thought.

"Yeah, it's my own little castle, but don't expect to be waited upon hand and foot. I've given the servants the night off," Adam cracked. Some of Michelle's tension broke as she and Adam shared the joke. Amy bristled.

"That's pretty classist." She wasn't smiling.

"Oh c'mon Amy, loosen up. Let's get started," Adam said as he reached for the most beat-up, taped-up six string Michelle had ever seen. Michelle was surprised that he didn't take everything as seriously as Amy, and could so easily tell this woman anything. It must be the benefit of having known her for close to ten years. I'll have to remember to ask him how he does that and get some lessons, she thought.

"Hell, where's my manners?" Adam shot up from the plywood table and got three beers and mugs.

"Yeah, really. I can't be expected to sing without a little throat lubrication." Michelle was warming to Adam quickly, but was still conscious of the fact that he was Amy's friend.

"Let's start with one of my favourites Adam," Amy asked. "You're going to need that other machine for it though."

"I thought we were going to give the banjo a rest for tonight?" He shot a look over at Michelle.

"It's okay, I think I can try to follow as long as Amy plays her guitar too."

The three of them dug into a rousing version of *I Never Will Marry* with Amy singing the melody straight ahead and Adam expertly plucking away while he tortured the harmony. Michelle tried not to laugh at him and at herself as she stumbled along trying to follow the chords of that song and several other unfamiliar tunes. Things got more and more challenging as several more beer chased down tokes from Amy's homemade pipe. The intoxication certainly wasn't helping her playing, but it was doing wonders for her confidence as she even attempted, sometimes more successfully than other times, some harmonies herself.

"Hey, isn't it my turn yet?" Michelle faked a pout.

"Whaddaya say there BB? Should we give the kid a chance?" Adam deferred to Amy's judgement.

"Sure. Why not? Besides, me and Lucille are getting a little worn out anyway." She patted her guitar while she leaned it against the wall, and smiled encouragement to Michelle as she re-stoked and lit her pipe.

Michelle closed her eyes and played her best version of Joni Mitchell's *Free Man in Paris*. To her own surprise, she managed to control her breathing in the second verse. This was usually a problem when she was nervous. Maybe she was loosening up. She had even pronounced "Champs Elysées" correctly. She was pleased with herself.

"All right Michelle. You've been holding out on us," said Adam in appreciation as he clapped.

"Yeah, really. Where'd that come from? You didn't play like that for me before." Amy was slightly annoyed that she hadn't been enough of an audience to see Michelle really play before tonight.

"I think that deserves another beer," said Michelle. "Are there any left?"

"Hey, like I said at the beginning of the evening, the servants have gone home. Help yerself."

Michelle got up and walked over to the counter. As she was taking the cap off her beer she glanced at one of the old black-and-white pictures on the wall. There were several people in it that Michelle didn't recognize, but off to the side there was a very young-looking Adam holding a protest sign. He had his arm around an even younger girl.

"Oh my god, is that you Amy? Do you ever look different. What's the occasion?"

"We were outside the gates of the naval base protesting on Remembrance Day. Or, as I call it, the 'Glorification of War Day.' That was about an hour before six of us were arrested for chaining ourselves to the gates. Sometimes I hate living in this military town."

Michelle bit her lip. They were dangerously close to having the conversation they had carefully avoided ever since she had let it slip that she had released from the navy a little over a year ago, after "being in" for seven years. Amy had said she had a problem being with someone who used to be in the military. She wanted to talk about some of—how had she put it?—some of Michelle's residual loyalties. Michelle had insisted there was nothing to talk about. She wasn't involved any longer and there was no love lost. That part of her life was over. She had stayed in a lot longer than she had intended, though. It was the security thing.

Michelle certainly didn't want to have this conversation now that she was drunk and in an unfamiliar part of town without any means of escape other than Amy's car. Besides, it had been such a great evening up until now. She had really enjoyed Adam's company despite her initial apprehensions about feeling like an outsider. Threes were always difficult, especially when two know each other better than the third. Judging by the look on Amy's face, she wasn't about to let it go this time.

"What was it like to work in a place where you always had to address each other by last names?" Amy took her first shot.

It had begun. Adam looked back and forth between his old friend and new and wisely remained silent.

Amy wasn't going to slow down for a moment.

"What was it like to work in a place that always denigrated women? What was it like to always give orders? What was it like to be in a place where there was never any respect for individuals, where people were reduced to copies of each other?"

"I can't answer that. Things weren't always that way."

"Well, how were they then? Oh yeah, I forgot. You were an officer. You perpetuated the system and played at class separation. You wrote propaganda for the admiral. You had a place of privilege. How could you possibly have known what it was really like if you never felt any hardships?"

"You're making an awful lot of assumptions about something you know nothing about. Besides, if you'd stop monopolizing all the oxygen in the room and let me get a word in edgewise ... "

"Hey look. You're the one who's been avoiding this. Well, now that you're on unemployment, maybe you'll find out how the rest of the real people live because money that should be fed into social programs gets shoved into inflated military budgets."

~

Michelle sat mute under the barrage. Well, she thought, I certainly can't refute that last point. Nor did she want to. Nor did she feel she had to defend herself. It had taken a real leap of faith to trust this woman and now her admission was being shoved back in her face. She had felt that condemnation before.

~

A few years ago, at the Women's Festival in New Zealand, Michelle's Canadian military ID card had fallen out of her wallet. The eight-woman crew she had worked with for three days setting up the children's play area had subsequently interrogated her and abandoned her as a pariah. She drank their Scotch and smoked their dope anyway.

She was agonizing alone on the beach about why, oh why, hadn't she just left the damn card at home, when a woman from Christchurch, with breasts she had secretly admired while bodysurfing earlier that afternoon, came and sat down beside her.

"Hey canuckie. How's it goin' then?"

"Oh, hi Pip. You know, I'm not really sure."

"Well, wrap yer laughing gear around this one and let's talk about it." She produced another joint.

"Thanks." Michelle lit up and took a long slow drag and released it just as slowly.

"I just spent a year travelling in the States and Canada. My ma died and left me all this money. I didn't know what to do with myself, so I just took off. This is the first time in a long time that I've seen a lot of these women. It's kind of like Old Home Week."

"I'm sure you're getting a warmer reception than I just got."

"Perhaps. You know I used to think pretty much exactly the same way they did about things until I went away. I wanted to tell you about this woman I met who's a U.S. army pilot. We had a bit of fun together. Y'know." She gave Michelle a bit of an elbow and a large sly grin. It coaxed from Michelle a similar smile.

"Here, gimmee that thing." Pip took her own drag and continued.

"I didn't know for awhile what she did, but when she told me, I had pretty much the same reaction as those other dykes did tonight. I felt she was being used voluntarily in this huge war machine that invaded other countries at will for economic interests. I reckoned she supported their views. I called her a trained killer, someone who advocated murder. I was pretty rough on her.

"When I asked her why she did what she did, she said she joined the army because it was the only way she was ever going to afford to learn how to fly. Besides, she said, she only transports supplies, she doesn't transport troops. I came away from her, figuring selling out is a matter of degree. We all do it. There's computer operators working for huge multinational corporations, or they're stuck in the typing pool. Whatever. Anyway, the thing that's necessary for their survival is so much larger than themselves that they don't have to claim any responsibility. I reckon that's all I wanted to say." Pip got up and walked away, leaving Michelle alone on the beach.

~

"What am I responsible for?" Michelle asked herself, back in Adam's kitchen. According to Amy, it was the incorrectness of her life experience.

Well, if that was so easily defended, why couldn't she answer Amy?

She wanted to say that she had called her bosses and co-workers in the navy by their first names just as in any other office. That is, unless the big boss was around. Then things reverted back to rank. She wanted to say that she was trained by women, had taught women. That she had been in a class made up of twenty exceptional women from across Canada and was one of the first five women to gain a bridgewatchkeeping ticket, which enabled her to navigate and manoeuvre the ship on behalf of the Captain. She had left the service after working her way up to the rank of naval Lieutenant. But she couldn't be proud.

~

Before she quit the navy all her "straight" friends had warned her not to be open about her sexuality, but it was pretty common knowledge anyway. Michelle had actually been disappointed that the Special Investigations Unit of the military police hadn't come knocking on her door in one of their infamous witch hunts for gays and lesbians. They had already done it to a lot of non-commissioned friends of hers.

The discovery of the "Shelburne Ring," the so-called "hard core lesbians" at the listening station in Nova Scotia had lasting effects. For years afterwards, the SIU had hauled friends of Michelle's into their offices and interrogated them for hours until they broke down and named names. The full weight of Canadian Forces Administrative Order 19-20—the Forces policy on homosexuality, sexual abnormality, investigation, medical examination and disposal—came into full effect. Michelle was never called into interrogation herself and could do nothing to help her friends, except refer them to civilian counsel. Eventually, it became clear she would never be called. She had fantasies about going out in a blaze of glory to make up for the suffering she had never shared with her friends. It never happened.

~

There had been that one time when she was in basic training and the woman training officer had called her into her office to talk, ostensibly about Michelle's request to remuster to another trade. After an hour of idle chit-chat, there was an uncomfortable silence.

"Is that all ma'am? Am I free to go?" Michelle had asked.

"No. Perhaps we should talk about the reason you're really here."

The training officer was having trouble speaking and had started to blush. Michelle felt her pulse rate increase and all her blood rush to accumulate in her legs. It was a stiflingly hot day. Why the hell wasn't the window open?

"You've been accused of making passes at some of the other women."

Oh shit. C'mon Michelle we can get ourselves through this one. For one thing, it isn't true. Yes, you're a lesbian, but we aren't going to tell her that the reason you aren't interested in any of these women is because you're already in love with someone. Never mind that she's two thousand miles away.

"What did they say?"

"You were too friendly. Looked at them in the shower."

"You're kidding ... I know you can't tell me who said it because you'd probably be afraid I would make some sort of retaliation. But I can assure you, these claims are untrue." Michelle made a face and delivered her best mock shiver. "Can you at least tell me if it's someone in my division? I have to live with them all summer."

It hadn't been anyone in her division but that hadn't stopped her from hating and mistrusting every woman in her dorm for the rest of the year. When she finally got to go home after summer training, she didn't care whether she saw any of them ever again in her life. For the whole summer, her first one away with the navy, she had been known on the base by reputation. So much for confidentiality. She found out five years later who had pointed the finger at her.

~

So it had all came down to one day. After years of deliberation, she just decided she'd had enough and walked into the office with all her uniforms and her ID card, shoved them across the counter top to the administration chief and said goodbye. No-one else was around and the Chief had looked confused.

"I'd feel irresponsible if I didn't even have at least a fifteen-minute chat with you about this, ma'am," he had said.

"Chief, in fifteen minutes I couldn't even tell you all the reasons, nor would I. I've thought about it for years. I'm sure."

It had been pretty anti-climatic. It certainly was not as confrontational as the situation in which she now found herself.

~

"Do you know how hard it was for me to even tell you I used to be in the navy? I stuck pretty close to my men friends at the club and it wasn't because I wanted to be celibate.

"Finally there I was, free to actually talk with other women. I didn't have to steal kisses in engine rooms and bathrooms. I didn't have to sneak my lover into the officers' quarters. I wanted to have friends and connect with other women and have something more in common with them than covering each other's asses.

"But I finally figured out that it was a lot easier to let the other dykes in the bar guess that I was a "fag hag" or a "fruit fly" than to have to explain—justify—where I used to work in order to be found acceptable. I got the distinct impression, after several attempts at friendship, that the past military calling-card was an icemaker in this community, not an icebreaker. I hoped all that had changed when I met you."

"Yeah right," said Amy, not giving an inch. "You've had it really tough. I guess we should feel sorry for you."

"No. I don't want your pity," Michelle retorted. "I suppose it was pretty naive of me to think things would be any different out here in the 'real world'—as you say—than in the military."

"Things are one hell of a lot different."

"No—they aren't. I lived for years tied down with sets of rules. Now it seems I should live by a new set. The only difference is that it's a new, unwritten, silent code. It's such sweet irony that you had asked me to be myself when we first met. Did you know that now, one year after releasing, when I tell people I used to be in the navy, the other response I get is extreme surprise? People say I seem so unscathed. I've denied that part of my history well. But it's not because I wanted to."

"I wish you didn't feel you had to be so defensive." It was an accusation.

"I wish I didn't feel I had to be so defensive either."

Amy looked over to Adam, who had remained silent during the entire exchange.

"So why do you want to have this conversation now?" Michelle's question forced Amy's attention back to her.

Amy looked back to Adam again. She might as well have looked to his photo on the wall. It spoke more to the subject at hand than he was going to offer that night.

Michelle still felt ambushed. Where the hell were her reinforcements? She got up to get her guitar.

It was going to be a long walk home.

THE PERFECT GUEST

CAROLYN GAMMON

The weather had turned mild at last. Too mild. The ski trails which had been packed to a fast sheen were now mush. For the fourteen lesbians gathered to celebrate the winter Solstice season at a country house owned by the university, it could have been a good moment to hold the snowdyke competition, but the low overcast sky and drizzle tempted few outside. Still, after the previous days of minus twenty-five with a minus forty wind chill, the mild weather was a relief to most.

Less wood needed chopping, the oil furnace could rest between intervals and more corners of the large wooden house became accessible for study, reading, love-making or chatting. It was nearly dark at five p.m. and Rachel was in the study room when she heard the dogs barking madly at the side door. Expecting the dogs' mistresses to subdue the racket, Rachel ignored it for awhile then yelled, "Pet, Mai-linh—get your beasts!" Still no effect. Wondering where everyone was, Rachel got up and hurried to the side door. A car was just pulling away and someone with a backpack stood peering in through the fogged double glass doors. Kaila, the largest dog, part Doberman, had her paws up on the pane and her jaws at face level but had stopped howling. Radclyffe, the Yellow Lab, sat quietly as Rachel opened the door to the new arrival.

"Hi," said the newcomer, "is this the lesbian Solstice retreat?"

Rachel laughed, having not heard it called so before—the university administration had made them use the generic "woman" on all the publicity. "Actually, it's a lesbian offensive more than a retreat, come in."

The new dyke broke into a fast smile. She was tall, stately even, Rachel thought as she helped her lower her pack to the floor. And that bright blond-white hair, Scandinavian maybe?

"Lil," said the lesbian, by way of introduction, extending her large and long-fingered hand.

"Your hands are cold," said Rachel.

"The heater in the car wasn't working."

"Where did you come from?"

"Montreal."

"Well, at least you hit a mild day."

"So what's your name?" Lil asked.

"Sorry about that, it's Rachel .... How'd you hear about the retreat?"

"Through Karen."

"Karen Stuckley?" Rachel asked.

"No, Karen Fielding."

"Do I know her?" Rachel mused aloud.

"She's lovers with Amanda who works at *Les livres lavandes*."

"Oh right, that new bookstore on St. Denis, does Amanda work there now?" asked Rachel.

"Since December."

"Were you on the list for the retreat?" continued Rachel.

"No," admitted Lil, "I tried calling Pet somebody ... "

"Petulia Rae, yeh, she's the organizer," clarified Rachel.

"... all I ever got was this weird busy signal," finished Lil.

"Hmmm, that's odd ... anyway, welcome and how long can you stay?"

"A few days," said Lil, "then my friends will pick me up again on their way back up from New York."

"Who's there?" Mai-linh had finally received the message that the dogs had needed calming.

"This is Lil, just arrived from Montreal," said Rachel, "Lil, Mai-linh."

Mai-linh had taken hold of Kaila's studded black collar. "Nice dogs," said Lil leaning to pet Kaila, "and nice collars," she continued, referring to the matching butch and femme collars for the two dogs.

"I designed them myself," Mai-linh said, pleased. Seeing that Lil was in good hands, Rachel, anxious to get back to her studies, asked Mai-linh to show Lil the free bunks upstairs.

The Hanukkah candles had been lit and sweetgrass tips burned, and everyone was seated in the communal eating area before they all met the new arrival. "Lil," announced Mai-linh.

"Lily?" asked one.

"Just Lil," she answered.

Mai-linh continued, "Meet Lark, Ginger, Pet, Jess, Hannah, Joann, Ingrid, Rachel, Beste, Lupita, Michela, Chris, Maryse."

"And you know Kaila and Radclyffe," said Mai-linh petting the dogs at her feet.

"Emre," yelled a small voice angrily from the corner.

"And Emre," said Mai-linh apologetically.

"He's the only man we let in, they've got to be small enough to crawl through the keyhole," explained Michela.

"Not a man yet, thank goddess," said Beste, Emre's mum.

"Okay, your turn for the names," Mai-linh said jokingly to Lil, but to everyone's surprise she managed to go around the two tables in the same order, this time including Emre.

"Qu'est-ce que c'est?" Maryse was peering into one high pot.

"Lentils," said Ingrid, next to her.

"And this?" Maryse continued down the food line.

"Latkes" said someone else, "try them with sour cream or apple sauce."

"Fine," said Maryse serving herself two, "but what are they?"

"Potato pancakes," Hannah looked up from her food.

After they had all overeaten, Ingrid asked who wanted tea or coffee. Before she could get up, Lil had offered her services to make a special coffee with cream she had brought from Montreal just for the occasion. The non-coffee drinkers were going to turn her down but Lil was convincing, said she had de-caf, and soon all agreed. The post-meal chat had hardly evolved to gossip or smut before Lil was back with fifteen steaming mugs of *café con concha*, as she called it.

"Coffee with cunt?" Lupita translated with a question.

"A friend showed me how to make it in Mexico, we called it that because it's *so* good," said Lil.

"And *creamy*," said Lark sipping it. And it was, creamy and thick, the cream infused with the coffee, a touch of chocolate and cinnamon on the top of each frothy mug. Even the teetotallers slurped it down. Lupita took her mug to sit beside Lil, "Soy de México, ¿quando estuviste?"

The *café con concha* kept them all lingering at the table and it finally took Lil's initiative to get the after-supper cleanup underway. "So the dishes do themselves here?" she asked, heading to the kitchen with two hands full of empty mugs.

"You shouldn't have to clean up, you made the coffee," said Michela.

"I don't mind," said Lil, already filling the sink with biodegradable suds, "it won't take long."

Bit by bit through the next few days, Lil turned out to be the perfect dyke to have on a Solstice retreat. She took the dogs for walks with Pet when Mai-linh was busy. Radclyffe was Pet's dog, blind from age three. Lil acted as seeing-eye human for 'Clyffe through the woods when the obstacles were numerous and she played endless bouts of fetch with puppy-hyper Kaila. Indoors, Lil was a second mum to Emre, who loved to sit at Lil's feet and cling onto her pant leg, waiting for Lil to swing him between her long legs, back and forth as Emre sang "ding-dong, ding-dong." She played a mean game of Pictionary and was valued on any team for telepathy with her teammates at crucial moments. At one point, Pet had drawn a picture of a mug of beer and beer hall and all teams were still stumped on an "All-play," with the egg-timer running out. Pet quickly drew a stick person with a stick cock.

"TAVERN!" Lil yelled immediately for the game-winning turn.

"She's friends with Amanda and Karen," Michela told Chris around the fire one evening.

"Amanda from the bookstore?"

"Yeh, we had a signup for the retreat there."

"Actually, I saw it at the Lab," said Lil coming into the den with a plateful of gingerbread.

"Where's that?" Chris asked.

"The Labyris, for heaven's sake Chris, you haven't been sober for that long!" Michela retorted, giving Chris a hug at the same time.

"Did we poster the women's bars?" Joann asked from another corner of the room. No one seemed to know.

"Well, I saw it there in the bathroom," said Lil.

"You didn't make this too?" Joann asked as she bit into the warm gingerbread.

"No, Pet di ... , I jus helfed out," Lil said, muffled by her own mouthful.

With her long, strong arms, Lil helped Rachel chop wood.

"Are you from Canada originally?" Rachel asked between blows.

"Yes, but my parents aren't, one's from Norway and one's from Trinidad," Lil answered, setting up another log.

"Really?" said Rachel looking at Lil anew, " ... but you're so ... "

"Blond," filled in Lil.

"Yes," said Rachel, slightly embarrassed.

"My parents are dykes," said Lil to explain.

"Fuck! No joke!? I can't believe it, you're the first dyke I've met with dyke mums! That's great! Oh *fuck*," Rachel said in earnest as she totally missed the next blow, landing the axe firmly in the shed floor. Lil extracted the blade and took over.

"So your biological mum's from Norway?" Rachel asked, still in awe.

"Scandinavian Amazon genes," Lil said matter-of-factly, slicing easily through a large piece of maple.

It was soon passed around that Lil had been a turkey-baster baby with two mums, so she spent a lot of time around the fire answering questions from the curious. "I didn't know they used turkey basters back then," said Ingrid.

"Actually I think they used a cake decorator," said Lil.

"Oh wow, sugary-sweet floral insemination ... " said Chris sucking off the first layer of her roasted marshmallow.

"Inovulation," Lil amended.

"So how'd they meet, your mums?" asked Beste, shish-kebabing three marshmallows on a branch she had found in the woods and whittled sharp.

"At a Daughters of Bilitis meeting in San Fransisco."

"Daughters of what?" asked Hannah looking up from her book.

"Bilitis," said Ingrid, "you know, they were one of the first—"

"*The* first," Lark broke in. "The first lesbian group in the States, like in the early '50s?"

"Your mums met at a lesbian meeting in the '50s??? That is just too much," Beste was amazed.

"But how'd they get there from Norway and Trinidad?" asked Rachel.

"Immigrants, the American dream and all that," answered Lil.

"Sounds like the American *lesbian* dream to me," added Beste.

"How does all that add up to Canada for you?" Rachel continued the demographics game.

"My mum from Norway first came to Canada as a nannie," Lil explained.

"Canada has nannies?" Chris asked, coming into the room.

"Where have you been Chris?" Rachel chided.

"In the smoking room."

Rachel rolled her eyes.

"She was hired by a family in Westmount, so she knew Montreal," Lil went on. "Then she travelled and met Martha, my mum from Trinidad, in San Fran."

"What's Martha do?"

"Mainly, she's a writer, she teaches some, at City University in New York now."

"How come you're not spending Solstice with them?" Hannah wanted to know.

"Actually, they split up a couple of years ago."

There were a few sighs and the ensuing silence suggested to Rachel that she change the subject. "Have you travelled much?"

Lil had dyke-travelled the world. She had been to all-womyn festivals from Amsterdam to Aukland. She had visited Trinidad with Martha and sampled the underground gay life there. She had stayed with her Norse grandparents in Oslo during the Feminist Bookfair there and met Norwegian and even a couple of Lappish dykes. Sure enough, on Ginger's asking, she turned out to be Sagittarian.

"And the Year of the Snake!" Mai-linh informed Lil excitedly after asking her birthdate. "A great sign! ... Great looking, cunning, seductive ..."

"We know, charming, sexy, and all that—same as Mai-linh," Pet said to Lil by way of explanation.

Lil sat one afternoon with Ginger listening to the significance of the cups and swords of Ginger's new Mother Peace cards but turned down the offer of a reading. "I know too much already," Lil said with a laugh. But she had a two-peaked almost breastlike quartz crystal to add to Ginger's altar. Ginger fondled it lovingly. "So much good energy in this one," she said, placing it beside her own crystals.

One cold rainy afternoon, Maryse took out the plaster of Paris and explained to all gathered how to wet the strips to make body masks—"*any* part," she stressed. While others had their faces, hands or breasts moulded, Lil lay flat on her stomach as five dykes worked on her firm white ass. They peeled it, painted it and flung sparkles at the finished work of art.

"Voila, ton cul, immortalisé!" said Maryse, holding it up with pride.

The next day the weather was transitional and the wet snow provided the perfect medium for the snowdyke competition. Beste helped Emre with a baby butch, Mai-linh and Pet sculpted a dog. But most, thinking of Lil's large, firm, white ass, sculpted a large, strong snow-amazon complete with milk-weed pod eyes, mud-grass pubes, full hanging breasts, hands on hips. From then on she was the Goddess of the Solstice and each morning dykes getting up would peer out the now frosted windows to see her. Outside, they would cup her breasts, touch her nipples until they became glassy. Returning from skiing one day with Maryse, Lil added a garland of freeze-dried goldenrod and wild cucumber vine about the Goddess' neck. Lupita, looking out the window, said to herself: "Ahora está perfecta."

Emre chased Kaila into the den one afternoon, nearly tripping over Joann, sprawled out across the carpet with the *Cunt Coloring Book*.

"Wha you dooooing?" Emre sat down with Joann.

"Colouring," Joann said, absorbed.

"Wha you col-ring?" Emre asked again.

"My cunt," said Joann.

"You cunn?" Emre asked.

"Yip," Joann said, continuing. Emre picked up a green crayon. "No, these ones," Joann said, handing him the browns, reds and blacks. Emre started scribbling on the periphery of the picture.

Lil walked in. "Domestic bliss," she said, sprawling herself likewise beside Joann, "wish I had a camera." She lay for awhile watching. "Look at this," she said, showing Emre how he could ball two colours at once in his fist and colour in stripes. Leaving her colouring to the disaster it was becoming, Joann withdrew to a sunlit corner of the room with Lil to chat.

"I've got to leave this aft," Lil said sadly.

"Ahhh ... how come?" Joann wanted to know.

"That's when my friends are coming through and I've told Amanda I'd go to their New Year's party."

"Phone them, tell them you've decided to stay with fourteen beautiful dykes out here."

"I'd love to, but ... "

Joann took Lil's hands, noticing for the first time the short, chopped nails on one and the grown out nails on the other. "Guitar," she thought.

"It's been so great to have you here, we'll have to get together again in Montreal."

"I'll leave you my number," Lil promised.

"Lil's going," Joann announced to the next person in the room.

"No!" said Hannah. "How come? She'll miss the workshop tonight."

"What's the topic?" Lil asked.

"Non-monogamy ... or polyeroticism." They all laughed.

"Forget the workshop, what about missing the broccoli soufflé?" said Joann in mock horror.

"I don't know which will be tougher to miss," Lil mused.

"When are you going?"

"Whenever my friends arrive."

"Lil's going," Joann and Hannah said simultaneously when Ingrid walked into the den.

"You'll miss the broccoli soufflé!" said Ingrid.

"We've tried that," said Joann.

"What about the non-monogamy workshop?"

"We've tried that too," said Hannah.

"But I wanted to show you my Michigan pictures," Ingrid said, looking at Lil.

"We can do that now if you'd like," said Lil and they were off upstairs. Joann cuddled up with Hannah. "What'll we do without Lil?"

"Don't know."

"What'll we do without *café con concha*?" Joann said, even more seriously.

"Make it ourselves, I guess." Hannah turned her face up for a kiss but Joann was looking to where Lil had left the room.

Later that day a car came and went, this time without the dogs registering their trespassing howls. The dykes were dispersed around the house or outside and only Rachel was there once again to see Lil off. "Your friends don't want to come in?" she asked.

"Probably, but they told me by phone that they're in a rush, sooo," Lil said reaching down to grab her pack. Rachel helped her with it.

"We'll miss you ... I'll miss you," Rachel said taking hold of Lil's hands.

"And I'll miss you," Lil assured her, "all of you." They kissed, their lips lingering that extra second of meaning.

"See you in Montreal!" Rachel called as Lil closed the car door.

That night at the communal meal, the concerted munching of Pet's broccoli soufflé served to mask the fact that the Solsticers were unusually silent. After supper, Lark suggested half-heartedly that she might make the *café con concha* but, checking the fridge, found they had run out of the special thick cream, and anyway, it seemed almost sacrilegious to have it without Lil. Despite a hopping k.d. lang tape, they straggled through the dishes.

"The workshop's supposed to start at eight," Lark said, a pile of dishes still stacked on the counter at five to eight.

"Change the time," someone suggested. Lark de-sudsed her hands and went to the den to write, beside the breasted Santa on the blackboard: "Non-M workshop 8:30 p.m." It was nine before tea was made and all seated.

"Who's facilitating?"

Silence.

"Whose idea was this workshop anyway?" someone asked with a whine.

"I wrote it on the board at first," said Pet grudgingly, "Mai-linh told me to."

"Sounds like you two should be discussing SM," said another.

"Okay, come off it, let's get something going," Rachel put her best organizational foot forward. "How about we all write on a scrap of paper some non-monogamous act we've done or would like to do, be it fantasy or reality, and then we discuss them anonymously?" With much discussion over how to guard anonymity and what constituted fantasy, the workshop finally got underway.

The first paper was drawn. "After three years in a steady relationship, I slept with another woman for one night only."

"That's a good one," said Pet enthusiastically. "Is it, or is it not the big Non-M?"

"If it's *one* night out of—what? Three hundred and sixty-five times three equals one thousand and something—I say no," said Michela emphatically.

"You have a vested interest, honey?" Chris said teasingly.

"I agree with Michela, what's a fling got to do with long-term commitment? I mean, we surely all admit to extra-marital attractions ... " Lark prodded. Most everyone nodded or mumbled agreement. "So what's a little fling? Let's go on to the next one."

Lark drew. "I would like two lovers at the same time."

"I'd like *one*!" Ginger cried. "This workshop doesn't even apply to me. How can I be non-monogamous when I can't even be *mono*-gamous?"

"This is beginning to sound like amoebas," Beste said.

"Or gene-pools," said another.

"Let's discuss the issue," Jess hauled them back on track. "Two lovers simultaneously, is non-m for sure."

"I object!" Rachel broke in. "I don't like that term, it makes monogamy the norm and it's a het throwback to men controlling women."

"Okay, okay," Pet mediated, "use polyerotic if it'll make Rachel happy."

"Thank you Pet."

"Then that's a polyerotic one for sure," Jess continued, "but think of the energy it would take! Think how much energy *one* relationship takes."

"Give me crystal energy anytime," Ginger concluded.

A third was drawn. "I want something on the side," read Hannah.

"Horseradish?" Lark snickered.

"Cranberry sauce?" Rachel threw in.

"Be serious," Hannah pleaded. "Here's someone who wants something on the side, an affair in other words."

"Isn't that like having your cake and eating it too?" asked Joann.

"Having your *pussy* and eating it too," said Lark.

"No, I don't think it's greedy," said Hannah. "I mean, the affair can keep the main relationship hot."

"You mean primary and secondary relationships and all that shit," said Michela.

"It's not shit," Hannah insisted.

"Abstain from value judgements," Rachel ordered in a courtroom voice.

Meanwhile, Joann had crawled into Hannah's lap. "Hey! That's your handwriting!" Joann had glanced at the slip of paper. "You drew your own!"

"That's cheating," Michela jerked the paper out of Joann's view.

"I'm just interested," said Hannah.

"You want something on the side???" Joann said in disbelief.

"It's just an exercise," Hannah reasoned.

"You want something on the side." This time Joann stated it as fact.

"Joann baby, you know I love you," Hannah cooed reassuringly, pulling Joann closer. They necked for a while, causing a domino necking effect around the circle. The singles got up to add logs to the fire or make fresh tea.

A second round of herbal and black tea, and a bowl of smarties, upped the morale. "Number four," Beste announced, drawing another slip: "A five-minute fuck—is it non-m?"

"What's that supposed to mean?" Jess asked.

"It means, is a fuck-'em-and-chuck-'em considered a fling even?" one answered.

"A toilet encounter?" Hannah suggested.

"How gross!"

"A feel-up on the dance floor?"

"What is a five-minute fuck?" Jess asked again.

"Use your imagination, Jess," answered Joann.

"Look," Ingrid spoke for the first time. "I'm tired of this, we're not getting anywhere. Either we change the format or I'm going ... "

" ... to have a five-minute fuck," Beste finished Ingrid's sentence.

"Seriously, I'll play one-woman Pictionary if this doesn't improve."

"She wants an Academic Discussion," Lark said in a hoity-toity accent.

"It's true, we're not going anywhere," Michela pitched in. "We all know what monogamy and non-monogamy are."

"You mean polyeroticism and non-polyeroticism," Pet corrected.

"Then let's talk real life," Rachel piped up enthusiastically, "like candid-camera, this happened to me."

"You can die-vulge if you want, I will not," Chris said emphatically.

"Neither will I," said Hannah.

"You see, it's only the coupled ones who won't," Lark accused.

"I will," Rachel offered. "Do you mind?" she added, turning to Ingrid. Ingrid shrugged, rolled her eyes and, at least, did not get up to leave.

"So go," Lark was anxious. The group seemed to perk up for the first time since Lil had left.

"Well," said Rachel, gingerly pruning her words, "let's say I've had a very brief fling once in the two years I've been with Ingrid." Ingrid rolled her eyes again and stared at Rachel.

"Define fling," came a request.

"Fling, flingette, short and sweet."

"How sweet, darling?" Ingrid said, trying to rally by grabbing at Rachel's crotch.

"I doubt it'll happen again, at least not with the same lover."

"How'd you take it, Ingrid?" asked Jess, concerned.

"I haven't heard about it."

"WHAT?"

"Till now," said Ingrid.

"Rachel," Lark reproached, "that is NOT NICE."

"It happened recently," Rachel justified.

"*How* recently?" Ingrid asked.

"Here at the retreat."

"No," came one audible gasp.

"Come off it, don't tell me you've all been pristine humpers here," Rachel surveyed the room.

"Who with?" Jess asked.

"I'm not telling," Rachel said.

"Obviously someone else isn't either," Jess said.

"I must protect the guilty," Rachel used her falsely deep courtroom voice again.

"Okay, well, so have I," said Beste.

Lupita looked at her, "¿Qué?"

"I've had a fling too,"

"Fling, what is this?" Lupita asked sharply.

"Una aventurita," Ingrid translated.

"¿Quando?"

"Here, at the retreat."

"Really?" Two or three voices spoke nearly together.

"With Lil," Beste was ready to hand over the information on a platter.

"¡Beste!" came Lupita's surprised voice.

"No ... " said Rachel, equally surprised.

"She came up to the room one afternoon when I was resting with Emre. We stuck him on the top bunk."

"You slut!" said Lark affectionately.

"Takes one to know one," Beste talked back.

"You had sex with Lil too then?" Rachel said directly to Beste.

"Too?" There was silence about the fire.

"When I was chopping wood ... " Rachel went on.

"In the wood shed? In the cold?" Pet was incredulous.

"She had a dildo on under her jeans."

"I would have run the other way if she'd pulled that on me!" said Chris, horrified.

"I have a soft spot for dildos ... " Rachel said by way of explanation.

"A soft, *wet* spot by the sounds of it," said Lark gleefully.

"*Spare* me the details," Ingrid said sourly.

"That Lil got around," Lark commented.

"Put another log on," Hannah told Joann.

"I'm going to bed," said Ingrid, getting up. Rachel tried to restrain her but ended up being partially dragged across the room. "Think I'll go too," she said, tripping out after Ingrid.

"I'm glad you're not like that," Beste said quietly to Lupita, folding herself into Lupita's lap.

The workshop broke up into video-watching—Lily Tomlin's *The Search for Signs of Intelligent Life in the Universe* for the fifth time. Some played Pictionary and others were off for a much needed fix to the smoking room.

That night in bed Mai-linh turned over to Pet, brushed her hair back tenderly, and waited a moment. "Pet, I can't sleep."

"Hmmmmmm," came a near snore.

"Pet-uuu-laaa I want to tell you something."

"Hmmmmm?" a bit of interest.

"I had sex with Lil too."

"Whaaaa?"

"After we took the dogs for a walk on that first mild day, we made love."

Pet was fully awake. "Where?"

"Here," Mai-linh said, nearly inaudibly.

"In this room?" Pet looked at Mai-linh with disappointment.

"She wanted to see me perform a Kata and I thought it would be more impressive if I stripped, so we came up here."

"In this bed?"

Mai-linh nodded. Dead silence for a few minutes. Pet broke the silence. Staring straight up at the upper bunk she said, "So did I, but at least not in this bed."

Now it was Mai-linh's turn to be surprised. "When?"

"When I was making gingerbread, she came up behind me. At first I thought it was you but of course she's so tall."

"In the kitchen?"

"No one was around."

"I can't believe it."

"Neither can I." They both lay side by side untouching until Pet reached out and intertwined her fingers with Mai-linh's. "I wonder," Mai-linh said thoughtfully, "how many others got together with Lil ..."

The next morning, a determined Pet set out to do a survey. They were all sitting in a row in the kitchen, bent over porridge, looking like they were doing time anyway, so Pet started in. "Chris ... did you sleep with Lil?

Chris looked angrily at Pet then glanced at Michela. "No," she replied at once.

"Did you, Michela?" A "no" came equally as fast. "What about you, Ginger?"

Ginger swallowed a sticky lump of oatmeal. "Pass the maple syrup please," she said.

"Ginger?" Pet persisted.

"Yeshh," Ginger said, with a spoon in her mouth. It had happened while she was showing Lil her new tarot cards. Lil had been looking over her shoulder and gone for an ear. "And my ears being the next closest in sensitivity to my clit ... " Ginger explained, and being single and all, how could she have refused?

During the second round of coffee, Hannah came in. Thinking of the workshop the night before, Pet asked Hannah, point blank, if she had got what she wanted on the side. Hannah played innocent until Pet told her the facts about herself and Mai-linh, Ginger, and obviously Rachel and Beste who had owned up at the workshop. Hannah said yes, it was while she had been cleaning the toilets, Hannah had yelled for someone to bring her an extra bottle of toiletbowl cleaner and Lil had shown up. "She came in with the cleaner and said 'Is this what you wanted?' and closed the door after her. It was her hands, you know, so long and strong ... " Hannah reminisced.

"I know," Pet commiserated. With over half of them confirmed as having had sex with Lil, Pet called a meeting as soon as everyone was back in the house.

"Okay," Pet began, "we've an epidemic on our hands—we wanted non-monogamy, we got it. It seems that Lil slept with everyone here."

"Oyyyy!"

"Slept with?"

"Had sex with," clarified Pet.

"Fucked," said someone else. The unverified singles and couples were looking at one another surprised, guilty, but mostly relieved.

Lark was the first to speak. "Lil came up to my bed one night, I think it was the second night she was here. I was asleep and woke to the softest, most expert caresses." Comparing nights, they figured she must have just come from Jess's bed where the same tactics had worked.

"For me, it was her nails, the way she drew them just hard enough along my thigh," Jess said, her eyes closed. "I thought I was the only one."

Lupita had been teaching Lil more Spanish vocabulary when Lil had asked to touch her lips to better feel the formation of the words. "Corny," was the only comment anyone ventured.

Ingrid hesitatingly admitted that she and Lil had fucked on the last day when they had gone upstairs to look at Ingrid's Michigan photos. Lil had told Ingrid how voluptuous she looked in the food line-up wielding a carrot. "I'm a sucker for flattery, what can I say?" Ingrid finished.

With Maryse it had happened in an abandoned barn off the ski trail. Pet was again astounded at the outdoor aspect of it. "It was sunny, and the hay was warm," Maryse explained. Lil had crowned Maryse with the vine wreath intended for the snow Goddess. "I wanted to thank her, so gave her a hug," Maryse continued.

"A hug?" someone asked rhetorically.

"Well, you *know*," Maryse would not elaborate.

Pet noticed during the confessions that Michela and Chris were whispering to one another. "Changed your minds girls?" asked Pet, referring to the breakfast denials.

"Well, you asked if we'd *slept* with her."

"Excuse my English, shall I try Sicilian?" said Pet.

"Did you sleep with her?" asked Lark.

"I *showered* with her," Michela said at last.

"Oooooh, showered how?" Lark pryed, delighted.

Michela squirmed as she spoke. "Showered, washed each another."

"Faces, arms?" Lark was relentless.

"Cunts?" Rachel joined in.

"Pubic hair and stuff," Michela wanted out of the hotspot.

"They ass-fucked," Chris said.

"Chris!" Michela implored, mortified.

"Michela's into asses," Chris added.

"And you're not?" Pet asked.

"Not really," Chris said.

"She did have a nice ass," Michela at last rallied to her own defence. She glanced at the glittery mould now propped against the Solstice bush. Some eyes followed, no one disagreed.

"What about you Chris?" Maryse turned the focus off Michela. It was Chris' turn to look uneasy.

"Tell them Chris," Michela said, resignedly.

"We were watching *Desert Hearts*," Chris said.

"When?" asked Maryse.

"Two, no three nights ago."

"So?"

"It was during the sex scene," Chris continued, "we were under the covers ... our hands were."

"How romantic—their hands met," Beste said. "I *love* these euphemisms!"

"With everyone in the room watching too?" Maryse was amazed.

"You were watching the movie, I should hope," Chris said indignantly.

"Come to think of it, I did see the blankets heaving," Beste teased.

"I thought the dog was under there with you," Lark added. Chris was blushing in despair before the teasing stopped.

They looked around; all dykes had owned up except Joann—Joann, who had been so indignant over Hannah wanting something on the side. Everyone turned their attention to her, appealing for the truth before she said, almost under her breath, "It doesn't really count, it was only five minutes."

"Ah-ha! The five-minute fuck!" said Lark.

"I thought you said last night's workshop was anonymous," steamed Joann, glaring at Lark.

"Sorry, go on."

"I was colouring in the *Cunt Coloring Book,* so I guess I was in the mood and somehow Emre took over and then Lil was there and we were cosy in the corner with the pillow-chairs."

"When was that?" Ingrid asked.

"Lil's last day, in the early afternoon."

"Goddess she worked fast ... " Ingrid said, calculating on her fingers how many lesbians, including herself, Lil went through in one day.

"I want smut, how did she come onto you?" Lark wouldn't stop.

"She asked to see the cunt I'd used as a model for my colouring."

"Of course," said Lark conclusively.

"And you let her?" asked Michela.

"Of course," said Joann.

"Why?"

"Well, why did you?"

"And why did you?" Michela said to Chris, Beste to Lupita, Rachel to Ingrid. They all stopped at once.

"We've been had," one said. "We've been fucked," added another. "Polyerotic and perverse!" Lark laughed. Even Joann cracked a smile, shaking her head in disbelief.

"So, who's got her telephone number ... *I want it!*" Lark demanded. No one spoke up. "Where does she live?" Lark persisted. No one could answer that either.

"She's friends with Amanda and Karen," said Rachel.

"And she hangs out at Labyris or she wouldn't have seen the poster for the retreat," added Maryse.

"Who'd she come with?" More silence.

"You saw the car Rachel," Jess continued the questioning, "who was driving it, what colour was it, licence plates, et cetera."

"I hardly saw it," Rachel protested, "and the windows were steamed or something so I didn't see who was driving."

"Were there any passengers?"

"I don't remember," Rachel answered meekly.

"Colour of the car? Was it an American or Quebec licence?"

"I don't remember, now *can* it," Rachel said forcefully.

"She's keeping information from us," Chris said.

"I am NOT!" Rachel exploded.

"Calm down!" Pet insisted, "I've had enough of this interrogation. Is it true that *none* of us know anything about Lil?"

"What's her last name?" No one knew.

"How long has she been in Montreal?" No one knew. No one knew her address, no one knew anything really except that she had managed to have sex with all of them. When they were at their wit's end, Joann offered resignedly, "Well, she did leave me her number."

Relieved and annoyed eyes circled the room to land on Joann as she pulled a purple piece of paper from her breast pocket and unfolded it. "Huh?" she said, confused.

Hannah, next her, inspected the paper. "It just says LOVE LIL," she announced.

"We exchanged numbers," Joann explained, "I just assumed ... " she trailed off.

"That's it," said Rachel, "I'm calling Amanda, now."

"It's long distance ... " someone yelled, but Rachel was already out the door. The amazed chatter continued until Rachel returned.

"I spoke with both Amanda and Karen." She paused for dramatic effect. "Neither of them know of Lil or even a dyke of that description ... they've never heard of her."

"This is beginning to sound like an Agatha Christie," Jess said ominously.

"Ten Little Lesbians," said Ingrid.

"Fourteen," corrected Jess.

"We've had sex, not been bumped off," said Hannah rationally.

"Who *is* this gal?" Lark was intrigued.

"You mean, who *was*," Beste finished.

~

As it turned out, no dyke in Montreal had ever heard of Lil. Most conversations in the bars, at the shelters, at the Lesbian Studies meetings, at dances, started and stopped short. Did anyone know of Lil of such-and-such a description? No, why? Oddly, not one of the fourteen who had been at the Solstice retreat would answer. "Oh nothing," the conversations would end. Maryse thought at one point she had found Lil's photo in a copy of *Our Right to Love*, but only Maryse thought it looked like Lil. Lark had a friend in California who wrote about meeting a Lil who seemed to fit the description but *that* Lil turned out to be a transvestite and they all knew Lil was not. Ingrid saw a dyke in the food line-up the next fall at the East Coast Lesbian Festival and reported back to Rachel that maybe it was Lil with longer hair. Rachel was determined enough to find out and the next time they saw the same lesbian, she went up and asked: "You're not Lil are you?" The lesbian signed that Rachel would have to do better than that if she wanted to communicate and Rachel panicked, shrugged "sorry" and left.

All leads led nowhere and the next winter's Solstice retreat found many of the same dykes thinking of the mysterious arrival and departure of the perfect seductrice. But no extra car came and all Solsticers were accounted for, paid up, and signed with telephone numbers.

"Hey! Listen to this," Lark said, looking up from a book. "Here's a biblical character called Lilith." A movie was on and Lark did not attract much interest. She read on to herself mumbling a series of yeses. "Listen," she said again, "who does this sound like to you?" A small audience around Lark became more attentive. She began to read: " 'Adam tried to force Lilith to lie beneath him in the 'missionary position' ... She sneered at Adam's sexual crudity, cursed him and flew away.' " Lark looked up expectantly but was still met with blank faces.

"What book are you reading?" Jess asked politely.

"*The Women's Encyclopedia of Myths and Secrets*," Lark was impatient to read on. "... let's see, it goes on: 'God sent angels to fetch Lilith back, but she cursed them too, ignored God's command and spent her time coupling with "demons." ' "

"I get it." Something was dawning on Jess at last, "*Lilith*, that's our Lil!"

"And we're the demons!" Rachel finished gayly.

Lark summarized: "She gave birth to a hundred children a day, seems to have had sex everywhere with everything. God had to invent Eve to get Lilith out of the story."

"Definitely not a good heroine for nice Jewish girls!" Hannah was entranced. "Lily comes from the same root, the Great flower-yoni ... "

"What's Yoni?" Michela wanted to know.

"Just a minute," Lark leafed through the book, "Yoni—Vulva ... the Goddess Kali, or Cunti ... cunt, what else but?"

"Finish up there on Lilith," Hannah urged.

"She disappeared from the bible, naturally, but her daughters, 'lilim' were, and I quote, 'lustful she-demons.' Daughters of Lilith were also known as Night-Hags, supposed to be very beautiful, expert at lovemaking," Lark closed the book.

"Night-Hags," Jess repeated.

"Expert at lovemaking," said Hannah.

"Definitely our Lil," Rachel concluded.

"*Eh, taisez-vous un p'tit peu* ... I'm trying to watch the movie," complained a voice from nearby. It was Claire, who had not been at the retreat the year before. "Just keep it down a little, please?" she implored, "and pass the popcorn." Lark went back to her book. Rachel passed the popcorn and sighed, snuggling into Ingrid's lap for the fourth rerun of *Anne Trister*.

"Hey you," Ingrid said softly.

"Yeh," came a nuzzled reply.

"How'd you like some ... " Ingrid broke off to wave a cunt-scented fingertip under Rachel's nose, *"café con concha.* I've brought the special cream."

"Hm-mmmmmm," Rachel hummed affirmatively and turning her face to Ingrid, sucked the tantalizing finger into her mouth.

"Now?" Rachel asked.

"Why not?" said Ingrid, "I've seen this before." They both got up and left the room.

THE JOURNEY

SHIRLEY LIMBERT

The two women sat companionably together as the bus rolled across the flatlands of the Prairies. Miles of yellow as far as the eye could see. Here and there a tiny speck slowly, very slowly growing larger and taking the shape of a grain elevator. Dotted across the landscape were sloughs left dry, white and powdery with no water for the cattle. Occasionally one of the sloughs had a mud hole, and dust trails marked where many hooves had trodden to find it. The summer of '88 had been even hotter and drier than usual.

One of the women dozed, her head resting against the window, nodding up and down with the rhythm of the bus, long legs stretched as far as possible under the seat in front of her and her hand, the one covered by the quilt on her lap, entwined in the hand of the woman by her side. She wasn't thinking, wasn't dreaming, she was in a state of solitude. Symbols rolled through her mind, pictographs, images of her being. She gave herself up to the motion of the bus and drifted on.

The other woman was more conscious of her dreaming, orchestrating, directing. She set her stage, allowed her players and wrote their script.

Two characters: one Sue, one Jeannie, both workers in a women's shelter. Sue is walking through the door of the big yellow house in which she works. Another sixteen hour shift is starting and in this house many women have re-created their lives and dreams. She walks into the office, aware of a subtle difference in energy. Usually Jeannie is dressed and ready for the morning's exchange of information, with a smile, a cup of coffee for her co-worker and a quick hug. This morning Jeannie is still in her pyjamas, her face drawn, dark circles under her eyes. She is standing by the phone, leaning back against the huge cluttered desk.

Sue involuntarily tightened her hold on her lover's hand as she remembered. The bus jolted on. The play continued as she closed her eyes. Disjointed scenes.

There had been an accident during the night. One of the ex-residents had called in—a crib death, a two-month-old baby born whilst her mother had been at the shelter. Jeannie speaks all of this with tears pouring down her face and soon Sue's arms are folding around her, drawing her close and Jeannie's head rests on Sue's shoulder. The tears continue and Sue can feel them soaking into her shirt. Sue also is crying.

A funeral parlor with a tiny casket at one end and half a dozen women players as family members. Sue and Jeannie arrive together. There is a difference in the quality of their companionship now. As they greet various women they appear to be at home with each other, conscious of each other and yet not needing to be in each other's line of vision. Something has happened, consolidating their friendship. The other actors are aware of the change and show signs of distrust that two women could seem to be so close, could appear to share something intimate. Sue and Jeannie behave as if unaware of the growing hostility. The funeral service starts, the minister intones, there is the sound of weeping, Jeannie leans against Sue and Sue puts her arm around Jeannie's shoulder comfortingly and rests her head against her friend's. There is whispering behind her, shuffling of feet and a woman clears her throat aggressively. Sue quickly removes her arm from Jeannie's shoulder and the two women sit rigidly in the chapel pew. More whispering and the sound of weeping continues.

The scene dissolved as the woman in the bus let go of her partner's hand and wiped her eyes. She looked at the other woman asleep against the window, her hair tousled, her face relaxed and her mouth slightly open. Why is all this coming back now, why am I needing to remember all this, she wondered.

Sometimes things come into our consciousness, scenes from the past to remind us and help us grow. She shifted uncomfortably in the hard seat. What did I learn from that coming together? Another jolt of the bus and she stretched her back, trying not to wake her partner as she moved.

The woman settled herself more comfortably. The sound of raindrops on the bus windows lulled her into her dream stage again.

A restaurant in a large town, candles on the table, food, wine. The two women, Sue and Jeannie, are sitting opposite each other at the table. They are on a date.

Sue looks into Jeannie's eyes over her wine glass. There is well-practiced dialogue in parts of this scene; however, the first few lines are a little different:

"Here's to yurts."

Jeannie smiles. "Yurts, how can we drink a toast to tents made of felt?" she asks. "Just because we've been to the museum for the afternoon and they happened to have an exhibition of Himalayan housing or whatever, you think you're expert enough to drink a toast to them?"

Sue nods, "It's either a toast to them or to us."

Jeannie is suddenly serious, "Well why not?"

She looks across at Sue who has been her friend for so long. Sue with the fair hair and quick smile. Jeannie's heart leaps. I could fall in love with this woman she thinks, amazed that it hadn't occurred to her before. Sue, she knows, is a lesbian, a strong independent woman, alone since the sudden death of her partner two years ago. Jeannie remembers the times they have spent together since the baby's death, eating lunch, talking about everything and nothing, laughing, arguing, getting to know each other on a completely different level and liking what they learnt. Jeannie looks again at Sue, sitting across from her, her glass still raised.

"Dreaming again?" Sue inquires. "Are we toasting yurts or us?"

"Let's toast us," Jeannie manages, "I think I'm falling in love with you."

Sue's eyes widen and she carefully replaces her glass on the little cloth-covered table. She leans across and takes Jeannie's glass and puts it down on the table also and then, in front of the entire restaurant, customers and waiters, she rises from her chair, leans over the table and kisses Jeannie hard on the mouth.

Both women were jolted in their seats as the bus came to a halt and they opened their eyes simultaneously as the driver started his monologue. The bus stop made a pool of light in the surrounding darkness and the women shivered as they made their way to the coffee shop. It wasn't so much the coolness of night, because summer still had a hold on the Prairies, it was the special excitement of being up and about in the midst of darkness, of being part of a special group who live their lives and do their business in the night.

Having swallowed some coffee and visited the washroom, they resettled themselves in the bus. One woman again rested her shoulders against the corner of the seat and the window. The other tucked her legs under her body, her head against the headrest and the quilt pulled up to her chin, and moved her hand across her lap and clasped her lover's hand, intertwining fingers. The bus rolled out of the station and into the night. The play continued.

Sue's apartment, tiny kitchen/living room leading to the bedroom. The two women, Sue and Jeannie, are standing at the entrance to the bedroom. They are face to face, their arms around each other, looking into each other's eyes.

"I want you to stay tonight, sleep with me, make love with me." Sue's voice is husky. Jeannie's eyes deepen and she nods.

Sue leans towards her and kisses the corner of her mouth. Jeannie sighs and smiles, returning the kiss. Sue continues kissing, nibbling and sucking around the edges of Jeannie's lips then very gently her tongue insists on an opening. Jeannie sighs again and Sue's tongue finds the opening; for a moment they stand quietly tongue on tongue and then passion carries them on. Sue's tongue explores Jeannie's mouth and her hands move slowly to unbutton her shirt. Soon her hands are inside the shirt cupping a breast, holding, gently teasing the erect nipple. Jeannie steps back.

"My legs will give way in a minute. Oh woman, let's go to bed."

The woman on the bus squeezed her thighs together. The warm sensation moved into her belly then down again between her legs. She squeezed again and felt a rush. The other woman moved restlessly and let her head drop onto her lover's shoulder. Again a change of scene.

The bedroom: pale pink walls, deep rose-coloured paper blinds on the large window and a futon on the floor covered by a fluffy duvet. On top of the duvet are Sue and Jeannie, naked and engrossed, faces buried in each other's thighs, soft murmurings coming from their throats. Now and then one or the other lifts her head, coming up for air, and kisses her partner's belly or slowly drags her tongue, soft and wet or pointed and almost dry across that belly, savouring the salty taste. Each face is warm and moist from exertion and from her lover's juices. Soon the two women are moving together. Each on her side, her head cushioned on the other's thigh, her mouth on her partner's cunt, tongue flicking, moving in and out, up and down until together their excitement carries them through passion to the door of light, then their cries mingle, their excitement mounts and they burst through, sobbing, laughing, rolling over and over until they end up on the floor, a tangle of arms, legs, tongues and cunts. Oh, the first time, how sweet, and the last time, how knowing. They lie together for a long time, bodies cooling in the night air, hair damp, lips bruised. Eventually they roll back onto the futon and cuddle together under the cover, knowing that as soon as they have rested they can again turn to each other and again and again.

The characters line up, as in a finale. First the bit players. Women from the shelter, workers and residents, friends and family, take their bow. They are acknowledged, each having played her part. Finally Sue and Jeannie, the stars of the play of Jeannie's first love. They take their bow also and make way for the author who carries the responsibility for the dream and for living other dreams based on this.

Again the bus jolted and the woman thanked the cast and opened her eyes. Her lover looked up at her and winked.

"Guess we're there, Jeannie."

They squeezed hands and unclasped them under the cover. Time to get their coats on and their bags out. Home at last.

Jeannie smiled fondly at Becky, her lover, the woman with whom she had spent almost half her life.

"Yes, I guess we're there," she agreed.

RHESA

SUSAN McIVER

DEAR BOXY,

This morning my mind is jammed with a million memories. I must share them with you. I know you've heard them all before, but then what are good friends for? Remember back in grade four when we built that first fort together? We've been telling each other our secrets ever since.

Five years ago today was my first appointment with Rhesa. My apprehension about seeing a psychiatrist wasn't lessened one bit by having to meet her at the mental health facility at 999 Queen Street, Toronto. As I went through the security gate at the entrance and past a couple of "reception" (read "control") desks on the way to Rhesa's office, my throat tightened. I wondered what I was getting into.

Yes, it took me a long time to tell you what prompted me to seek professional help. I was really ashamed of my behaviour the night before my mother's visit early that fall. I got drunk and ran around the house yelling, "I hate you. I don't want you to come. You never loved me. Just leave me alone." I was really on the edge.

I will never forget that first visit. Straightaway I told Rhesa why I had come: consistent heavy drinking, alienation from my family, and general depression. She asked me what I assume are the usual questions shrinks ask new patients. When we got to the part about sexual experience, I swallowed hard and said, "I'm a lesbian."

She hesitated, glanced at my well-turned-out appearance, and in her heavily accented English asked, "You mean you have tendencies?" Now, having stated clearly that I was a dyke, I wasn't sure what I was supposed to do to get the idea across, jump her? Instead I responded, "It isn't a matter of tendencies. I am a practising lesbian." I felt like I should whip out a government licence stating that I was qualified to practice lesbianism.

From the beginning I knew that Rhesa's attitude toward lesbians would be crucial to my continuing to see her. I was perfectly aware that many of us have suffered at the hands of psychiatrists—the lavender couch and all that. Rather than query her directly, I decided to see how she responded to what I said, sort of practice rather than theory. She won her first high marks from me at the end of a long session about Phyllis. I told her that when we had finished our Ph.D.s in Boston, Phyllis had opted for an unhappy marriage to Fred and not joined me in Toronto as planned. As you know, Boxy, my inability to break free of Phyllis' clinging to me after her marriage was a big factor in the early development of my drinking problem. So I told Rhesa about all that stuff, including the depressing letters I was getting from Phyllis. I could sense that Rhesa wanted me to summarize, pick out the essence, do something. Then it clicked. I said, "The moral of the story is that it is better to be a well-adjusted pervert than to live unhappily in the midst of mainstream society."

Rhesa smiled and said, "Got it." We both laughed. I began to trust her.

In time I learned that Rhesa had fled Iran with her husband and children in the early part of the revolution that brought the Ayatollah Khomeni to power. She had been a general practitioner. Upon coming to Canada she did a residency in psychiatry and was establishing her own practice when I started going to her. Eventually she got a posh office in the Annex, but for the first six months we met at the mental institution.

I used to sneak away for my weekly appointments. Disappearing, even for a few hours, is not easy for a busy university administrator whose personal secretary keeps close tabs on her whereabouts. In the Tuesday afternoon slots of my appointment book I would put down a set of initials. Never once did I give my secretary, Helen, an explanation about who A.H. or P.D. or G.F.W. was. Sometimes I used the same initials for several months and other times for only a week. Helen must have thought I was having the most wonderful affairs! Much to her professional credit, she never once asked, never even hinted, about what I was doing.

Some really funny things happened during those three years I went to see Rhesa. Psychoanalysis certainly was hard work, but there were light moments also. Rhesa got off a great quip in the midst of one of my exceedingly well-organized, thoroughly analyzed lectures on something. She interrupted and stated flatly, "I bet you are professor and chairman in bed." At appropriate moments since then I have asked my bed partner if she finds me to be "professor and chairman." So far the answer has been no.

Oh yes, then there was Rhesa's use of pronouns. She frequently got "he" and "she" mixed up. This could be most disconcerting. In the midst of telling her about an intimate lesbian episode, she might ask, "What did he say then?" At first I thought she was playing little tricks on me, but then realized that indeed "he" and "she" are very similar words and how confusing they must be for someone learning English.

I almost forgot the grand joke on myself. In the beginning I didn't know a heck of a lot about the psychoanalytic process. Somewhere I had picked up vague ideas about transference and countertransference. Also, I sort of knew you were supposed to fall in love with your shrink. Now Rhesa is good-looking, meticulously and beautifully groomed, but she is straight and I just knew I wasn't going to fall for her. I thought of our relationship as strictly professional, you know, one professional woman helping another. Then I began to find every woman I met with Arabian features to be so lovely and attractive. Of course, I had fallen in love with Rhesa!

There were also the not-so-funny times when I shed my quota of tears. When Candice's fourth book was published, the one containing the poems she wrote during our break-up, I took it, along with her earlier book of love poems about me, to Rhesa. I read poems and sobbed. Yeah, I told Rhesa all that shit about how Candice had split with the American drug dealer in Guatemala. Good ole staid pillar of the community me, gets dumped for a fucking criminal, male at that! My fifty-minute cry, even if it did come two years after the fact, cleared out most of the garbage I had about Candice.

The biggest struggle, as you now know, was with the drinking. God, when I think back on how I used to drink myself into a stupor almost every night, I get cold, cold chills. It was a wonder I survived, let alone was so damned successful. Just think, I excelled as a research scientist while drinking myself blue! When I became department chair, things got really bad. I felt so terribly alone and feared I would never have a personal life, someone to love, a home. Somehow living a fulfilled lesbian life and holding a professional position seemed incompatible. It turned out that way for me. I hope it isn't for other women, but there was no way I could stay in that revolting department. For those turkeys a "lesbian event" would be a burning, not a Holly Near concert.

Back to the booze story. I struggled for nearly two years after I began seeing Rhesa. I had cut down drastically on the amount I was drinking but just couldn't seem to stop completely. Then the miracle happened. I was participating in a small group-dynamics class and had just spent a week locked up for six hours a day with eight other people, talking about power in groups. What is it? Who has it? How do you get it? My thesis was that knowledge is the ultimate power, an appropriate enough stance for a professor. Somehow my opinion didn't seem to carry much weight with the group.

All week the consultant had been asking, "Who has the power in this group?" We had discussed this question in terms of profession, gender, race and other differences amongst us. In the last meeting of the course, he was still asking, "Who has the power in this group?" No one would answer.

Looking my way the consultant said, "The leader in this group is a homosexual." I stared intently at my folded hands and said to myself, "He couldn't mean me. How would he know? I'm dressed in my most conservative, Presbyterian-blue suit. Maybe there is someone else in the class?" There was more discussion. With only ten minutes left he asked again. "Who will speak for the group?"

Then I said, "All week I have contended that knowledge is power and I still believe that. But for people to have power, to be good leaders, in the best sense, they must also care about the others in the group." I looked slowly around the circle meeting each person's eyes. "You've got to link up the head and the heart."

Silence. All eyes were riveted on me. Tears began to flow silently down my cheeks. After some time, the consultant said to the others, "It is also fine to be a neck."

Immediately after the session ended I went to the washroom. While I was in the stall, a voice unlike any I have ever heard before said, "You don't have to drink anymore." And I haven't. That day made the rest of my life possible.

Four days later I told Rhesa what had happened. I ended with the proud announcement that I hadn't had a drink since the previous Thursday night, the longest period I had gone without alcohol in fifteen years. Yes, Boxy, I did expect a big, gold star from my trusty shrink. Instead a look of alarm came over her face. She asked imploringly, "Why didn't you tell me you were going to stop so suddenly?"

How in hell was I supposed to know what was going to happen between 11:50 a.m. and 12:25 p.m. last Friday?

She continued, "When people with long term problems stop drinking suddenly, they may have psychological reactions that can cause loss of consciousness or even seizures. You still aren't safe. Be careful driving home and for the next few days." I was touched by her concern, but disappointed that I hadn't received my anticipated praise. That came later, many times over.

The next spring I took a course in England on authority and leadership in organizations. In the large study group of about seventy people the topic of freedom came up. A space seemed to open within the group for me to speak. In a strong, emotion-laden voice I said, "It wasn't until I looked deep inside of myself and faced the presumed most-terrible thing, my being a lesbian, that I was able to stop the drinking I was using to kill myself. Once I faced the blackest of the black, my life turned around, toward the light, and I was free." It is impossible to capture in words the atmosphere of a moment. I can only say that my statement had a profound effect on the group. Also, I got my first experience as a public lesbian—one quarter of the group congratulated me on my courage and honesty, one quarter actively shunned me, and the other half did not comment nor alter their behaviour.

When I returned to Canada, I related my recent experiences to Rhesa. After making appropriate comments, she told me about similar courses in which she had participated. We discussed the various types of courses, conferences and workshops that explore group psychodynamics. On the way home I realized this was the first time we had simply talked about a topic of mutual interest. Our relationship had changed subtly. We never dropped the roles of therapist and patient, but from that time on their edges were softer.

Just before I went to England, the most wonderful thing happened. Anne and I acknowledged the love developing between us. I loved a wonderful woman who loved me and wanted to spend her life with me. How I had longed for just that! To me, April is a month bathed in the orange light of miracles. The previous April I had stopped drinking and the following one Anne and I became partners. I shared the happy news with Rhesa. A few weeks later Anne went with me to meet her.

Our newly found love and my year-old sobriety were about to get a stiff test. Boxy, that was when the mess in the department began to hit the fan. As I told you in my letters then, it became apparent that, regardless of tenure, full professor rank, and all the trappings of success and prestige I had, those bastards would make my life so miserable, it wouldn't be worth living. Anne stuck by me and I didn't once think about drinking. After we decided to move to B.C., Rhesa confided that she was about to tell me to leave the university. The other day I ran across a piece of graffiti at our local pub that expresses how I tried to act during those last months: "If you are going to get run out of town, get out in front and act like it is a parade."

Since coming to Nelson, I have thought often of Rhesa. I wrote to her after we bought the bookstore. It seemed important to let her know that we were getting our new lives in order. The only other time I have written to her was a month ago. I ended that letter with "You will receive this letter just a few weeks shy of my first appointment five years ago. It has been a tough, good five years. I knew that by beginning the process of looking inside of myself, I would change in unforeseeable ways. I suspect I have only begun."

Well, Boxy, that about takes care of the memories. Thanks for listening again, as you have done so faithfully over the years. I must scram and get some lunch. I have the afternoon shift at the store.

Take care and write when you get a chance.

LOVE,

JEAN

FULL CIRCLE

KATHRYN ANN

It happened at the Sapphistry dance at the Baby Grand. I was sitting in the foyer, smoking, and glanced up to see Jos walking toward me, smiling. She asked me to dance. She'd never asked me that before, and after three years of platonic acquaintanceship, you don't expect surprises, right?

Jos and I had spent one of those years working in tandem at the local shelter for battered women, and during that time had established the parameter of our relationship: broad enough to include a mutual liking and respect, limited enough to leave the details of our lives on the periphery, if not excluded altogether. Well, Jos was straight. She had a common-law husband and a male child, whereas my only commitment was to keeping myself uncommitted. After work, she went to self-help groups and sat on politically correct boards; I went to parties and sat in bars. She liked women. I loved them.

Once, over a cup of orange pekoe at the shelter, Jos told me all about the support group she went to once a week. It was for feminists who had male partners. I nodded a lot and made inarticulate affirming noises, but all I could think at the time was how strange it must be to need a support group as an adjunct to the most intimate relationship in your life. A more cynical thought occurred to me when Jos admitted to me that five out of the seven members of her group recently initiated sexual relationships with women.

"What you really need," I said, "is a support group for feminists with male partners who become intimately involved with lesbians." I took a generous swallow of tea and set my cup carefully into its saucer. "So who's the other hold-out?"

"Most of them," Jos said, ignoring my levity, "described being with a woman as a glorious homecoming. Some said they couldn't imagine why they hadn't done it sooner. I wonder," she added musingly, staring into her teacup, "if it'll ever happen to me."

As we threaded our way through the dancers, I reached behind my back and found her hand there, waiting, even reaching, to be held, led.

Perhaps she'd been living with it for awhile, this miniscus, this tension rounding the surface of her life, this small but inescapable rebellion against containment.

As we danced, I felt her hand, lightly affixed to the small of my back, moving a soft, scant inch upward, then down. I pulled a little away and looked into her eyes, raising my brows, asking my woman's non-verbal question of her.

Is this something, Jos? Are you feeling something new?

I saw the helpless glance from her blue, myopic eyes, then a swift, shy veering away. I nudged the tip of her nose with mine—to smile, to laugh, to say without the words she would find it impossible to hear at this point, *It's alright, Jos. I care for you. It's alright.*

The music stopped, and in one of those protracted periods between songs that only seem to occur at women's dances, we stood facing each other, a polite three feet apart.

"I hope it'll be another slow song," Jos said.

"The last one wasn't slow."

She glanced at me with an unlikely hybrid of fear and wonder in her eyes. "Seriously?" she said.

I scuffed the floor with the toe of my tennis shoe.

You've got to be kidding, I thought. *Just who's the dyke here?*

We walked, after the dance, through the icy Kingston streets. Jos reached out and slid her arm through mine. She said it was because of the treacherous sidewalks, and I said nothing, only gripped her forearm in the crook of my elbow and did my best to keep the two of us upright.

I warned myself to be careful, especially careful, with this one. She was experimenting, and I sensed with some cellular, non-specific level of awareness, that she might provide too little, ask for too much. I didn't want to spend the rest of my life noticing Jos wasn't in it.

I've wondered since why I didn't just walk her home, give her an encouraging, affectionate hug, and let the whole thing blow over like a dream made poignant by its peculiar context and dispersed in the light of dawn. I didn't, though.

I asked her back to my apartment for tea.

"I ought to get home," she said. And then, "Yes."

I shouldn't have done it, but I was curious, and that seemed enough of a reason at the time.

Jos, you didn't mean to.

Isn't it so for us all? We never mean to harm, do we? Our desire crashes through the resistance, even the sensibilities, of others, like an avalanche gathering force. We bowl over everything in our path until, impetus spent, we settle down and survey the damage we've done.

You couldn't describe desire as a gentle force, could you, Jos?

After our slippery walk to my apartment, Jos perched upon the edge of my sofa and sipped a glass of water.

I lighted a cigarette, made myself comfortable in the armchair, and wondered whether it would be advisable to pour myself a drink. I'd had one beer at the dance and was feeling distressingly sober, considering the surreal nature of my circumstances.

"I haven't felt this way since I was sixteen," Jos said. "I feel sixteen."

I puffed on my cigarette and decided to forego the drink.

"I'm wet," she added. "We're not even touching, and I'm wet."

I wasn't wet, but the idea that my presence could inspire this deluge in her, without a word or a touch, piqued my curiosity even further. I got up and slipped Beethoven's *Eroica* into the tape deck.

"Oh Christ," Jos said a moment later. "Now I feel as if I'm six."

"Watch out," I said, leaning forward and mashing my cigarette into the ashtray on the coffee table. "Pretty soon you'll be embryonic, and then what'll we do?"

"I should go," she said.

I watched as she pulled her sweater over her shoulders, reached for her boots and laced them, then knotted her purple scarf around her throat. She picked her gloves off the coffee table and shuffled them from one hand to the other.

What could I do, Jos? Let you stand there indefinitely like a stoplight stuck in amber while cars lined up in all directions, hooting and honking and revving their engines?

Someone had to make a move.

I made it, though I don't quite remember how that happened. In my memory, I feel the warmth of your skin as my palms drift over your cheeks and turn your face up to mine. Your eyes, before you closed them, looked as if they were filmed with tears. I ran the tip of my tongue over the V in your upper lip, and in a momentary flash of clarity realized this was a softness you had not yet experienced. A woman's skin, a woman's hair, a woman's touch—all textures you knew nothing about.

We forgot the danger, didn't we, for a moment. We forgot willingly, because for that moment we remembered who we are. We remembered that we belong together because we are women, and because we know beyond a doubt that we belong to ourselves.

I inhaled the faint, yeasty smell of your skin, the comforting clean detergent of your sweater, and tasted the residue of brown rice and whole grains on the inside of your mouth. We articulated our intent right there, mouths touching, not needing to question or explain, just that, all that was important—our homecoming.

But life never stops in the right place, does it? It goes on, plodding away, moving toward its own extinction.

Jos pulled away from me and sighed. She gazed at the carpet for a minute, not seeing it, then up at me.

"I can't," she said, and then her words spilled out like a flood, explaining, presuming, apologizing.

I watched her, watched the words tumble around her body until she was surrounded by an almost tangible scream of sulphurous yellow.

I reached for her again, whispered in her ear, stroked her shoulders and arms until she was quiet. She slid her arms around my waist and held on tight.

I stood at the door, barefoot and shivering, when she left that night, as she disappeared down the street bundled in her layers of clothes, less afraid of the night, the darkness and its possibilities, than of giving in to her love for me. Or—and here my lips got as far as framing the J in her name before I pressed them together and stepped back and closed the door—or of giving in to mine for her.

I paced for awhile, then poured at least three fingers of Scotch over an ice cube, carried my glass to the couch, and sat down where she had been sitting. I sipped and let my thoughts drift over the evening's events. I couldn't figure out the exact point at which I had ceased being an observer in our drama, and had become a participant. It was impossible for me to tease one emotional stage from another. I had the dissonant sense that our passion had always, somehow, been inherent in our friendship. As if this seed had its own integral life, had pushed a fragile leaf above ground, and was destined to shrivel in a climate of necessary neglect. I mean, not everything gets a fair break.

I stared at my feet splayed over the coffee table, gulped down the rest of my Scotch, and went to bed.

What I didn't count on was her tenacity, her reluctance to forfeit a dream for the hard-packed earth of reality.

We ran into each other at a potluck a few weeks later.

I saw Jos as soon as I walked through the door. Her eyes found mine, and didn't leave. I pulled my boots off, then my socks, balancing precariously upon one foot, then the other, and stared back at Jos throughout the entire operation.

She was talking with a couple of women, but walked out of the conversation in mid-sentence as I approached her.

We began to dance. We danced as if we had known each other for lifetimes. We were not proficient so much as familiar, touching easily, gauging each other's feelings with the tactile intelligence of our bodies, arbiters of a sensory duet. Somehow, we knew when to draw closer, when away.

We didn't notice or care how we might have looked to the others in the room. All we cared about was exploring this understatement of erotic energy flowing between us, this ill-timed eruption of lust. And for that moment, we were honest.

Jos guided my hand to her lower back and held it there, lightly. I started to say something—I don't remember what—and her lips shut me up in the middle of the sentence. After that, I forgot. I just forgot.

Later, I walked her partway home. She wouldn't let me take her to the door. It might have been twenty below. I was shivering, shaking, both of us were, but it wasn't entirely from the cold. We stopped and kissed under a streetlight, not caring a damn who saw us or what they might have to say about this display of passion between two women. All I could hear in my heart and hers was yes, yes, and oh, yes.

Finally Jos pulled away and ran down the hill towards her house, whooping at the top of her lungs. I strode away in the opposite direction, laughing out loud, hoping she wouldn't up-end herself on the icy sidewalk.

She didn't.

She up-ended me.

She telephoned me two days later while her male partner was at his bi-weekly support group for spouses of feminists, and told me she couldn't see me anymore. She asked me not to call, not to connect.

I said yes, and yes.

In that moment, with the receiver pressed hard against my ear, I understood what becomes of love when its natural expression is denied. It consumes you while you still live, breathe, see. If you let it.

"I'm sorry," Jos said before she hung up. "I'm so sorry."

Of course I gave her exactly what she asked for—nothing. As I would have given her anything else.

She's phoned me a few times since then, always in the morning, from work, never from home, and each time has managed to interject a clue, a hint, a word or phrase that tells me in code she's been counting the days since our last meeting. And each time I wonder what for.

What does it mean to you, Jos, to remember the calendar details, the beginning and ending and the tyranny of time? Time after all, is what you have with your partner, your man. Time to pay off the mortgage, time to renovate the house you share, time to raise your son with his red-blond curls and his child's shy awareness of his right to say no, taken on trust, the trust you afford him. Time to look in the mirror and watch your need for security rearrange the soft contours of your face.

It's understandable, though, even to me. I mean, what *is* passion compared to a floor under your feet and a roof over your head, food in the cupboards, a surety of what tomorrow will bring.

Anarchy, that's what it is.

Did I ever tell you, Jos, that anarchy is the most freeing of concepts? Anarchy is that instant when you've lifted one foot from the rung of a ladder to mount the next. If you focus only upon it, you forget your other foot is still firmly planted. What terror in that moment of transition. I don't blame you for hesitating, for sticking with what you know.

And I'm hardly one to speak, am I, with no one to consider except myself? But I choreographed my life that way, Jos, against all other temptation. I choreographed my life so I would forever be lifting one foot or the other to a higher rung. Always unsure, always in transit, always susceptible to criticism from my more sure-footed consoeurs. Always open to the notion of spontaneous combustion, that finger-in-the-socket mode of enlightenment.

Perhaps nothing else stood between you and me except that frisson of possibility which opens my eyes each day to a new and unexplored universe—the one that you open, then close your eyes to.

This morning I lounged in bed sipping a cup of coffee and ruminating. The telephone rang. I glanced at it, but didn't bother answering. I suppose there are times in everyone's life when there's nothing left to be said, or listened to.

And perhaps during moments like these—the in-between moments—we have a chance to carve out a new perspective for ourselves, and with it, humour.

Before the phone had stopped ringing, I was turning over the idea of starting a support group for lesbians who love feminists who have anchored themselves to men, but who have fallen in love with dykes.

Oh, endless possibilities.

... THEN TO FUCHSIA

LEE FLEMING

When the Fuchsia Woman (as I came to call her) miraculously arrived in my life, I was living alone, about thirty-five kilometres from the city where I worked. I'd moved to the country to hide for awhile. Even though I'd always been a city dweller, I reasoned that the peace and quiet I got at night and over the weekends was more than worth the ride to the city every day. Now I know that I just couldn't deal with my abysmal ending with Greta—that I was healing from a relationship that should have ended years before, so marked with boredom and unhappiness it had been. I did not socialize, had no consuming hobbies or passions; in fact, I was in a rut.

I ate sporadically, and mostly out of boxes and cans. My wardrobe hadn't changed in five years, and I had the same haircut as when I'd graduated from university twelve years earlier. My job as a prof in the biology department provided me with financial security, and a certain kind of status, but I knew I was a closeted, conservative lesbian. I was desperately wishing I had the gumption to break free and live the vibrant, risk-taking life that only visited me in rare, half-remembered dreams. In retrospect, where truth is so much easier to swallow, I realize that I was hoping for some (to stretch a metaphor) fairy godlesbian to make my life whole for me, to kiss awake my sleeping amazon ...

One chilly, grey Friday afternoon, after a hellish week of marking papers, getting my period, and fighting over the phone with Greta (with whom I hadn't had a civil conversation in the year and a half that we'd been officially separated), I drove home from work, vowing to trash my career and *really* move back to the land. I'd pursue the wool dying and weaving that I had never given serious time to. As the city receded, I ruefully admitted to myself that this was escape-fantasy number thirty-one in the past month alone. I pulled onto my muddy dirt road and headed the last mile home. Seeing the flag up on my mailbox, I pulled over, and semi-expertly executed the country art of removing my mail while remaining seated in my car. I was not really expecting any personal mail, having let correspondence lapse with the friends and lovers of my earlier, wilder days, before I'd become "one" with Greta.

This day, along with bills and junk mail, I found a small package neatly wrapped in lovely thick pink vellum. Placing it on the seat beside me, I drove up the long lane to the house, parked the car and let myself in by the kitchen door, as I did every afternoon. The one bright spot in my life was my house, purchased after the break-up. It was small, comfortable and homey—the previous owners had seen to that.

Jerome, of the long whiskers and mewing needs, was, as usual, screaming for food and affection. I did my familial duty, then got a fire going in my old Franklin stove. Finally I settled into my worn, living room rocker to study my mystery package. I noted the local postmark, dated the thirteenth. My name was written boldly and neatly in a fuchsia-coloured felt marker on the front. No return address.

My bitchy mood gave way to curiosity. I carefully opened the package with my little-used letter opener (a gift Greta had given me three years back that now reminded me of a sharp dagger) and unwrapped a cassette. It was marked on the "A" side, in the same fuchsia-coloured marker: "To the Rainbow Woman from Angelica." Hmmm, Rainbow Woman? And who on earth was Angelica? No one from the University, that was for sure. I was the only Angela I knew, and Angelica seemed much rarer a name. In fact, I hadn't heard the name Angelica since reading that godawful *Angelica in Love* trash-fiction series during my pre-lesbian teens.

And no one had made me a music tape since my first big lesbian romance with the exchange student from Paris, with whom I'd become infatuated during my undergrad studies. But I didn't want my reminiscing to follow that line. I was so young then, so naive, idealistic and romantic. Qualities all sadly buried in my present cynicism. Yet, sitting there holding the cassette, I felt a rush of excitement and a sense of an adventure about to unfold.

Somehow I knew *this* tape wasn't music. I went over to my stereo and slipped the tape into the player.

"Rainbow Woman" she began. "I want you to sit back, close your eyes and let me enter your life. I want you to surrender, to allow yourself to feel anything and everything that my voice compels you to feel." All this in a low, sensual cadence. Thirty minutes of delicious suggestion about exactly what she'd like to do to me followed. Somewhere in the dim reaches of my sexual yesteryear I remembered having an erotic imagination, a sparking sexual vocabulary. But I didn't remember anything like this. Nope, this was magnificently original all right.

I sat glued to my rocker, listening with a mixture of pleasure, disbelief and fear. Who was this woman and how did she know me? Furthermore, what did she want with me? Boring, retreating me? And "Rainbow Woman?" She obviously couldn't know me in my present incarnation. She'd rightly assumed that I'd be in thrall to the very end, that I'd receive this cassette as a no-strings-attached fantasy. No demands made, nothing required. So why was I so terrified? As the tape finished, she told me that if I wanted to hear from her again, I should paint my mailbox. I'd bought one of those utilitarian unpainted grey (like my life) aluminum ones when I'd moved in, with a little red flag that the deliverer raised when I had mail.

The next three weeks passed with me in a veritable frenzy. I endlessly litanized: "Who is she? Do I know her? Where did she get my address? Why me?" I'd whip home from work, put on the tape and make out on the rug while a bemused and impassive Jerome looked on. I realized that I hadn't taken the time to sexually pleasure myself for years. In fact, I hadn't been very self-loving in general. Soon this stranger's voice became an intimate lover, and I relaxed more and more every time she invited me. Rather than becoming bored, I found myself elaborating and enlarging on her suggestions.

Three Fridays later, I took the plunge and stopped in at the hardware store to purchase a can of brown paint and a brush. Saturday morning, I was up bright and early to paint my mailbox. It required two coats. Feeling energized, I decided to use the rest of the can on my outside kitchen door—the first chore I'd done around the house since the fall before.

The following Friday, I arrived home and noticed my flag was up. Inside was another little package, identical to the first. I zipped up the driveway, fed Jerome a special treat of gourmet cat food and then examined my new offering. Still no return address, the same lovely fuchsia-coloured handwriting, the local postmark again dated the thirteenth. "To my Rainbow Woman from Angelica" was marked on side "A." A-ha. So now it was *my* Rainbow Woman. I lit a candle, even though twilight was another hour off, closed the shutters, put the cassette on, and settled into my rocker.

The same sexy voice, but more outrageous, more presumptuous, as if we'd met, were now lovers, and she was free to take even greater liberties. I began to appreciate this woman's chutzpah. She'd obviously given this seduction much thought. Her confidence was awesome, despite her anonymity. I felt my body come alive as her words penetrated my walls of self-loathing. It was the best sex I'd ever had.

Before my mailbox seduction I'd had strict "types" of women who I deemed attractive to me—usually they were thin and femmy. After cassette number two, I realized that if she'd come knocking on my kitchen door, I would have been down on my knees begging for her, whatever her looks. Her words evoked women with curves and flesh and hair and breasts of all kinds, all colours. I, who had predictably acculturated hatred of my own physical being, began to see myself as beautiful, worthy of love and desire. I could actually feel the appreciative gaze of my Fuchsia Woman as she wooed, lusted, and commanded me with her words.

After cassette three, I sent an order to the sex-toy store in the States that I saw advertised in my *Lesbian Connection* mag. My Fuchsia Woman told me what to get and what to do with my order when it arrived. She now called me

Angie, or Angie baby; she seemed to intuit what pleased me, or that a certain commanding tone would be exactly right. She had no inhibitions, allowing her voice to be dramatic, or crooning, or anything at all really. I felt that she somehow knew me, was observing my pleasure and the changes in me. She was so sure of herself.

My lover revealed herself as a widely-read, travelled and experienced woman. She would choose exquisite erotic quotations from obscure writers, sending me searching at the antiquarian bookstore for the complete text. She'd make epicurean references—food was obviously an entire erotic exploration unto itself for her—that had me shopping at the food emporium and rare wine store. One day I had my hair cut in a style, that was for me, quite daring. Even my colleagues noticed when I arrived at work with a sexy new wardrobe and a glow in my cheeks. Jokes got thrown around in the faculty lounge about the "new, mystery man in my life." I just smiled.

By cassette four I had painted my mailbox from brown to blue to green then to red. I was getting some pretty curious stares from my local neighbours, who observed all the goings-on within a thirty-two kilometre radius. Folks even started chatting me up at the Food Co-op to glean a little info from me. One elderly farmer managed to make me blush to my roots by asking, "Are you planning to paint a rainbow on that mailbox of yours soon?"

For cassette five I decided to paint my mailbox yellow, a colour that had never really appealed to me. Spring was coming on, and yellow was to herald the event. Angelica constantly referred to colours, with names that I'd rarely heard or used. She used language as if it was food, colours to express emotion or erotic longing. I started to dream in vivid colour, and some were so original that I bought a journal and began to write them down.

Still, there was never a sign from my mystery lover. I figured that she had to drive by my mailbox to see if I'd painted it, but I never saw her. I'd given up asking if anyone knew an Angelica. Besides, somewhere inside me I was enjoying the privacy that this anonymous lover extended to me.

In the fifth month of my seduction, I received a tape that was nothing less than a no-holds-barred gift of brilliance. There I was on my couch, allowing the tears that I'd so long repressed, to flow like healing waters as her voice made love to me, as she loved me. Then after a long pause, she very quietly but firmly told me that this was the last tape I'd receive from her. That I was on my own now—that I was ready to live and love again, when and how I chose.

I sat in shocked denial. Anger, betrayal, loneliness, and the familiar voice of self-loathing coursed through me. It was as if I'd been dumped by a kindly but patronizing older lover. Now the tears flowed unrelentingly. I had released a grief more profound and locked up in me than I had ever known was there.

The next month passed with me in a kind of stupor. University had ended for the year, and I had too much time on my hands. I wallowed in an obsessive denial—making two or three walks to my mailbox a day—thinking that my lover would change her mind and contact me. I still played the tapes, but I felt an emptiness that would not be sated even by my Fuchsia Woman's knowing voice.

The summer passed. My grief gave way to a kind of quiet resignation. She really was gone, but there was no blame to cast or absolve. Angelica had been nothing but loving, and had never asked for anything but for me to be the same—to myself.

By late August, my first-ever garden, planted in that spring of my sexual reawakening, had come fully alive—thriving and demanding attention. Despite myself, I found a peace and tranquillity working with the soil and the plants. One Friday, as I worked solitarily, an abundance of vegetables sitting in baskets at the side of my garden, the sun broke through the clouds, catching the now massive sunflowers in the north row. A blaze of realization came to me. Although Angelica, my anonymous lover, had nourished me with her sexual, sensual imagination, it had been my own self-loving that had opened me to myself. She'd been an erotic guardian angel, but more importantly, an aspect of my own being.

The next day, a beautiful autumn Saturday, I drove into town, and went straight to the art supply store. I purchased a can of rare fuchsia paint and a new brush, then headed home.

CONTRIBUTORS

KATHRYN ANN

My stories have been published in *Prairie Fire, Room of One's Own, Fireweed,* and *Dykewords II.* I have also written hundreds of the world's worst poems, penned a novel which has wisely been relegated to a drawer, composed countless songs that never got air-time, painted the portraits of a number of ex-friends, and am presently drawing a series of cartoons about abused children that will likely never appear in the dailies. My multi-faceted talent is matched only by my unbounded optimism.

LUANNE ARMSTRONG

I presently teach writing at a native college in Merritt, B.C., but my background is varied. I was an organic farmer in the Kootenays, have raised four kids, mostly as a single parent. I have run newspapers and been a "paid worker" in the feminist movement as an organizer—the wild and varied background of those of us who have learned to survive and flourish in the cracks of the patriarchy.

BRENDA BARNES

I am a mostly outrageous, risk-taking, twenty-nine-year-young lesbian who escaped from my home town and finally ended up playing guitar, swimming to relieve stress, and working as the Current Affairs Director at CKDU-FM in Halifax. My journalistic writings have appeared in several newspapers, and in gay and lesbian, women's, and media analysis periodicals. This is my first piece of fiction. I also used to be a naval reserve officer.

KAREN BOEGH

Karen Boegh graduated from Carleton University in May, 1991. She spent two months backpacking in Europe, before resettling in B.C., after living for some time in Ottawa.

BRENDA BROOKS

Brenda Brooks currently lives in Toronto but spends most of her time driving elsewhere. She does most of her writing at truck stops along the way. She has had a book of poetry published, *Somebody Should Kiss You* (gynergy books) and contributed work to other publications and anthologies including *Fireweed, Rites,* and *By Word of Mouth* (gynergy books).

HEATHER CONRAD

Heather Conrad lives with her domestic partner in Berkeley, California. She supports herself as a bookkeeper and is completing a Masters in Creative Writing at San Francisco State University. Her first novel, NEWS, was published in 1987. She is currently working on a new novel, as well as short fiction and poetry.

NANCY DARISSE

The last two years of my life have transformed my perceptions of what it means to be productive. Immobilized by Chronic Fatigue Syndrome, my active life collapsed into a dreary, unpredictable experience, in and out of a numbing sleep. A great sense of isolation and powerlessness haunted me as I learned how I had been defining myself by my capacity to "do", to act. The writing of my short story offered me the power to redefine myself. I wrote for myself, I acted solely for myself and that was empowering ... that is productive.

ANN DECTER

Ann Decter grew up an urban prairie girl in Winnipeg, Manitoba. She has published two books, *Katie's Alligator Goes to Daycare* (for young children) and *Insister* (gynergy books) and her work has appeared in anthologies and periodicals. She lives and works in Toronto, where she is currently co-managing editor at Women's Press.

JYL LYNN FELMAN

Jyl Lynn Felman is an award-winning short story writer whose stories, prose and review essays can be found in many journals such as: *Bridges, Sinister Wisdom, Sojourner, Tikkun, Lambda Book Report* and in anthologies including *Word of Mouth, Speaking For Ourselves, The Tribe of Dina* and *Korone Vol. IV.* She received her M.F.A. in Fiction from the University of Massachusetts, where she was awarded a Writing Fellowship.

LEE FLEMING

My heart's desire is to be playing music full-time, but I find that my day-to-day life is all tied up with film and video producing, editing and, most recently, marketing books. My long-term goal is to be an aging rock'n roll star. ... *then to Fuchsia* is dedicated, with love, to Heidi. With courage and humour, she inspires me to "live and change."

BETH FOLLETT

"I am a woman running into my own country ... Do not let them kill me before you speak to me, touch me, hold me." (Meridel le Sueur)

CAROLYN GAMMON

Carolyn Gammon, a recovering *Anne of Green Gables* look- and act-alike, lives in Montreal, where she pursues polyerotic polemics. Her politically correct dildo collection is one of the most fashionable in the city.

GARBO

Garbo lives in Columbus, Ohio, where she divides her time between writing and massage therapy. She contributes regularly to the "Entre Nous" column in Chicago's *Windy City Times*. She is the author of the novel *Rusty* (Big Breakfast Publishing) and a novel-in-progress, *Doctor Fell*.

GABRIELLA GOLIGER

Gabriella Goliger lives in Ottawa where she works part-time as a freelance writer/editor and part-time on short stories. Last year she took an excellent creative writing course at Concordia University with Robert Majzel who taught her, among other things, to appreciate self-conscious fiction. She lives a quiet, inoffensive life, spending many hours making paperclip chains and thinking about herself in the third person. Singular. (Potentially interesting compulsive character? Save to disk? No, too close to home. Erase! Erase!)

CANDIS J. GRAHAM

I live in Ottawa and work part-time as a bookkeeper to support myself and my writing habit. *Tea for Thirteen*, a collection of some of my stories, was published by Impertinent Press in 1990. "Because" is dedicated to Mountain and Tamarack, who work so hard for change.

FLORENCE GRANDVIEW

Florence Grandview is into motorcycles (byke pride), and has published elsewhere under another name.

JAYNE HOLOWACHUK

I was raised in Ontario's "fruit belt," and now reside in Ottawa, where I am a laterally mobile, marginally-employed Bohemian. I studied Biology and English Lit. at various universities, without concocting a degree in either. This is my first attempt at short fiction—I'm usually a poet.

JOANNA KADI

Joanna Kadi is an Arab-Canadian, working-class lesbian feminist. She is a writer and political activist, with a B.A. in women's studies from University of Toronto and an M.A. in feminist ethics from the Episcopal Divinity School in Cambridge, Massachusetts. This is her first short story.

K. LINDA KIVI

I am a happy Kootenay (B.C.) country dyke recovering from the urban jungles of Ontario. I live on eighty acres of mountain, forest and field that will soon become cooperative women's land. There is no lingonberry jam for hundreds of miles, but I dream of the day when I will meet other Estonian lesbian feminists (one will do!). In the meanwhile, I walk this land, write erotica and stew over my first novel.

SHIRLEY LIMBERT

Shirley Limbert is a lesbian feminist who lives in a small house by the sea on Prince Edward Island. She shares her home with a lover and a cat. Shirley spends time with loving friends when she's not writing, painting, house renovating or doing Kripalu yoga.

SARAH LOUISE

I would like to dedicate the story in this collection to closeness and love between women—which always requires great courage—and to the cherished women in my own life.

SUSAN McIVER

For twenty-two years Susan McIver was a research scientist and university professor and administrator. She and her partner left the university system and now live on Salt Spring Island, B.C.

LEAH MEREDITH

I was born in Ajax, Ontario, and raised in Calgary. I then moved to Vancouver to pursue an acting career. Soon after finding out what the movie industry was all about, I quit and returned to college. Through a Women's Studies course I learned that we all have a writing voice—it's just a matter of finding it. "Ice-Time" is my first published piece and will hopefully be followed by many more. I am currently living in the West End of Vancouver with my partner and our guinea pig, Buckwheat.

RHONDA JAYNE OLSON

I'd like to see or leave the world in a sail boat, with Corinne, my family, all my friends, books forever, pens and papers, plenty of good food, beverages, and just a few cigarettes.

FRANCES ROONEY

Frances Rooney is editor of *Our Lives: Lesbian Personal Writings*, published by Second Story Press. Her biography of photographer Edith Watson (1861-1943) will be published in 1992. She and her cats live across the street from the only farm in downtown Toronto.

BETSY WARLAND

Betsy Warland has published several books of peotry. Her most recent book, *Proper Deafinitions* (Press Gang) is a collection of essays and prose. She also recently co-edited *Telling It: Women and Language Across Cultures* (Press Gang) and edited *InVersions: Writing by Dykes, Queers and Lesbians* (Press Gang). She lives off the coast of Vancouver, on Salt Spring Island.

PAT WOODS

Pat Woods lives in San Diego, where her conspicuous lack of a partner and a cat classify her as an anomaly in the lesbian community. She frequently can be found at local women's bars, desperately attempting to engage lesbians in conversations about their pets.

EDITOR

LEE FLEMING is the editor of *By Word of Mouth: Lesbians write the erotic*. She is a film/video producer. Her latest project *Skip To the Beat*, is an educational film for young women. She moved to Prince Edward Island in 1987 from Ottawa, where she worked as a feminist bookseller. She occasionally sings and plays her music on regional stages.

NEW AND RECENT RELEASES FROM *GYNERGY BOOKS*

◊ **By Word of Mouth: Lesbians write the erotic,** *Lee Fleming (ed.).* A bedside book of short fiction and poetry by thirty-one lesbian writers from Canada and the United States. $ 10.95

◊ **Don't: A Woman's Word,** *Elly Danica.* The best-selling account of incest and recovery, both horrifying and hauntingly beautiful in its eventual triumph over the past. $ 8.95

◊ **Double Negative,** *Daphne Marlatt and Betsy Warland.* An innovative collaboration that redefines boundaries and images of women from a lesbian feminist perspective. $ 8.95 / $ 7.95 US

◊ **Each Small Step: Breaking the chains of abuse and addiction,** *Marilyn MacKinnon (ed.).* This groundbreaking anthology contains personal narratives by women at various stages of recovery from the traumas of childhood sexual abuse and chemical dependency. $ 10.95

◊ **Fascination and other bar stories,** *Jackie Manthorne.* These are satisfying stories of the rituals of seduction and sexuality in the otherworld of lesbian bars—fascinating fiction for lesbians. $ 9.95

◊ **getting wise,** *Marg Yeo.* Women-loving poems of resistance and triumph. Marg Yeo shares hard-won truths and "the fine delight there will always be for me in poems and women." $ 8.95 / $ 7.95 US

◊ **The Montreal Massacre,** *Marie Chalouh and Louise Malette (eds.).* Feminist letters, essays and poems examine the mass murder of fourteen women at Ecole Polytechnique in Montreal, Quebec on December 6, 1989. The writers express a common theme: the massacre was the extreme manifestation of misogyny in our patriarchal society. $ 12.95

◊ **Somebody Should Kiss You,** *Brenda Brooks.* An intimate, humorous and bold collection of poetry that celebrates the courage of lesbian lives and loves. $ 8.95 / $ 7.95 US

◊ **Tide Lines: Stories of change by lesbians,** *Lee Fleming (ed.).* These diverse stories explore the many faces of change in lesbian lives—instantaneous, over-a-lifetime, subtle or cataclysmic. $ 10.95

gynergy books is distributed in Canada by UTP, in the U.S. by Bookpeople and Inland and in the U.K. by Turnaround. Individual orders can be sent, prepaid, to: *gynergy books*, P.O. Box 2023, Charlottetown, PEI, Canada, C1A 7N7. Please add postage and handling ($1.50 for the first book and 75 cents for each additional book) to your order. Canadian residents add 7% GST to the total amount. GST registration number R104383120.